THE MAKING OF US

DEBBIE HOWELLS

Boldwood

First published in Great Britain in 2024 by Boldwood Books Ltd.

Cover Design by Alexandra Allden

Cover Illustration: Shutterstock

A CIP catalogue record for this book is available from the British Library.

Paperback ISBN 978-1-80415-041-2

Hardback ISBN 978-1-80415-040-5

Large Print ISBN 978-1-80415-042-9

Ebook ISBN 978-1-80415-043-6

Kindle ISBN 978-1-80415-044-3

Audio CD ISBN 978-1-80415-035-1

MP3 CD ISBN 978-1-80415-036-8

Digital audio download ISBN 978-1-80415-038-2

Boldwood Books Ltd
23 Bowerdean Street
London SW6 3TN
www.boldwoodbooks.com

For Georgie and Tom
with love

If you are alone for a long time,
soon you will accept loneliness.
You will never know your potential
if you are afraid to be alone.

— LAO TZU

PROLOGUE
STEVIE

It wasn't so long ago that I had no idea that the worst possible thing to have happened in my life was a precursor to what was probably the best. But unless you've discovered the art of hopping between far-off parallel universes, the existence of time means there's an order in which events have to unfold. Even so, there was an other-worldly familiarity to what I was feeling as I sat in the departure lounge at London Gatwick that March day.

It was the first time I'd flown from here, yet it felt as if at some point in time, I had been here before. As it happened, I didn't pay it the attention it merited. Instead, my mind was filled with thoughts of everything I'd recently lost. But in a world defined by grief, I was yet to become that person who was open to the magic the universe holds; who could see beyond the trifling matters that govern the structure of our days. All I knew was that something was missing. Simply going about my days putting one foot in front of the other, I didn't, in all honesty, expect anything to change.

That day at the airport, I was just a girl staring at the book on my lap, staving off the feeling of fear that was eating relentlessly away at me. Trying not to think about all the people around me, my head was filled with thoughts of the flight that lay ahead – just a short hop, I kept telling myself. London to Limoges in south-west France wasn't far. Not to most people.

But Limoges might as well have been on the other side of the world. Even though for now, my home was there – technically speaking. The home that was still a shell, my heart remaining firmly in denial, nomadically searching, as all hearts do, for somewhere in this world where it belongs.

1

STEVIE

Sitting at the boarding gate, I stare with a macabre sense of fascination as another aircraft takes off, my stomach churning with nerves as it lifts into the sky. If anything happens now, if the aircraft malfunctions, if the laws of physics were to change suddenly, for everyone on board, it'd be too late.

Feeling my heart start to race, I twist my fingers together, trying to focus on breathing, my tried and tested method of dealing with irrational fear. It works – sometimes. Just not always.

Feeling myself calm slightly, as I reach into my bag to take out my drink, out of the corner of my eye, I notice this guy walk in. For some reason I can't take my eyes off him. Not because there's anything particularly remarkable about him – there isn't. Carrying a battered retro barrel bag, his jeans look as though he's slept in them, while his hair is dishevelled as if he couldn't be bothered to comb it this morning. He's wearing dark glasses he clearly thinks are cool, which in the shade of the departure lounge are completely unnecessary.

Finding an empty chair, he perches on the edge of it and feels in his pocket for something. Producing his phone, he slides his sunglasses on top of his head, and I see the real reason he's wearing them. He's hiding what looks like the mother of all hangovers.

Studying the screen, he sits there smiling to himself, his face lighting up for a moment before, oblivious to everyone else, laughter erupts from him. But, as he gets a set of headphones out of his bag and puts them on, the smile is gone as he sits back and closes his eyes.

Immersed in whatever he's listening to, one of his feet taps to the rhythm, then his fingers. Then as I watch, slightly fascinated, he seems entirely lost in his musical world as his whole body seems to get taken over.

Aware I'm staring at him, I turn my attention to my book. But as I open it, my flight is called. This is where I forget about everything else, my mind instantly filling with doomsday scenarios as I think about boarding, fear making my body start to shake. It's a short flight, I remind myself. *But distance is irrelevant*, my inner voice goads me. *Once you're off the ground anything could happen – as well you know.* My sense of impending doom is not helped by the aversion I have to confined spaces; to being crammed in with too many people.

It's one short hop between here and Limoges, I remind myself. *After, I need never do this again.*

Clasping my hands tightly, I force myself to think about something else. But as I try to get up, it's as though I'm frozen, unable to move, when I hear a voice.

'Excuse me, but are you OK?'

Startled, I look up to see the guy with the dark glasses standing there.

'Of course,' I say briskly, the fact that I've been noticed by him galvanising me into action. Glancing towards the gate, I watch the last two passengers going through. 'I was miles away.' Standing up, I pick up my bag.

He grins at me. 'Cool. It's just that if you're heading for Limoges, everyone else has boarded.'

'Yes.' I take a deep breath. 'Don't let me hold you up.'

Nodding, he turns, loping away in the direction of the gate. I wait until his passport has been checked and he disappears onto the air bridge. And that should most definitely have been the end of that. I mean, there are at least 140 seats on this Airbus A320 – and when I booked mine, the ones next to me were empty.

But for whatever reason, today the plane is almost full. After boarding, I find the seat next to mine taken – by the guy. Staring towards the window, he appears deep in thought.

'Um, excuse me.' My cheeks are suddenly hot.

Turning, he looks surprised when he sees me. 'Oh! It's you! You made it, then.'

'Yes. I'm sitting there.' I point to the window seat.

'Oh – of course.' He stands up to let me pass.

'Thank you.' I breathe in a faint waft of a woody cologne as I slide past him. After sitting down and taking my book out of my rucksack, I place my bag under the seat in front of me, aware of the guy putting on his headphones again, before he starts quietly humming to himself.

Minutes later, the aircraft doors close and there's a jolt before we push back, then taxi slowly out to the end of the runway. Trying to still my nerves, the humming of the guy next to me starts to grate.

Unable to subdue the panic I'm starting to feel, I gaze out of the window. It's a beautiful early spring day, the sky broken only by small, fluffy white clouds. It should be a perfect day for flying, but as the aircraft starts its take-off roll, fear engulfs me.

Clenching my hands together, I close my eyes. Planes crash – as I know too well. Maybe I should have listened to my intuition and I shouldn't be on this flight. Then the worst thought of all as the aircraft lifts off and the ground falls away – *If anything happens now, it's too late.*

'Shit,' I mutter. Unable to resign myself to my fate, I start to hyperventilate.

'Are you OK?' The guy next to me sounds concerned again.

'Yes. No.' Overwhelmed, I squeeze my eyes more tightly shut, telling myself to breathe, counting each breath, drawing them out, until at last they slow.

When I open my eyes again, the guy is still watching me. 'You want me to call one of the cabin crew?'

'No,' I say quickly. Then add, 'I thought I could do this.' My voice is shaking.

'Try not to think about it,' he says brightly. 'Safest way to travel, I always tell myself. I'm Ned, by the way.' He holds out a hand.

'I'm Stevie.' As the aircraft lurches, instead of shaking his hand, I grab at it; in spite of myself, I'm unable to ignore the tiny spark between us.

'It's OK – just a little turbulence.' Ned looks at me slightly anxiously.

The spark is instantly gone. It's all very well him saying that – and I know he's trying to help. But in my mind, 'little' and 'turbulence' don't belong in the same sentence.

'That's the point. And unless you're a pilot or something, you're guessing. You don't actually know.'

'It's already stopped.' Ned's still looking at me. 'So where are you headed in France?'

'To a small village – in Corrèze.' I tell him the name. A stone's throw from its border with the better-known Dordogne, it's what some people would describe as the middle of nowhere.

'Nice part of the world. I know it well – though I would have thought it was a bit quiet for a holiday.' He looks nonplussed, as though he can't see why anyone would want to go there.

'Not for camping. I used to go there as a child, with my parents.' I don't tell him that I live there. That, after leaving Matty and clearing out my parents' place, since moving to France, the tiny village house is the only thing I have in the world. That my sole reason for travelling back to the UK was to settle the last of the paperwork to do with my late parents' estate, such as it was.

But he doesn't need to know that. In fact, there's little point in pursuing this conversation and I turn to the window again, struggling to keep my fear under control as I gaze outside at the clouds, then at the shades of blue in the far-reaching sky.

My world is small, I muse, listening to the engines drone. But I still remember when it wasn't. How it was a bright, expansive place of infinite hope. Of dreams, where anything was possible... Where I believed in the magic of beginnings; in love, too.

That's how it was until that fateful day when, out of the blue, my world came crashing down. To be fair, it wasn't the world itself that crashed. It was the small twinprop plane in the depths of Africa that stopped defying the laws of gravity for long enough to fall out of the sky, taking with it the two people I loved most in the world. My parents.

With no one else in my life I turned to Matty, my boyfriend. But in the midst of my grief, it was about to get worse. In what felt like the cruellest of coincidences, I discovered that he'd been summoning up the courage to tell me it was over between us. He'd met someone else.

This coming so soon after losing my parents, I was left rootless, lost, struggling just to get up every day. It felt as though I'd lost the foundations of my life. It also made no sense that when my parents had been selfless, dedicating their lives to charitable causes helping children in war zones, their lives had been brutally cut short while millions of shallow, feckless people just like Matty carried on living, trampling over other people's hearts, leaving a wake of destruction behind them.

It was a chapter of my life that left me traumatised. After weeks of therapy I worked it out, that I'd morphed into one of those people who have become stuck in life, the shock of losing my parents leaving me half-metamorphosed. There was no going back. Yet emotionally, I was unequipped to move forward.

Life doesn't treat all of us the same. And some of us are destined to be alone, I've realised. But there's a thing about being alone, I'm discovering. It's safer. If there are no people in your life, you can't lose them.

Ned's voice stirs me from my thoughts. 'How are you doing?'

I turn to look at him. 'Sorry?'

'It's just that I noticed you haven't been reading.' He glances at the unopened book on my lap.

'Oh. I was thinking,' I say defensively.

'You're into birds?' He sounds curious.

'Birds?' I glance at the book on my lap, entitled *Birdwatching*. 'It isn't so much about watching birds,' I tell him. 'It's more about seeing life from different points of view – for example, traditional, indigenous... And from a bird's, of course. The bit I'm reading at the moment is about Buddhism.'

He looks surprised. 'Sounds interesting.'

Suddenly I'm curious about him. 'What brings you to France?'

'Family.' He glances away. 'My parents live there – by chance, not far from your village.'

I stare at him as he says *parents*. Plural. Does he have any idea how lucky that makes him? 'That's nice,' I say too quickly. 'Where do you live? In England, I mean?'

'London,' he says. 'It's where I ought to be now. But duty summons!'

'Oh?'

He smiles. 'It's my mother's birthday. And seeing as we don't get together very often, my father's organised a party. It's a flying visit – no pun intended.' For a moment, he looks impressed with his wit. 'I fly back to London on Friday.'

Suddenly I have all these things I want to say to him – about making the most of his time with them. How you never know when your family are going to be ripped from your life, never to be seen again; how suddenly everything can change. But instead, I try to smile. 'I hope she has a nice birthday.'

Engrossed in my book, the rest of the flight passes uneventfully and it isn't long before the aircraft starts its descent. As the engines throttle back, my catastrophising mind runs away with me again. But my worst fears are unrealised and twenty minutes later, we're on the ground.

As we taxi in, Ned glances at my book again.

Closing it, I hold it out to him. 'Why don't you take this?'

He looks taken aback. 'I can't do that.'

'I've read it five times already,' I tell him. 'Call it a thank you for being so nice to me – about my ludicrous and unfounded fear. I mean, here we are – and in one piece.'

'It isn't ludicrous.' His eyes are warm.

'Honestly...' I'm still holding the book out. 'You'll be doing me a favour. It will encourage me to read something else.'

He looks amused. 'OK. In that case, I will. Thank you.' His eyes are dancing. 'You must be relieved the flight is over.'

I nod. I am – more than he'll ever know. 'Have a nice stay – with your family.'

'Thanks.' But I can't help noticing he looks distracted.

2

NED

As I take the book, I can't help staring at Stevie. Her eyes are beautiful, a brilliant blue that's almost turquoise, setting off perfect skin and long copper hair.

'Will you be OK now?' Something in me wants to spin this out, to keep her talking.

'Now that we're on the ground, I'll be fine.' She has a composure about her that wasn't there before.

I put her book in my rucksack. 'I suppose I better get moving.' Behind me, passengers are chivvying to get off. 'Good luck,' I say, immediately feeling stupid. I mean, FFS. What kind of idiot says that to a total stranger?

'You, too,' she says, her eyes briefly meeting mine before darting away.

And then I'm swept along towards the aircraft door by the milling passengers behind me, leaving her sitting there; for reasons I can't explain, wishing I weren't. After disembarking, I catch a fleeting glimpse of her as I make my way through passport control, then again while I wait in baggage reclaim. Alone, she looks slightly lost. Turning away to haul my case off the carousel, when I look around, she's gone.

* * *

I walk through the automatic doors into the arrivals hall, a smile stretching across my face when I see Nina, my sister, waiting for me.

'Hey.' I walk up to her and kiss her on the cheek. 'Thanks for coming to get me.'

'Someone had to.' She's cool, Nina, with brown eyes and toffee-coloured hair streaked with blonde. She smooths an errant strand of it behind one of her ears. 'Did you bring me some ciggies?'

'I forgot. Sorry.' It's only half a truth. The other half is about my refusal to be complicit in her poisoning herself.

'You're a terrible liar.' Nina sounds pissed off. 'You know I'll buy them anyway.'

'They're almost as cheap in the shops here,' I remind her. 'And at least it won't be on my conscience when you're dying from lung cancer,' I warn her.

'Shut the fuck up,' she says amiably. 'Anyway, a few cigarettes aren't going to kill me.' Pausing, her voice is different as she goes on. 'So what have you been up to, little brother?'

'The usual.' I shrug. 'Work, play, sleep...' Though probably not enough of the latter. Or the former, come to that.

'How's Jessie? Shame she couldn't join you.'

'Jessie's great,' I say brightly, leaving out what Jessie said about how deadly boring rural France was. 'She's just been promoted.' Jessie's my girlfriend of the last three years; while my career seems doomed not to get off the ground, her star is rising.

'Again?' Nina sounds surprised. 'How does that work with you guys?'

'It's OK.' I'm evasive. Relationships are about balance – it can swing either way, though ours has become somewhat weighted in one direction. And though I've been denying it to myself, Jessie and I are not what we used to be.

But Nina knows me too well. 'She's cool with that? The struggling musician and the high-flying consultant?' she says more quietly.

I'm silent for a moment. It's not just the lack of balance that's a problem. It's the growing absence of passion between us. 'We've been together three years. Things change, don't they? Believe it or not, I think I'm finally settling down into adult life,' I try to joke. But I'm thinking of the party Jessie went to without me, which turned out to be more of a grown-up kind of dinner party; how she said it had been nice not getting completely pissed – which is totally understandable, except that Jessie is an all-or-nothing kind of girl – mostly all. Plus, it wasn't just the one party.

Nina's silent for a moment. 'Don't sell yourself short, will you, Ned?'

Uncomfortable, I change the subject. 'So, about Mama's party,' I say casually. 'What's the plan?'

'The usual,' she says coolly. 'A hundred guests, outside caterers, a truckload of Philippe's vintage wine…'

'Great,' I say, my lack of enthusiasm tempered by the single fact that our neighbour is a superlative winemaker.

Beside me, Nina snorts. 'Sorry. Not fooled, little brother. I did suggest that you should play some of your music.'

Before I can stop it, a ridiculous sense of hope rises in me. 'What did they say?' But I should know better. My parents' opinion of my music career is common knowledge – and expressed far too frequently.

'They'd already booked some fricking harpist. Chantelle something or other. Haven't a clue what she's like. Sorry, Ned.' Nina sounds regretful. 'I tried.' Her voice changes. 'I'm really glad you're here.'

'Me too.' But even to me, my words are unconvincing. Comforting myself that I only have to be here a few days, days that no doubt will be eased by Philippe's wine, I lapse into silence. I rarely come back to France. My father has never accepted my music as a career and too many conversations have turned into heated confrontations about when I'm going to get a proper job; how music will never make me any money. It has added to the growing rift between us, which is why when he called a few weeks back, I put him off.

'*I'll call you back, Dad. I'm in the middle of something.*' The some-thing was actually a boozy pub lunch with my band.

'*Ned, this won't take long.*' He'd sounded irritated. '*It's your mother's birthday. She'd very much like it if you could be there.*'

I'd resigned myself to being summoned back to the fold, but the familiar sense of not belonging is back. Put simply, my life has moved on, while as Nina turns into the driveway, on the surface, everything here is just the same. The big old French manor house surrounded by neatly clipped shrubs, the lawns mown in stripes, the gravel drive immaculate.

Nina parks around the side, next to my father's Mercedes. After sitting there for a moment, I get out. After the constant noise of London, there's a silence I can only describe as deafening, until I walk towards the door and the dogs come tearing out to greet me, falling over themselves in their race to be first.

'Hey, boys.' Crouching down, I hold out my arms. Excitedly woofing and trying to lick me at the same time, it's no wonder they're happy. They've mastered what humans lose sight of.

Yesterday forgotten, tomorrow unknown, all they know is this moment.

Maybe we should all be more dog, I'm musing, as my father comes to meet me. 'Good of you to come, Ned.' His face is stern, his hand gripping my shoulder. 'Your mother will be pleased to see you.'

The gripping hand that's the closest we ever come to a hug feels less than welcoming. *It's as though I've become the family black sheep*, I can't help thinking, feeling oddly displaced as I walk along the familiar passageway that leads towards the kitchen, my mother's voice drifting towards me, clearly beseeching one of her many friends.

'You must come, *chérie*. Please, I am counting on you... You know it won't be the same without you.'

As I go into the kitchen, she turns. Seeing me, her eyes light up.

'I must go. *À bientôt.*' Blowing a kiss down the phone, she puts it down and holds out her arms. 'Ned.'

I walk into them. As they go around me, I hug her back, slightly awkwardly. As always, she's stylishly dressed, her make-up perfect, but she seems smaller, I can't help noticing – and a little older, the strands of grey in her long hair expertly blended with blonde. But a year has passed since I was last here; we are all getting older.

'Happy birthday, Mama.' I kiss her soundly on the cheek.

'Thank you. Oh Ned... It is so good to see you.' She holds my face in her hands, her eyes warm as she gazes into mine. 'How is your life in London? How is Jessie?'

'It's good. Everything's good.' Gently pulling free, I pin on a smile. 'I have a gig coming up. It's why I can only stay a couple of days.'

'Naughty boy.' She frowns at me. 'You are away for a year, and you have only two days to spend with your mother?'

Suddenly I feel guilty. 'I'll come back again soon. I promise.'

I'm saved as Nina comes in. 'Mama? The florist has just arrived with a whole ton of flowers. She wants to know where you want them all.'

'I am sure I told her this afternoon.' Looking mildly irritated, my mother sweeps out of the kitchen in a waft of Chanel's Coco while Nina makes us coffee.

Passing me a cup, her eyes pause on me. 'I know that look.'

I'm taken aback. 'What look?'

'Guilt.' She shrugs. 'Pointless emotion, Ned. You haven't done anything wrong, remember? But hey, I'm forgetting. You don't do emotions.'

'I do guilt,' I say wryly. 'And to be honest, she has a point. It's been a year.'

'She could go and see you in London,' Nina points out.

'I know.' But it wouldn't be a good idea. And it isn't just the thought of our mother being shoehorned into my and Jessie's tiny flat. It's the prospect of my life under her close scrutiny, asking uncomfortable questions I'd rather dodge.

But that aside, time seems to be passing at an ever-increasing speed, only adding to my guilt. Not wanting to dwell on what I haven't achieved with it, I drink my coffee. Then as Nina goes off to make a video call for work, for no reason I'm thinking of Stevie, the girl on the plane. Whether it was one of those chance meetings that will fade into the past, forgotten by both of us. Or whether fate will conspire and our paths will cross again.

* * *

Early that evening, I call Jessie.

'Hey. I miss you.' It's something I say less and less – that, if I'm honest, I feel less and less. But lounging on my bed, hundreds of miles away, I feel very alone.

It's a sentiment she clearly doesn't share. 'I can't talk for long, Ned. I'm about to go out.' It's obvious from her voice she's in a hurry.

'Oh.' This isn't at all what I'd hoped for from her. 'Anywhere nice?'

She hesitates. 'Just to a bar.'

'Nice. Who with?' I try to sound interested.

'Some friends,' she says vaguely. 'When are you back?'

'In a couple of days – for the gig, on Saturday.'

'Right.' She pauses. 'Look, can we catch up properly then? I'm sorry, but I really have to go.'

She ends the call, leaving me lying there in silence, somewhat bemused, contemplating that there was no love in her voice; no affection. She didn't even ask how I was – or my parents. But what's stranger still is that I feel nothing.

But it probably isn't strange at all. As Nina said, I have an inexplicable talent for being unemotional and that evening, with my mother's pre-birthday celebrations about to kick off, it isn't the time to be preoccupied. Going downstairs, I take a deep breath and pour myself a large glass of wine.

At a dinner table set for twenty, the food is sublime, the wine freely flowing, the company surprisingly entertaining, and very soon, the last person I'm thinking about is Jessie.

'You must play at my daughter's twenty-first, Ned.' Geneviève, one of my mother's oldest friends, corners me after we've eaten. 'The girls—' she raises perfectly arched eyebrows '—they will love you.'

'Thank you.' Gazing at her with the gratitude that follows consuming four glasses of my father's finest Bordeaux – Philippe's wine being reserved for tomorrow – I forget my promise to myself. *Only make decisions when you're sober.* 'Thank you very much. I would love to. I'll give you one of my cards.' I feel in my pocket for a business card, frowning, reaching deeper, before remembering. 'Sorry. In my jacket pocket. Upstairs.'

'Ned.' Geneviève brushes an imaginary fleck of dust off my shirt, before her hand gently pats my cheek. 'Do not worry about a card. I will speak with your mother.'

Not sure if she's being flirtatious, I reach for another glass of wine from a passing waiter just as Nina comes over.

'Been propositioned, little brother?' She raises an eyebrow at me.

'To be honest, I'm not sure.' I gaze after Geneviève's retreating back. 'But I suppose, in one sense, yes. I have. She wants me to play at her daughter's twenty-first birthday party.'

'You're brave.' Nina sips her wine. 'Have you met Persephone?'

'Persephone?' I splutter on my wine. 'Is that her name?'

'It is.' Nina lights up a cigarette. 'She and her friends got arrested in Paris not so long ago – for taking something illicit to a party.'

'What's wrong with that?' I look at her, mystified. 'I mean, doesn't everyone?'

'I think it was something to do with the party being thrown by the French foreign minister's son – at his official residence.' She exhales a small cloud of smoke. 'Apparently, it was quite a rowdy party. The neighbours ended up calling the police. Of course, it didn't help that his father was out of the country – visiting Ukraine, I believe. Persephone was found guilty of possession... Blah blah blah. It was all hushed up, of course. Money buys everything, doesn't it?'

'Shit.' I'm starting to regret saying I'd do the party. 'You'll have to come with me – as backup.'

She shakes her head disbelievingly. 'You have to be kidding, Ned.'

* * *

I awake on the morning of my mother's fifty-seventh birthday to the sound of birdsong outside my bedroom window, my eyes turning to Stevie's book, on my bedside table. Sitting up, I wince, my head thumping as a few blurred memories of last night come back.

I get up, go downstairs and put the kettle on before letting the dogs out. Standing on the doorstep, I take in the grass sparkling in the sunlight, the first of the cherry blossom starting to flower, the delicate warmth of the sun, all of them signs that spring is coming.

'Ned, darling.' My mother bustles into the kitchen. In a pink silk kimono over her pyjamas, she comes over and plants a kiss on one of my cheeks.

'Last night was fun, was it not?'

'It was a great night, Mama.' I watch her pour herself a strong coffee. 'Did you enjoy yourself?'

'Last night was your father's idea.' She's silent for a moment, her eyes resting on mine. 'Do you know what the best thing is?' She sounds uncharacteristically wistful. 'Maybe it is because I am getting older, but it is having my children here. Together – even if it is only for two days.' Sounding more like herself, she says it pointedly.

I frown slightly. It's as though there's something she isn't saying. I open my mouth to ask her, but then I put it down to growing older; the way it changes how you think.

'It's good to be here.' I hold her gaze, for the first time meaning every word.

Just then my father walks in. 'Ah. Ned. Just the person. I need the cars moved. Give me a hand, would you?'

That was it, I think, when I look back later. That single brief moment alone with my mother – before everything changed. Potentially the reason I came here, to be with the woman who brought me into the world, who raised me to become the musician she's less than proud of. To be unashamedly myself, whatever that is.

But none of us are perfect. After going out to help my father, the day passes in a whirl of beautifully dressed guests, more exquisite food, trays of champagne proffered by silent waiters, Philippe's promised vintage wine one of the high points, the other being my mother's speech.

'Thank you to all of you for coming to share this day – especially those who have travelled a long way.' Her eyes rest on me for a moment. 'Maybe being older makes me a little wiser – at least I hope so! I think it also gives me the right to be outspoken...' As she pauses, there's a ripple of laughter. 'But what I'd really like to say, is what matters most to me is the people in my life.' She falters, but only for a moment. 'It means the world to have you all here! I would just like to say, from the bottom of my heart, thank you.'

As she finishes speaking, there's a silence, before clapping starts. Then my father steps in and kisses her on the cheek. '*Bon anniversaire.*' Turning to everyone, he raises his glass. 'To my beautiful wife. Aimée.'

I watch as all the guests stand to toast my mother. Briefly I catch her eye again, noticing her face soften as she holds my gaze.

'What was that about?' I say to Nina. Our parents' parties are known for being glam and riotous, rather than poignant.

My sister looks just as puzzled. 'I don't know.'

Frowning, I can't help thinking that like me, Nina's picked up on something.

* * *

We find out the following morning that our sibling radar, though woefully out of practice, when put to the test, is still bang on. In the kitchen, we're making coffee when our parents join us.

'Sore heads?' my father enquires.

Nina shakes hers. 'Not me,' she says firmly. 'Ned drank my share. Ask him.'

'Rubbish.' I muster as much dignity as I can. 'I'm absolutely fine.'

When our father falls silent, Nina and I glance at each other, as our mother steps forward.

'Darlings?'

It isn't just the paleness of her skin, the troubled look in her eyes. It's palpable, the feeling around us, that something is terribly wrong.

* * *

It's the moment our lives change forever. When the carefreeness of youth, the assumption that life can be taken for granted, come to an end. The knowledge that cancer can happen to anyone is no longer a theory. From this point on, it's an integral part of all our lives.

'The thing is, there's no such thing as *just a small tumour*, is there?' Across the garden, Nina and I sit on the swings under an old beech tree that have been there since our childhood.

'I can't believe she went ahead with the party.' Nina's voice is tight. 'If it were me, I wouldn't have been able to.'

'Me neither.' I'm silent for a moment. 'I can't believe they didn't tell you.'

'Me neither.' Nina's face is ashen. 'I mean, I live here for frick's sake.' She's silent.

'Shows how good they are at hiding things, doesn't it?' I swallow the lump in my throat. 'Don't beat yourself up.'

'I still should have known, Ned.' Nina's eyes glitter with tears as she looks at me. 'We both should have. What happens now?' She sounds like a little girl. 'How do we know if it isn't more than just a little tumour? What else haven't they told us?'

* * *

There's quite a lot, as it turns out, including the fact that it's secondary breast cancer, after an initial diagnosis that was picked up years ago. Caught early, she didn't even need chemo. But this time around, as she tells us the prognosis isn't good, the reality sinks in that time is running out.

It's as though I'm caught between two worlds when I catch a flight back to London for the gig that weekend. There's guilt I've never known the like of at leaving my parents and Nina; yet the fact is, life goes on, or so I keep telling myself as I gaze out of the window at the clouds.

But it feels even less real when I get back to the flat. If I'd been hoping for any comfort from her, Jessie is oddly subdued. 'I'm sorry about your mum, Ned.' She hugs me, but it's the polite kind of hug you'd give a distant friend, rather than compassionate. Then she tells me there's a dinner party we're invited to.

I sigh. 'I'm really not in the mood, Jess. I was hoping you and I could have a quiet evening in.'

'I didn't expect you to come with me.' She doesn't meet my

eyes. 'But Alice organised this weeks ago. I can't cancel now – you know what she's like.'

I do indeed know what Alice is like. But this is my hour of need. Going over to Jessie, I put my arms around her. 'These are pretty exceptional circumstances. I'm sure she'd understand if you told her why.'

But she pulls away gently. 'I'm sorry, Ned. I can't do that.'

It's obvious that Alice's party is more important to her than my mother's illness, and in the event, Jessie goes out early, her hair freshly washed, wearing a dress I haven't seen before and spritzed in an unfamiliar perfume.

Alone in our flat, I go to the box room. It's more like a large cupboard and arguably the least tidy part of the flat. But it's where I feel most at home; the place where my creative genius gets unleashed. Putting on my headphones, I go through the music for tomorrow night's gig. The gig's a thirtieth birthday party at a posh hotel – the kind of gig I've been striving for; that if I get right, could lead to many more. It seems the cruellest irony that for reasons I can do nothing about, my mind is elsewhere.

Losing track of time, the evening rapidly passes. I'm on my fourth beer and still working when Jessie pushes the door open.

She's obviously had a good time. Her face is flushed from wine, her eyes sparkling brightly. 'You're up late.'

'Just getting ready for tomorrow.' I pause. 'Did you have fun?'

'It was OK.' Turning away, she stifles a yawn. 'Alice sends love, by the way.' She stretches up her arms. 'I'm going to bed.'

Her lack of affection leaves me sitting there, slightly stunned. Has she always been this cold or is it just that I haven't noticed before? As she closes the door behind her, I can't decide.

* * *

The following morning, I lie in bed, listening to the city coming to life. At some point, Jessie's phone buzzes and she stirs, yawning as she picks it up and glances at the screen.

As she's holding it, her phone buzzes again. Reading the message, she types a reply.

'Everything OK?' Lying there, I stare at the ceiling.

'It's just Alice.' Stretching luxuriantly, she yawns again. 'I'd better have a shower.' Throwing the duvet back and getting out, she pads naked to the bathroom.

I take in her tanned legs and soft skin, the tangle of long hair; wonder again how it is that I feel not even slightly aroused. But I have other things going on, I remind myself. My mother's illness, still forefront of my mind – not to mention this gig tonight. Sighing, I get out of bed just as Jessie comes out of the bathroom. As we pass, I brush against her damp skin; yet again, thinking how odd it is that it does nothing to me.

* * *

If timing lies at the heart of luck and great fortune, of the most brilliant synchronicities, it stands to reason that it's also the orchestrator of our greatest downfalls, never more clearly demonstrated than when I ask Jessie if she's coming to the gig. Despite the distance between us, she's always been my staunchest supporter, so it hasn't crossed my mind that she might not want to. Plus, if it goes well, as I'm hoping it will, this could be the start of redressing the imbalance between us.

'You're playing at a private party, Ned,' she objects. 'It's not for you to invite people.'

'You can be my roadie,' I joke. 'No one will argue with that. And I don't suppose anyone will even notice.' I pause, frowning at her as I work it out. Back in the day, she wouldn't have given it a second thought. 'Be honest, Jess. You don't want to, do you?'

'It isn't that.' Standing there, Jessie looks awkward.

As it sinks in that this is about far more than the gig, the blood in my veins turns to ice. 'What do you mean?'

She shakes her head. 'I wasn't going to say anything.' But as she sits on the edge of the bed, her composure vanishes. 'This is hopeless.'

'What is?' I say stupidly.

'Pretending, Ned. Us.' Sounding distraught, Jessie doesn't meet my eyes. 'I know the timing is terrible, but we don't do anything together any more. We don't even like the same things.' At last, she manages to look at me. 'Why can't we both be honest with each other and admit we're avoiding the elephant in the room?'

'Elephant?' It sinks in that she's talking about the void between us; a void I've noticed myself, but kind of got used to; that even has an odd familiarity to it. But after my mother's bombshell and the week I've just had, suddenly I can't face it. 'You're right about one thing – this is terrible timing.'

'I know. But what's the point in going on like this?' she says sadly. 'You and I... It used to be different, Ned. You used to have dreams. I believed in you. I really thought you were going to be one of those musicians who made it. But all this time is going by...'

Her words sting. 'It's never too late. And I still have dreams,' I say obstinately. She's not putting all of this on me. 'And don't forget it's you who's always shoehorning in dinners and parties and galleries and shopping – not to mention evenings at the theatre and with...'

'It isn't that, Ned.' Jessie's face is pale.

I freeze. 'What is it, then?'

She sighs. Then the words start tumbling out of her. 'Your

music is great... I love it. You know I do. But the fact is you may never get a break. Not everyone does. Meanwhile, you won't even consider doing anything else.'

Gobsmacked, I shake my head. 'But you've always supported my music.'

'You're right. I have.' She looks away. 'For quite a long time. No one would be more delighted than me if it took off.' Her eyes fill with tears. 'I suppose it would be nice if things were on more equal terms. If now and then, it were you taking me out, rather than the other way around. If we could plan an extravagant holiday... Buy a nice car...' Getting up, she folds her arms around herself. 'You don't have to tell me how shallow it sounds.' Desperation flickers in her eyes. 'But it feels like everything's down to me. Like we don't have any balance in our lives.'

It's the same word Nina used. *Balance*. 'This is only for now,' I say defiantly. 'It won't always be like this.'

'You don't know that,' she says.

I'm silent for a moment. 'I can't believe we're having this conversation – right now, when my mother is ill.'

She looks uncomfortable. 'I didn't plan to, Ned. But when it comes to something like this, there's never a good time. And I can't go on putting my life on hold.'

Standing there, it's like I've been punched.

But Jessie hasn't finished. 'You're a great guy. But...'

'But what?' I prepare myself for the next blow; the *but* telling me everything I need to know.

Jessie looks exasperated. 'It's your feelings – or lack of them, rather. Your emotions, Ned. I can't read you. Your mother's ill, for frick's sake. And you're acting like everything's the same.'

'What am I supposed to do?' I stare at her. 'Life goes on. And I have a gig, remember? Has it occurred to you that just maybe I'm trying to hold things together?'

'Is that all you can say?' She looks at me incredulously. 'Wow, Ned. If that's what you think, you really do have problems.' She pauses. 'Do you realise that in the three years we've been together, not once have I seen you cry? Take yesterday, for instance. When you told me about your mother, you were completely unemotional.'

'It might have looked like that,' I bluster. 'But you've no idea how I feel inside.'

She sighs. 'Just for once, can't you be honest with yourself?'

My body tenses. 'I'm not hiding anything from you.'

'You can't even see it, can you?' She looks at me sadly again. 'You've been doing it so long, you don't know any different. And that's the thing. I'm beginning to realise I don't even know who the real Ned is.'

'This is the real Ned,' I say urgently. 'Standing right here.' Then I stop. 'Are you saying you want us to break up?'

In the silence, as we stand there, her phone buzzes again. A look of something like guilt crosses her face.

As I gaze at her, I realise that just like that, it's over between us. 'You've made your mind up, haven't you?'

'I didn't plan for it to be now.' Jessie's voice is shaking. 'I wanted to be here for you.'

'You have a frigging odd way of showing it,' I say tightly. Suddenly it's too much. 'Look, I can't deal with this. Once I've done the gig, I'm going back to France. I want to spend some time with my mother – while I still can. I'll take as much of my stuff as I can. I'll arrange for someone to collect the rest.'

Going to the wardrobe, I get the case down from on top of it and start to pack, before remembering the book Stevie gave me, which I'd brought with me to carry on reading on the plane. Seeing it on the floor next to the bed, I pick it up.

'What's that?' Jessie eyes it with interest.

'A friend gave it to me.'

'A friend?' She frowns. 'Is there something you're not telling me, Ned?'

'Absolutely nothing,' I say wearily. Is it really so alien to her that I should have a friend? 'I met a girl on a flight. She lent me her book. She thought I needed a distraction.'

'You mean you actually talked to her?' Jessie looks confused.

'It was nothing.' But as her phone buzzes again, suddenly I realise it *was* something. But the real reason for Jessie's interest in the book is to deflect from whatever it is she isn't telling me. 'Don't try and put this on me, Jessie. We both know it's you who's met someone else.' Right on cue, her phone buzzes for the third time. I meet her eyes. 'That isn't Alice, is it?'

* * *

Somehow I keep myself together for the gig. My performance is less than perfect, but buoyed up with beer, in the circumstances, I think I pretty much excel myself – and it helps that almost everyone at the party is pissed. Jessie isn't there when I get back to the flat. Packing the rest of my stuff, all that remains are some books I don't really want any more and some musical paraphernalia that will have to be sent on separately.

When I've finished, I gaze around the flat, at the calm, neutrally painted walls, the enormous sofa that nearly didn't make it up here; then at the views of the Thames, the lights of aircraft making their descent into Heathrow, wondering how Jessie and I have come to this; how three years of my life can be over, just like that.

Leaving my key on the side, I drag my cases downstairs and take an Uber to the airport. When I check in my baggage, the cost is eyewatering, but in the context of everything else that's going on, I just pay it.

When I analyse it, all I'm leaving is a flat I don't love and a woman who doesn't love me; a career that isn't going anywhere. But if anyone had told me that endings can be beginnings, I'd probably have punched them.

Topping up my caffeine levels sufficiently to keep me awake and buying some Red Bulls just in case, three hours later, I board my flight. After take-off, I am one of those passengers who has a gin and tonic for breakfast – I know. Don't judge me. But it has the desired effect of numbing the sense I have that I'm leaving behind one of the most significant chapters of my life.

3

FAY

As I stand in the arrivals hall in Limoges, I'm not sure where it's come from, this sense of feeling detached from my life; that I'm just another woman who's getting older, for whom the years are speeding up; that all this unaccounted-for time is passing me by. Maybe it's watching all the people coming off the plane: the hikers, the young couples, the families being reunited. The optimism that comes with being young; the brightness of their eyes.

I've always found it fascinating trying to guess at other people's lives – like this young man, for instance. With sunglasses on top of his head, he has slightly long hair, a guitar case slung over his back and several cases on his trolley. His eyes are red and he wears the look of someone who hasn't slept. Probably burning the candle at both ends, I'm guessing, thinking of my own children. And probably arriving to embark on the adventure of a lifetime.

He looks up as a girl of a similar age calls out. *Ned*, I think I hear her say, before he turns and starts walking towards her. He hugs her and the two of them head for the exit.

Standing there, I wonder if anyone notices me. Fay, devoted

wife and mother of grown-up children, owner of a lovely old French house and immaculate garden. Except it's not my money that's paid for the house – it's Hugh's. Ashamed though I am to say it, I am the characterisation of a woman who's become defined by her husband.

Seeing my oldest friend appear in arrivals, a feeling of relief comes over me. I wave at her. This is exactly what I need – a few days with Marcie bringing me down to earth, banishing these self-indulgent thoughts over a glass of fine wine as we put the world to rights.

But in the event, it doesn't quite work out like that. March in south-west France is fickle. It can be blessed with warm days and unbroken sun. It can also bring cold winds and heavy rain that fills the ditches and floods the narrow lanes. For the duration of Marcie's stay, it's mostly the latter.

The first day, when we drive down the lane towards the village, I slow down, then stop as we come to the water flooding the only road to our house. 'I'm so sorry, but we're cut off.' Wondering when apologising became my default setting, when I have no control over the rain.

'Aren't you worried?' Marcie flaps. 'What if one of us is ill?'

'I don't suppose we shall be,' I say firmly, more concerned about some of the older villagers.

'Yes, but you don't know. Surely it has to stop soon,' Marcie frets, as she gazes out of the window at the rain.

'Hopefully.' I cross my fingers as I reverse and turn the car around.

'I was hoping we could go into Limoges for some shopping.' Marcie sounds disappointed.

It's the only time I thank my lucky stars for the rain. Limoges is an eighty-minute drive, and while there's the unresolved problem of a twenty-first birthday present I need to buy for Persephone, the daughter of one of our closest neighbours, with Marcie's stay bookended between two airport trips, I've no desire to add a third. I try to distract her. 'I have a rather nice bottle of white wine in the fridge. Let's open it when we get home.'

It works, and after a glass or two of wine and reminiscing about the old days, Marcie's back to waxing lyrical about France. 'You know, if I had a place like this, I'd move here. It must be wonderful in the summer when everyone comes out on holiday.' That she seems to have forgotten how she felt earlier is maybe the surest sign of a good wine.

'There are the children to think of,' I say, even though the children are grown-ups. And although I never used to, I prefer France without the crowds. 'We're lucky, to have the best of both worlds.' And Hugh would never consider moving here for good. He likes our suburban life in Surrey as much as he does golf, loudly and embarrassingly holding forth at dinner parties about our house in France. 'But you know, I *would* like to spend more time here.' I've come to savour the sense of space; the simplicity to life that's absent at home in England.

'Why don't you?' Marcie studies me for a moment. 'And I'm not talking about what Hugh doesn't want to do. I'm talking about you.'

It's a rare moment of connection between us, one I'm not expecting, and unaccustomed tears prick my eyes. For the first time in I don't know how long, someone has considered what *I* might want. Blinking, I force a smile. 'Thank you. You're a good friend, Marcie.' But I still can't help thinking it isn't that simple; that regardless of what she says, I do have to think of Hugh.

That night, I'm unable to sleep. Thoughts fill my head – unsettled, restless ones, about my life, my marriage, my family, while I try to work out why what's always been enough suddenly isn't;

where my unease has come from; why it's suddenly taken centre stage.

Now and then, the hoot of an owl breaks a silence that doesn't exist in Surrey, where the rumble of traffic is constant. Lying there, I think of our home, imagining Hugh in bed, completely oblivious to the rest of the world. Oblivious to how I'm feeling, too.

The following day, to my relief, the clouds have cleared, leaving a watery landscape bathed in sunlight. After driving to a nearby village, we park on the outskirts and walk along a path by the river. It's beautiful here, on either side the sloping narrow streets filled with higgledy-piggledy little houses, a central area that in summer is a mecca for picnickers and markets. But at this time of year, with holidaymakers absent, to Marcie's disappointment, the single bar is closed.

'There must be somewhere else.' She stares at the bar's shuttered windows, the man halfway up a ladder outside it, holding a paintbrush.

'I'm afraid not,' I say gently. 'But never mind. The cellar at home is stocked with wine – and there's a rather nice piece of fish I was going to cook.'

'No offence,' she says. 'But it isn't the same, is it?'

I'm taken aback. It isn't that long ago, I remind myself, that I would have felt exactly the same. After all, it's what France is known for – the pretty shops, the bars and restaurants in picturesque settings. But for me, the allure of these has faded; I have a yearning I can't describe for something more.

You're a spoiled, bored housewife, I scold myself, *who doesn't know how good she has it. Get a grip, Fay. Countless women would bite their hands off for a fraction of the time you're lucky enough to have here.*

* * *

When Marcie goes back to London, after taking her to the airport, I spend a leisurely afternoon in Limoges looking for that present for Persephone. With Hugh still in England until the weekend, I have a rare few days to myself; unbroken time alone I'm suddenly relishing.

Maybe it's the changing of the seasons, the days starting to warm, but I find myself more and more drawn towards the garden. When we bought the house, after the building work was done, Hugh had the pool installed and the garden expensively landscaped. Typically low maintenance, it's mostly lawn that he pays someone local to mow once a week, with shrubs that someone prunes – somewhat brutally – once a year.

But today, as I stand outside, I'm seeing what I've never noticed before. Pale green shoots appearing through the earth, the faintest hint of colour on the trees, a vibrancy to the birdsong that would usually pass me by.

How come I haven't seen all this before? Turning to look at the house, for the first time I notice the bare stems that have been trained around the windows, that in summer flower prolifically with roses. In my mind, that's how I've always pictured our house: rose-covered. But today as I walk closer, I notice tiny shoots forming on the stems that will later develop into leaves, then buds – the part of the cycle of life that has to happen before a rose can flower.

When it comes to planting anything, I wouldn't know where to start. And anyway, Hugh wouldn't want me to. Almost immediately, I start to feel frustrated. When everything's decided by Hugh, paid for by Hugh, where in all this is something that's mine?

I sigh. It's never bothered me before. It's been as much my choice as Hugh's, I remind myself. *But when did you actually stop and seriously think about it?* I find myself asking. And it isn't Hugh who's changed. But as I look at myself, I see a woman locked into what's evolved into a rigidly defined pattern of us; half of Hugh-and-Fay, so much so I've forgotten how it feels just to be me.

That evening, Hugh calls me to tell me there's been a change of plan and he isn't coming out to France this weekend. Something to do with the golf club in Surrey he's a member of.

'But there's the party, Hugh,' I remind him. 'Persephone's twenty-first. Geneviève's expecting us.'

'They're hardly going to miss us, Fay. You know what those parties are like. In any case, it can't be helped.' Going on, he tells me that he's booked me on a flight home tomorrow.

As I think of returning to England, resentment washes over me. Hugh's always booked our flights. But why, for once, couldn't he have asked me? As he goes on talking, suddenly I'm realising that nothing he has to say is remotely of interest to me.

Yet still I say nothing. After the call ends, I pour myself a glass of wine. I think about calling Geneviève to make our excuses, but put it off, a strange feeling taking over me as I pick up the copy of the local paper on the side.

Usually I wouldn't give it a second glance, but tonight, as I leaf through the mostly banal and trivial features, a photo catches my attention. It's of an elderly man with smiling eyes, sitting on a beaten-up chair, holding a bunch of brightly coloured flowers.

Curious, I read on. It seems he runs a kind of gardening commune, similar to what the British would call allotments. He goes on to explain that people have the freedom to grow whatever they choose to there, taking advantage of the sheltering walls and rich soil; the sun. The location is just a couple of miles from here, and as I read on, the seed of an idea begins to form.

After another restless night, the following morning, I wake early. I make a cup of coffee and take it outside. Breathing in the cool air, the peace is tangible and I feel it sink into me.

It's a peace I wouldn't notice if Hugh were here, or anyone else for that matter. As I try to work out why that is, it's shattered by the sound of my phone ringing in the kitchen. I go inside and pick it up to see Hugh's face on the screen. Hesitating, I'm guessing it's about something trivial – such as collecting his dry-cleaning on my way back from the airport later today, or picking up some food. My heart sinks at the mediocrity of it all. The expectedness. The realisation that there is no room for spontaneity, that in the grand scheme of things, none of it really matters. That Hugh simply sees me as someone to meet his needs; as no more than a useful extension of himself.

After letting his call go to voicemail, I switch my phone off. Then picking up my coffee again, I go outside.

Sitting on one of the chairs, I'm oblivious to the damp from last night's dew seeping through my pyjamas as it strikes me I haven't begun to close the house up; to pack. As the sun's rays reach through the branches in the silence, it's like my whole existence is under a spotlight.

Who are you, Fay – apart from the mother and wife? I've been hiding behind the pretence that my children still need me, when they have their own lives; that Hugh wouldn't function without me when, in all honesty, a cook and cleaner would fulfil his needs.

When we're only here for a finite number of years, years we could do anything with, what do I have to show for mine? It's a brutal question, one I can't not ask. The world needs all kinds of people, but when so many people do great things with their lives, apart from raising my children, my sixty-one years seem utterly meaningless. It's the banality of my daily routine, the insignificance of what I fill it with. The absence of anything that benefits anyone other than Hugh.

You're supposed to be packing up and flying home, I remind myself. *To the dull grey of England, with its congested towns and crowded roads. To pick up Hugh's dry-cleaning, do his washing-up; be the dutiful wife he expects you to be.*

But if I were to be really and truly honest with myself, what I want right now is to stay here.

I breathe out slowly. Am I brave enough? Apart from Hugh's objections, I can't see any reason why I shouldn't. I feel a fleeting moment of courage. This is my life, after all.

With some trepidation I call my husband. 'Hugh? Sorry I missed you this—'

He interrupts me. 'Bring some of that red home, will you, darling? And my jacket's at the dry-cleaner's in—'

It's my turn to interrupt. 'I'm afraid you'll have to pick it up yourself, Hugh.' I try to sound matter-of-fact. 'I've decided to stay on a bit longer.'

There's a stunned silence. 'Nonsense. I've booked you a flight.'

'Maybe you should have asked me first.' I try to stop my voice shaking. 'After all, we were expecting to be here this weekend. I've already made plans.'

'Plans?' He sounds outraged. 'I'm sorry, but you're going to have to change them.'

Suddenly it's crystal clear. This is lunacy, I'm suddenly realising. Hugh expecting me to change my plans just because he has. 'Because you're playing golf?' I say calmly. 'Have you stopped to think about what I might want? The thing is, Hugh, that while you're at the golf club with your chums all day, I'll be at home on my own. Surely it doesn't matter if I stay here?' When there's silence, I go on. 'If you're worried about the state of the kitchen, I suggest you either clean it yourself or pay someone to do it for you. You could ask Angela for her cleaner's number.' Angela is our neighbour.

'What's going on?' he says suspiciously.

'If you really want to know...' I take a deep breath. 'I've been thinking I'd like to do something – with the garden. It hasn't changed in such a long time... I was rather thinking I'd like to grow something.'

'You've never grown anything in your life.' His tone is scathing. 'And I'm not at all sure it's a good idea. I spent a lot of money having it done.'

'I know, Hugh. But that was years ago. The kids were young. We don't need acres of lawn any more. I was thinking...' I hesitate. 'I was thinking of planting a vegetable garden.'

'It's a terrible idea,' he says brusquely. 'You're not there half the time. And it would need watering and weeding.'

'Well...' I take a deep breath. 'That's another thing. I've been thinking I'd like to spend more time here,' I say, slightly nervously. 'I can't see any reason why I shouldn't, really. You're usually either working or playing golf. And I... I suppose I want a new challenge in my life.'

'We'll talk about this when you're home,' he says sharply. 'Assuming you are coming home?' There's sarcasm in his voice.

'Of course I am. I'll let you know when I've booked a flight. Goodbye, Hugh.' My hands are shaking as I end the call, then I switch my phone off again before he can call me back and change my mind.

The conversation does little other than to affirm in my mind that Hugh's view of me is as someone without autonomy; whose life path exists solely to complement his own. But however shocking a realisation it is, I can't deny I can feel something shifting inside me.

Usually, after an altercation with Hugh, I'd feel terrible – and guilty, seeing it as all my fault. But today, I'm oddly calm, wondering how it is I haven't reached this point before.

There's something liberating about the prospect of a few days alone and after a morning poring over gardening websites, in the afternoon, I pull on a jacket and set off in the direction of the village I went to with Marcie.

The sun is warm, enough that before long I push my sleeves up, the soft air layered with birdsong as I feel the faintest of breezes against my skin. As I walk, I pass houses that are locked and shuttered, waiting for the first days of summer to arrive. I know, because it's how our house used to be. Dormant until July, when for a few short weeks, we'd throw the windows and shutters open, filling it with life, until we closed it up and were gone again.

Such happy days... A pang of nostalgia hits me for a part of my life that's gone forever, when I was a mother, a homemaker. But the passing of time is an inevitable part of life. Children grow up, I tell myself. Things change.

Being out in the countryside seems to magically clear my head. Of course, I've always wanted my children to have wonderful, independent lives. And as I think of my call to Hugh this morning, I have no regrets. Of course, it would have shocked him that I'd go against his wishes, and yes, it would have been better to speak face to face. But there were things that needed saying – and sometimes you just have to say them. And you can't always predict a crisis point.

Is that what this is? Because unless he starts listening to me, it potentially is, I'm realising, slightly shocked. A crossroads – at least for me it is. In the context of many years of marriage, quite a major one.

He'll say I'm thinking only of myself. And though it appears this has come out of nowhere, it's been brewing slowly, so that in a sense, there's an inevitability to it.

What do I want? I ask myself. But as I try to work out what it is that I'm missing, I'm taken aback as I realise it's something along the lines of freedom.

You've only yourself to blame, I scold myself. *It was you who let it go. You could have kept your independence, got a job, even. Hugh wouldn't have liked it, but he would have got over it. Eventually.*

I follow the lane around a bend, past a farm where several generations are gathered at a table outside in the sun. The image of family united; as mine used to be. Would it make a difference if it still were? Unable to answer my question, I keep walking.

On the outskirts of the village, beside a weathered door in a stone wall, I notice a sign I've never seen before – *Jardin partagé*, underneath which has been added, in smaller letters, *À louer*.

I stare at it, translating it. It means allotments for rent, as suddenly I realise, whether subconsciously or deliberately, I've found the garden I was reading about.

Curious, I push the door open. As I step inside, I find myself in what feels like a secret garden. Edged with high walls and trees that are coming into blossom, there is little in the way of lawn. Instead, the entire space has been divided into what appear to be randomly planted flower beds.

It's the antithesis of my and Hugh's garden. Following one of the narrow paths, almost immediately I stop again. Everywhere I look are signs of life – green shoots poking through the soil, artfully arranged frameworks which I'm guessing are for plants to climb up; a few early flowers in which bees are bumbling, amongst banks of last year's flowers gone to seed.

Glancing around for the man in the magazine, I follow one of the paths, breathing it all in, as suddenly I know with certainty that this, right here, is what I've been searching for.

4

ZEKE

I notice the woman before she sees me; out of the corner of my eye, watching her as she surveys everyone's gardens. Not for the first time, I curse the magazine for bringing me the wrong kinds of people because on first glance – no offence – I'd hazard a guess that's what she is.

OK, so I'm making an assumption here, based on clothes that look more suited to wandering around the shops, hair that for a woman her age almost certainly isn't natural. You old hypocrite, I tell myself, feeling a smile spread across my face. Judging her, when I'm always telling other people that none of us should judge.

But it isn't her appearance that puts me off. It's the attitude most folks seem to have, about wanting everything to be instant these days – and that includes gardens, money being the means for them to achieve that. Looking at the lady again, I wouldn't mind betting that cash isn't something she's short of. But part of the beauty of gardening is the time it takes for things to grow – at least, that's what I tried to explain to that journalist woman who wrote the article. Plants are like people. Give them poor soil, or block the light out, and they won't have a chance. Nurture them, give them time for proper strong roots to form, and they will grow.

Too often these days, time equates to money, which is kind of sad. We forget to live in the moment; that time is undervalued, one of our most precious commodities. But that's something we only learn when we're old enough to have wasted too much of it, I reflect ruefully. When we become aware that we don't have indefinite reserves of it.

'*Excusez-moi.*' I turn to see the woman walking towards me. Despite her attempt at French – not a bad one – she's English, as I guessed from her clothes.

'Good afternoon to you.' Speaking in English, I stand up and raise an imaginary hat. 'Can I help at all?'

'It's you, isn't it?' She stares at me. 'Sorry. I mean, I saw you in the paper. At least, I think it was you.' An anxious look crosses her face.

Throwing back my head, I laugh. In my experience, laughter is the balm to most social unease. 'If you're talking about that old rubbish the journalist wrote, then yes. That's me. Name's Zeke.' I hold out my hand. She hesitates, before taking it.

'I'm Fay.'

'So how can I help, Fay?'

'I saw the sign on the lane. I was really hoping...' She hesitates, looking around. 'That you might have a spare allotment.' She hesitates again. 'I suppose I'd just love a little piece of land to grow things on.'

'You would?' I don't hide my surprise. Women like her usually have other people to do their own gardens. She has a manicure, for starters.

She looks put out. 'Is that so unlikely?'

'Have you had a garden before?' I say more politely.

'Yes.' She pauses. 'As a matter of fact, we have a large garden –

with shrubs and trees and lawn. But...' She sighs. 'I suppose I've never had a garden that's completely my own. I want to grow things,' she repeats. 'Flowers, carrots...' she says vaguely. 'Anything, really. And my husband is quite against the idea of any changes to our own garden. He says I don't know what I'm doing. He's right, of course – but I want to learn – which is why I'm here.'

'I see.' Studying her, I take in the unhappiness in her eyes. It's often a reason people turn to gardening. There's something healing and life-affirming about it. But I'm forgetting something. 'I should have taken the sign down. You see, the last space has just been taken.' Seeing her face fall, I explain. 'There are only half a dozen of them – that journalist lady forgot to put that in. But how about I show you around?'

'Thank you,' she says humbly. 'If you have time?'

'Time is one thing I'm not short of.' I beam at her again. Then glance at the heels on her boots. 'You wouldn't happen to have anything a little more, er...'

'Robust?' she suggests, blushing slightly. 'I'm afraid not. But these are fine. I walked here in them – from our house.'

I raise my eyebrows slightly that this lady considers these to be walking boots. 'Not to worry. Shall I lead the way?'

As I show her around the garden, she says little, just takes it all in. 'What's all this?' She points to a small, glorious mountain of compost.

'Ah. That's what's going to feed everyone's vegetables this year.' I nod towards a row of wheelbarrows. 'Give it a couple of weeks, and I wouldn't mind betting the whole lot will be dug in.'

'Two weeks?' Her eyebrows disappear into her hair. 'That soon?'

'Time is of the essence. Any later will be too late,' I say firmly. 'In two weeks, we'll all be planting.' I pause. 'No offence, but are you sure you'd be up for this?' I can't help asking. 'It's hard work –

in all weathers. If you don't keep on top of it, you'll end up fighting a losing battle. Where there are flowers, there will always be weeds...' Stopping short of telling her gardening plays havoc with your hands, it's what I say to everyone who comes here. Nature's a fierce adversary, as I know too well.

'I'm sure it will be no problem,' she says firmly. 'I can learn, can't I?' She clearly isn't put off. 'And everyone who grows things here... they had to start somewhere, didn't they?'

'True.' I hesitate. 'What does your husband think about you doing this?'

Her cheeks colour faintly. 'I haven't told him.'

I'm quietly impressed; liking that under her elegant exterior, there's steel. 'That doesn't bother you?'

'No.' Stopping, she looks at me. 'And I don't think it should. I mean, if he weren't so utterly unreasonable, I'd be digging myself a veg patch at home.' She says it with feeling, before looking slightly shocked with herself. 'Only I have to say, I rather like the idea that he'll never come here.'

Nodding, I'm silent. I'm old enough to know not to get involved in other folks' marital glitches.

'So which is yours?' she asks.

'Over there.' I nod towards the path. 'Come on. I'll show you.'

I'm proud of my garden. More blood, sweat and tears have gone into it than anyone on this earth will ever know. As a result, there's something to harvest every season of the year. Reaching it, I stop. 'This is it. Of course, at this time of year, it's a little sparse.' But it's the time of year the prep goes in.

She stands there in silence, studying the frames in place for this year's peas and beans to clamber up, the neat rows of onions and leeks, another of spinach, the last remaining stalks of Brussels sprouts. 'I don't know what to say,' she says at last.

'Erm...' I'm not sure what she's getting at. 'Haven't changed your mind, have you?'

'Oh no. Not in the least.'

'These are what's left of last year's sunflowers.' Reaching out a hand, I touch one of the tall, dried stems. 'I leave them for the birds.'

'They like the seeds?'

'Indeed they do. We have a philosophy around here.' I pause. 'We grow in sympathy with nature. Take the soil: after harvesting a crop, it's only right to give back to the earth. At this time of year, that's about manure, like I said.' I point to some low clumps of green. 'These herbs have done well.' Picking a leaf from a mint plant, I pass it to her.

She tastes it. 'You forget everything doesn't come in jars, don't you?'

I raise my eyebrows. I've never been one to take for granted the fruits the earth gives us. 'There's years of goodness been dug into that soil. But the pay-off is worth it.' I pause. 'You're still not put off?'

'Quite the opposite.' She looks slightly dazed. 'I think it's exactly what I need.'

I sigh. It saddens me to let her down. 'I'm just sorry I don't have any space I can offer you.'

She looks disappointed. 'I'd forgotten that. Well, is there a waiting list or something I can sign up to?'

'There is.' The list is more trouble than it's worth, because if I've learned anything in the years I've been here, by the time a space comes up, there's a good chance people will either have changed their minds or moved on. 'It's a bit on the long side, but I can add you if you like.' I go into my shed, find my clipboard and write her name down. 'Want to give me your telephone number?'

Before she can reply, my mobile buzzes. Now, it's rare I get any calls, which is why when I do, I answer them. 'Sorry. Would you mind if I take this?'

She nods. 'Of course.'

I pick up my phone. 'Zeke here.' Turning my back on her, I listen. And that's when something completely extraordinary happens.

'That was Delilah,' I say to Fay when the call ends, still taken aback by the timing of this. 'She was calling to tell me her mother isn't well. She's moving back to England to look after her.'

'Oh.' She looks at me blankly. 'I'm sorry.'

I realise I haven't explained. 'Delilah has one of the plots here. It means she's going to have to give it up.' Which means I'm going to have to start trawling through my list again. Unless... I pause, looking at Fay. 'Do you believe in synchronicity?'

She looks confused. 'I'm not sure.'

'It's about being in the right place at the right time.' I watch her face. 'And, well... Maybe that's what's happening right now. You, being here, just as an allotment comes up...'

Her eyes widen. 'What about your list?'

I burst out laughing. 'It's my list – I can do what the hell I want with it!' Instead of checking who's been on it longest, I've always tended to base my choice on degrees of need. Right now, Fay needs this – I can tell. More than that, I have a hunch she's going to fit in here. 'Welcome, Fay! If you want it, Delilah's allotment is yours.'

A look of utter shock crosses her face, followed by one of delight. 'Thank you.' She still looks slightly disbelieving. 'Is there some paperwork I need to sign? And I imagine you need a deposit from me.'

I shake my head. 'I need nothing of the sort. We have what I guess you'd call an honesty box – back in my shed. You pay what you think is reasonable, and I see the money ends up where it's meant to. Does that sound OK?'

'It really does. Thank you.' Still looking dazed, this time she smiles properly. 'Honestly. I can't tell you how much this means to me.'

* * *

I'm still thinking about Fay long after she's gone, suddenly realising I forgot to ask her if she lives here or if she's one of those second-home owners who comes and goes. But no matter, my gut tells me I've done the right thing – and that's good enough for me.

Smiling to myself, I think how there's been a flow to the day, from the timing of her coming here, just as Delilah called, to the deal I struck on Fay's behalf to buy the tools in Delilah's shed. As I dig up a bowlful of potatoes, I can't help thinking it's been a while since something like this has happened in my life.

Across the garden, I notice Rémy coming towards me. I've known her for years. One of the first to take on an allotment here, she lives in the nearby village.

'Afternoon.' Raising my arm in greeting, I wince.

Rémy shoots me a disapproving look. 'You have been digging again, haven't you, Zeke? After the doctor told you to rest, too,' she scolds. 'When will you learn?'

I quite like Rémy fluffing over me, but only in small doses. 'There's nothing wrong with me. You planting today?'

She shakes her head. 'Still digging in all that manure. Anyway, it is far too dry. And I'm running out of water.'

'You'll be fine after the rain we've just had. But if you don't have enough, help yourself to mine.' I nod towards the barrel that's been filled by the rain.

She looks at it, mystified. 'I will never understand why your tank is full, Zeke, and everyone else's is empty.'

I laugh at her. 'You know that saying about being in the right place at the right time?' I wink at her.

'You have the luck of the devil.' Looking disapproving, she goes on her way.

Left alone, thinking of her comment about luck, my smile fades. My smart reply would be that we make our own luck. But things have happened in my life that were out of my control. Bad things. They're things no one knows about. But there's no need for them to know. We all have things we keep to ourselves.

* * *

The following day, Fay is back bright and early. Wearing pristine white trainers, and carrying a brand-new basket and a pair of secateurs, she looks every bit the rookie gardener.

'Morning,' she calls out. 'I can't wait to get started. I bought some seeds yesterday, when I left here.'

'They won't stay like that for long.' I nod towards her trainers.

She blushes slightly. 'I hope not. They're awfully white, aren't they?'

After putting down my mug, I get up. 'Why don't I give you a hand? Just till you get the lay of the land.' I lead the way to what used to be Delilah's allotment, smiling as I glance into her basket at the packets of seeds she's bought.

Over the next hour, I talk her through what's already growing and what she needs to do, at the end of which she looks slightly shell-shocked. 'There's more to learn than I'd realised.'

I nod. 'You'll be fine. And it won't take long. I have a book I can lend you. It'll teach you the basics. After that, read your seed packets. The instructions are all there!' I smile at her. 'There's rainwater in there.' I point to the water butt beside the small shed that comes with the allotment. 'Not a lot, though, so use it sparingly. The only other prerequisite is a healthy amount of patience.' I touch my imaginary hat. 'Any questions, you know where to find me.'

I leave her standing there, slightly nonplussed. There's a whole lot more I could teach her. But that isn't the point. She's here because she needs to do this for herself.

Over the rest of the day, a handful of people come and go. We're an eclectic little bunch, all here for different reasons, but mostly for the peace here. As I've learned, gardening offers an escape, a place to heal. Hours later, when Fay leaves, her eyes are bright, the trainers already losing their pristine whiteness.

'It's started,' I chuckle as she walks past.

She frowns. 'What has?'

I nod towards her shoes. 'You, turning into a proper gardener.'

'Oh.' Glancing down, there's a ghost of a smile on her face. 'That's good. I'm off. I'll see you tomorrow, Zeke.'

'Have a good evening.' I watch her walk towards the road. There's soil on her jeans and wisps of her hair have escaped her ponytail. But I wouldn't mind betting that already, this place is starting to work its magic on her.

After locking my shed, I make my way home. It's only a short distance along a narrow path through a gap in the hedge along the farthest edge of the garden. As I reach the other side, my house comes into view.

Gazing at it, I sigh. It's a rambling old farmhouse with shutters on which the paint is peeling; too big for one person; that used to be a place of love and laughter. But that was a long time ago, and there's no point dwelling on the past.

Bending down, I stroke the straggly looking cat that's recently moved in. 'Hey, cat. Hungry?'

Yowling, he rubs against my legs and follows me inside. He's a skinny creature who arrived out of nowhere a few weeks ago.

As I feed him, Fay comes to mind. I wonder if apart from her husband, there's something else she's escaping from. Maybe in time, she'll tell me. And if not, that's fine too. As I've always believed, there are no rules about these things.

The cat fed, I turn my attention to my own meal. Tonight, it's going to be an omelette made with eggs from my neighbour's chickens, with a salad freshly picked from my allotment – beet tops, some shredded crinkly cabbage leaves, a lettuce. But as I crack the eggs into a bowl, there's a knock on the door.

Going to answer it, I find a young woman standing there. Clutching her hands, she looks distressed.

'I'm really sorry to bother you.' She sounds flustered as she pushes her long red hair off her face. 'My car's broken down – it's blocking the road. And I can't call anyone because my phone's run out of battery.' There's desperation in her voice; in her eyes, too. 'I don't suppose there's any chance I could use yours?'

'Of course.' I stand back. 'Where's your car, exactly?'

'Only a few metres away – up there.' She points up the lane. 'It stopped where the road is flat, otherwise I could have rolled it onto the verge.'

'I wouldn't worry – we don't get too many cars around here.'

She shakes her head. 'But what if someone needs to get by?'

'I wouldn't worry, if I were you. These lanes are often blocked up by tractors and sheep and the like.' And if someone does need to pass, there's another lane around the village. 'Would it help if I gave it a push?'

'I'm not sure.' She looks at me doubtfully. 'I'm mean, you're very kind. But it's a lot to ask. And I'll still have to find someone to tow it away. Then I need to get it fixed.' Her eyes glitter with tears before she blinks them away.

'Not having the best day, are you?' I say kindly. 'Why don't we try and get it off the road? Then I'll help you find someone to tow it away – if you'd like me to, that is.' I pause, watching her. 'I'm Zeke, by the way.'

'Are you sure? I'm Stevie.' Still on edge, her eyes are like those of a rabbit caught in headlights.

'Nice to meet you, Stevie. Come in for a moment.' I lead her through to the kitchen. 'Is yours an iPhone? I have a charger around here somewhere.' Finding it in a drawer, I pass it to her. 'Why don't you plug your phone in? Then we'll go and take a look at your car.'

She doesn't speak as she follows me out again, walking quickly up the lane as I try to keep up, until an elderly Fiat comes into view. 'Here it is.'

As she said, it's completely blocking the road. Between us, we manoeuvre it into a gateway. 'It'll be fine here for now,' I tell her. 'Come on. I'll make us a cup of tea. Then we'll make some phone calls.'

On the walk back, I discover that Stevie moved here six months ago. That she leads a quiet life. 'It's how I like it,' she says apologetically, before glancing timidly at me. 'Have you lived here long?'

'Oh, about forty years now.' It's actually thirty-nine years, nine months and twenty-eight days, a detail etched into my ageing brain that's meaningless to anyone else. 'Do you have family around here?'

'No.' When she twists her hands together, I sense there's something she isn't saying. But I know better than to ask.

Back at the house, I put the kettle on, then place a jug of milk on the table. 'Do you take sugar?'

'No – thank you.' Her eyes scan the walls, resting for a moment on one of the photographs. 'Do you live here alone?'

My personal life is exactly that – personal. And I prefer to keep it that way. I pour us both a cup of tea. 'Let's just say there are fewer passing through than there used to be,' I say, passing her one of the cups. 'So how do you like it around here?'

'So far, it's good.' She wrinkles up her face in a frown. 'It wasn't what I planned, though.' She's silent for a moment. 'You see, I used to come on holiday here – with my parents. We stayed at a campsite on a farm. My plan was to camp there for a while until I worked out what to do next, but when I arrived, it had been closed.'

'That was bad luck.'

'That was what I thought – at first. I was going to leave. But then I bumped into the farmer who used to own it and he offered to rent me the house that used to belong to his grandmother.'

'Sounds like you were meant to stay,' I say promptly.

'I hope so. I think I was lucky,' she says quietly. 'You know, meeting him the way I did. The house is really small – and everything needs painting – it's been empty for years. But there's this feeling about it, like it needed me.' She looks surprised. 'Anyway, I think I knew straight away it could feel like home.'

'That's the thing about plans, isn't it? Life has this way of surprising us,' I say gently. 'I kind of like that.'

She nods. 'If he hadn't offered it to me, I don't know what I would have done. After my parents...' Breaking off, her face turns visibly pale. 'I couldn't trouble you for a biscuit, could I?'

'No problem at all.' Getting up, I'm slightly concerned as I fetch an unopened packet from the larder. 'Are you OK? Only you're a little pale.'

'It's a blood sugar thing. I haven't eaten today.' It looks more like she hasn't eaten for a week as she swiftly devours a biscuit, followed by another.

'All day?' I frown at her. 'That's not good.' But it's hardly surprising, given there's nothing of her. 'I was just about to make an omelette. I don't suppose you'd like to share it with me?'

To my surprise, she accepts, sitting in silence as I cook the omelette and serve it up, adding a basket of freshly baked bread.

'That was so good,' she says, once she's finished.

'It's the difference when you use fresh ingredients. The veg I've grown myself, while the eggs are from a neighbour.'

'It's how I like to cook,' she says shyly. 'Or rather, used to.'

My ears prick up. 'Used to? You mean, you don't cook any more?' I'm attempting to be humorous.

Her cheeks flush slightly pink. 'I used to be a chef.'

'Well.' I stare at her, wondering how on earth a chef ends up not looking after herself. 'Given you're in France, you should do something with that. The French love their food.'

'I have a part-time job in the bar in the village.' She frowns slightly. 'But I suppose I'm not what you'd call a traditional chef – at least, not the way the French cook.'

'So what would you call yourself?'

She hedges. 'I don't know. It isn't exactly ground-breaking, but I suppose I like recipes that use seasonal food – like your omelette, for example. And plant-based. A lot of people don't know how easy it is.' She hesitates. 'And I like foraging.'

'The best kind of food, if you ask me.' Though as she said, not your typical French diet. Looking at her, I frown. 'You were about to say something just now.' I hesitate, wondering what she was going to say. 'Something about your parents.'

She looks startled and I wonder if I've said the wrong thing. 'I don't usually talk about them...' She pauses. 'You see, a year ago, they were in a plane crash.' Her voice wobbles as her eyes meet mine, before looking away. 'They... they didn't make it.'

'That's terrible.' I'm truly shocked.

'It was. They were such good people. They did all this charity work... They were on a small plane taking them to a remote African village when it happened.' Her voice peters out.

'You must really miss them,' I say quietly.

'Every day.' She wipes a tear away.

My heart goes out to her. 'There's no one else in your life?'

She shakes her head. 'Just after it happened, I broke up with my boyfriend. I found out he'd met someone else. We had a house together – but after that, I couldn't stay.'

'Of course you couldn't.' I hardly know her, but I feel outraged on her behalf. 'What did you do?'

'I moved back to my parents' house. It made sense – I had all their stuff to sort out. But once that was done, I decided to leave.'

I watch her. 'Do you have some food at home?'

'Some beans,' she says vaguely, taking another biscuit.

'Well, I can help with that. Then we need to find someone to sort your car,' I say decisively. 'Now, I don't know if you have anyone in mind, but if not, I know someone.'

Clutching a biscuit, her hand freezes midway to her mouth. 'You do?'

I'm thinking of a friend of Rémy's, who's helped me out in the past. 'He's a good guy. He has a tow-truck. And I'm sure he'll give you a good rate.' Picking up my phone, I call him. 'Billy? Zeke here. What are you up to right now?'

When I explain what's happened, he offers to come straight over. He's like that, Billy. Always there when you need him.

'He's on his way,' I tell Stevie, glancing at my watch. 'Now. About some food...' Finding a bag, I put together some of the veg

I've grown, and a box of eggs from my neighbour, before passing it to her. 'This is for you.'

She stares at the bag. 'I can't take that.'

'Well, you've got to eat something. And from what you've said, I'm pretty sure this is the kind of thing you like.' Pausing, I hear a vehicle pull up outside. 'I'm guessing that's Billy.'

'Already?' She looks astonished.

'He only lives a mile away.' Hearing a knock on the door, I go to answer it.

'Evening, Zeke.' There's an easiness about Billy as he stands there.

'Thanks for this,' I say. 'I owe you.' I turn to find Stevie behind me. 'This is Stevie. It's her car that needs rescuing.'

She steps forward. 'This is so kind of you,' she says shyly.

'No worries. I'm always happy to help a mate out.' He catches my eye. 'So where's the car?'

I nod towards the lane. 'A little way up the road. Just a moment and we'll show you.'

I go back to the kitchen and pick up the bag of veg for Stevie, as an afterthought adding the half-empty packet of biscuits, before taking it out to her. 'Shall we go?'

It's a glorious evening as we walk up the lane, a chill in the air now that the sun is setting. After Billy tries and fails to start her car, he winches it onto his truck.

'I can't believe this,' she says quietly as she turns to me. 'I mean, you charging my phone and cooking me supper, then calling Billy... I can't thank you enough.'

'You're welcome.' I smile at her. 'I'm happy to help.' Then because she looks so serious, I laugh. 'And don't worry about it! Sometimes, it's just the way things go. Being in the right place at the right time... One day, you'll do the same for someone else.'

'I guess so...' she says.

I stand there watching as Billy drives away, and a strange feeling comes over me. It isn't just Stevie's life that's quiet. These days so is mine, more by chance than design. Yet these last couple of days have been surprising. I mean, firstly meeting Fay, then Stevie. Deciding there must be something in the air, I find myself wondering what tomorrow will bring.

5

STEVIE

April

'He's such a nice man,' I say quietly as Billy drives us away.

'Salt of the earth,' Billy says. 'So, what are we doing with this car of yours?'

I sigh. 'Very good question. As you've probably noticed, it's a bit of a disaster waiting to happen.'

'No offence, but I think the disaster's already happened,' Billy says cheerfully. 'Look, why don't I offload it over at my place? I'll take a look at it over the next couple of days. Then if I can fix it, would you like me to?'

I shake my head. 'It's too much. You've already been so kind.' Alarm shoots through me as I think of the ever-decreasing balance of my bank account. 'What do I owe you for today?'

'Nothing.' Billy turns off the main road up a track.

My eyes widen. 'You can't do this for nothing.'

Billy shrugs. 'Let's take a look at it first, and go from there.'

I'm silent for a moment, thinking of Zeke's generosity, then of the photos on his wall; how evasive he was when I asked him if he lived alone. 'It's none of my business, but did something happen with Zeke's family?'

Billy frowns. 'I'm not sure. But if it did, he doesn't talk about it.' He pulls into a yard, in front of a couple of small barns and a cottage. 'Here we are. It won't take long to unload your car.'

Getting out, I stand there watching, as he expertly manoeuvres it off the truck and out of the way.

'Right. How about I drop you home?'

I stand there, flabbergasted. My car breaking down felt like the end of the world, but since it happened, I've been inundated with nothing but kindness. After a long day, I'm too tired to protest. 'If you're sure it's OK, then thank you.'

However nice Billy is – Zeke too – I've become used to my own company and back at my house, as I close the door, relief fills me that I'm alone.

Placing Zeke's bag of veg on the side, I then push open the kitchen window and stand there for a moment taking in the view.

The window looks out over the river that meanders through the village. At the moment, it's quiet here, half the houses empty, the handful of residents mostly keeping to themselves, which suits me fine. Except that today has left me with a different feeling, that maybe it isn't so bad having a few people in my life once again.

As I told Zeke, I moved here six months ago. After my parents died, and with no one to keep me in England, I'd felt compelled by nostalgia to retrace my footsteps back to the village where we used to come on holiday, fantasising that once I got here, my memories would make me feel close to them; that maybe I'd even stumble across some intangible connection between us.

After loading up my little car in England and giving up the

keys to the house they rented, I'd driven across France. But as I found out when I got here, reconnecting with the past doesn't instantly solve your problems. It simply opens the door to a whole set of new ones, while the same realities follow you: even hundreds of miles from my old life, I still had to earn some money and work out what to do next.

Healing takes time. And it's about small steps, I've kept telling myself. In navigating grief's ups and downs, there are no shortcuts.

But moving has been its own kind of therapy and six months on, the old clutter that filled my little house has gone, while the kitchen wears several coats of bright white paint, with pots of herbs arranged on the newly sanded windowsill.

I've also met Nicole and Olivier who run the Petit Bar a short walk away in the village. Dynamic and in their early thirties, Olivier is the calm to Nicole's storm. I work for them on an ad hoc basis, which in winter amounts to occasional weddings, parties, and funerals. Given how remote this part of France is and how few people live here, it's very occasional in winter, but it still earns me enough to keep the roof of my tiny, incredibly cheap house over my head.

Meanwhile, I'm learning to appreciate the small things in life. Going to the cupboard, I pause to admire the polished brass handle I acquired at a local *vide-grenier*. The contents are sparse, the tins of beans unappetising, as is the box of breakfast cereal. But then I remember the bag Zeke gave me. Opening it, I find some newly dug potatoes covered in a fine dusting of earth, a lettuce, a few beetroots and carrots, then at the bottom, a box of mismatched eggs.

Today has been unexpected – and most definitely an anomaly. Firstly, I'm not usually comfortable talking to strangers. Secondly,

I never, ever, talk about my parents. But today, for whatever reason, I've done both.

It's as Zeke said, I can't help thinking. There are times life really can be surprising. Stifling a yawn, I put away Zeke's vegetables. Today has been a good day. The thought leaves me wondering what tomorrow will bring. If maybe, at long last, I'm reaching some kind of turning point.

* * *

I'd imagined living here would assuage the need I have for solitude, for privacy, assuming it's how it is when you live in a small village. I'd pictured people keeping to themselves, but when I think about how I found my little house, then met Zeke and Billy, I realise how wrong I was.

People here are easy-going and life is simple, but there's also a sense that they look out for one another, as I find out the following afternoon when I hear a car come up from the village, then stop outside. A minute later, there's a knock on the door. Breaking off from the omelette I'm preparing, I open it to find Billy standing in the doorway. In faded jeans and a black T-shirt, there's a smudge of oil on one of his cheeks.

'I came to let you know your car's almost fixed.'

'Already?' Guarding my privacy, I edge towards the door to the sitting room, pulling it closed so that he can't see how untidy it is; my feeling of relief that my car is OK vanishing as I imagine the cost. 'Thank you so much. When shall I pick it up?'

'How about tomorrow evening?' His eyes turn to the eggs Zeke gave me and the salad I've made with some of his vegetables. 'Wow. That looks good.'

'It all came from Zeke. You should have some.' Pouring the eggs into the pan, I watch as the omelette starts to bubble, before flipping it. It's a movement I've practised many times – I started watching chefs at work long before I started training. Cutting a piece, I slide it onto a plate and pass it to him. 'I'll get you a fork.'

Going to one of the drawers, I get one out and hand it to him.

Standing in the doorway of my tiny kitchen, he takes a bite. 'This is amazing,' Billy says through a mouthful.

'It's just an omelette.' Cutting another piece, I slide it onto his plate.

'Well, it's the best I've ever tasted.' He pauses. 'Aren't you having any?'

'I might,' I say. 'Later, though.' I have a ritual about setting the table precisely, dividing my food into equal portions in a way other people don't. That's why when I eat, I prefer to be alone.

But it pleases me to see him enjoying it. And given the contents of my kitchen, I know right now it probably doesn't make sense, but like I said to Zeke, I had this idea once, about teaching people to cook.

'Thank you.' Billy puts his fork on his empty plate. 'I'm not sure how you made that so tasty, but it's like no omelette I've ever had before.'

'Good ingredients,' I say quickly. Fresh eggs and vegetables; cold-pressed, extra virgin olive oil instead of the butter the French use in literally everything. You can't go wrong.

He looks at me. 'I'm guessing you can cook more than an omelette.'

'Occasionally,' I say.

He raises his eyebrows. 'Is it all this good?'

'Mostly,' I say, not in a bragging way. I'm just being honest.

He looks as though he's about to say something, but thinks better of it. 'I suppose I'd better get back and finish fixing your car.'

* * *

True to his word, Billy is back the next day. Gazing at my car, I barely recognise it.

'You've cleaned it.' I stare at it. 'It actually looks quite nice.'

Billy smiles. 'Don't sound so surprised. It's actually not a bad little car.' He passes me the keys. 'I've given it a tidy-up inside, too.'

Opening the driver's door, I'm stunned. My mess has gone, the windows and dashboard are clean. 'I can't believe you've done all this.' I gaze at him, slightly embarrassed. 'How much do I owe you?'

He looks awkward. 'It didn't cost much.' He names a figure that's ridiculously cheap.

I look at him anxiously. 'It doesn't sound enough.'

'I'm not out of pocket, if that's what you're worried about.' He pauses. 'Zeke said something to me once, when I first met him – about paying it forward. You know, the idea that you do something for someone, and at some point, they'll do something for someone else... Anyway, it stuck with me. Maybe someday, you'll be in a position to help someone out. I like to think it's how the world works.'

I open my purse and take out some cash. 'It isn't enough,' I say to him. 'But maybe I could buy you a drink sometime?'

'That's kind of you.' He pauses. 'Any other time, I'd have taken you up on it. But I'm about to go away for a few months.' He grins. 'Maybe I'll see you in the summer!'

After he leaves, I go for a walk. Taking in the rays of sun through the trees, I'm slightly surprised to find I'm disappointed that someone I'd considered might become a friend isn't going to be here. But I need to stop having preconceived ideas of how things are going to work out. Nothing's the same, any more. As I walk up the lane away from the village, I know things will never return to how they used to be. But that's how life is. It moves on – as it does here in the village. As Nicole has told me more than once, it isn't going to be long before the bar opens; then when summer arrives, the tourists and second-home owners flock from miles around for lunch by the river, sheltering from the sun in the shade of the plane trees. 'It gets crazy, Stevie. You would not believe it. In the summer, we all will be rushed off our feet,' Nicole had said when she offered me the job. But it all slows down again as autumn comes – until it's quiet and sleepy again, as it was when I arrived last winter.

I think of Billy, then Zeke; how in the last two days, they've come out of nowhere into my life; wondering if there's a reason beyond the obvious. I used to believe things happen for a reason – until my parents died.

I still believe that people come into our lives when the time is right. But is the time right? And if so, for what?

At the end of the street, I pass Madame Picard carrying a bag of shopping. '*Bonjour.*' I smile at her.

'*Bonjour,* Stevie,' she says, but her usual smile is missing. Putting the bag down, she sighs.

I stop. '*Ça va?*' An unspoken understanding has developed between us that I try to speak French, and she speaks the little English she knows.

She sighs. 'I am not good today.'

I'm torn between wanting to carry on walking and wanting to help. But then I think of Zeke and Billy, the difference the unexpected kindness of a stranger can make. A new philosophy to me, but for too long, I've been living such a small life.

I pick up her bag. 'Why don't you let me help?'

And that's the moment. A small, apparently insignificant one, but one where I start to find my way back to life, to myself. It's like a light has been switched on, even if only a dim one. But as Madame Picard takes my arm, it grows brighter.

The following day begins with a last-minute thing. But it's always a last-minute thing with Nicole and Olivier at the Petit Bar in the village. It's how they are. Flamboyant and wonderfully vibrant people, their energy goes into the creativity they are renowned for, meaning organisation isn't their strong point.

Closing the door behind me, I set off down the road towards the bar. The village is quiet, sunlight glistening through the branches of the plane trees.

This is what I've come to like about living here: the isolation, the absence of traffic; that apart from Madame Picard, there are no people who know who I am – that is, until I get to the bar.

'*Ciao*.' Nicole kisses me on both cheeks. 'You are a little English angel, Stevie.' Pausing, she strokes my hair back. 'An angel with the most beautiful hair I have ever seen. No one should have hair that colour.'

Feeling my cheeks grow hot, I try to deflect her. 'What would you like me to do?' I tie an apron around my middle. From what she's already told me, she doesn't have time to look at my hair; there's a mountain of work ahead.

'Vichyssoise.' She pushes a knife and chopping-board in my direction. 'After, we must prepare choux for a hundred. My God. Why couldn't they have ordered something simpler?'

Nicole has a penchant for stress and panic and I tune her out, losing myself in the repetitive chopping of vegetables into precise dimensions, only stopping when I notice her watching me.

Suddenly, I'm anxious. 'Is something wrong?'

She comes over and slowly picks up a piece of leek, followed by another. '*Non*.' She looks at me quizzically. 'It is perfection. Each piece… it is perfection, Stevie.'

I feel uncomfortable. 'I was taught it is all in the process. I'm sorry if it's wrong.'

'Wrong?' She raises perfectly arched eyebrows. '*Oh non, ma chérie*. It is so perfect I could cry.' For a moment, her voice wavers. 'It is just that it is a *crime* to blend them into a soup.'

Nonplussed, I have no idea what she's talking about. 'You *do* want me to make soup, don't you?'

She sighs. 'I suppose.' She waves her hands around. 'Of course I do. I just wish you would be less of an *artiste* – and that you'd cut the vegetables more… badly, I think the word is.'

Still gesticulating, she goes to find Olivier, leaving me none the wiser. But she doesn't understand that I have my own way about these things. You see, I believe that the care that goes into a dish is reflected in the eating experience; that if you rush and cut corners, you make mistakes, a point that's proven when Nicole ends up burning a pan of crème anglaise.

'Now I have to start again.' There's panic in her voice. 'Why does this always happen to me?'

'I'll do it,' I say calmly, taking the pan and scrubbing it out before starting again.

She shakes her head. 'But you must make soup.'

'It's done. Where is the vanilla?'

Throughout the day, Nicole keeps breaking off to answer her phone in animated French, and by the afternoon her degree of panic reaches fever pitch. 'So many people,' she flaps. 'We will never get everything done.'

As always, even though it takes an extra hour, we do. Relieved that my part in the proceedings is over, I take off my apron. But as she stops talking on the phone, I already know from Nicole's face I'm not going to like what she's about to say.

'That was Adèle. She was going to waitress tomorrow, but her little daughter is sick. It means I need to find someone else.'

As she speaks, my heart sinks. Nicole knows about my aversion to large crowds of people. Seeing her face, I start to panic. 'I can't. I have plans.'

'Really?' Standing there with her hands on her hips, Nicole raises one of her dark eyebrows. 'What plans exactly?'

Now the reason I love my job at the bar is because in the kitchen, I'm the washer of pots, peeler of potatoes, preparer of meals. In short, I'm the performer of the tasks that most customers never think about; invisible to the world. And I like it that way. The thought of being a waitress is almost as terrifying as boarding a flight.

'It is just a very simple lunch, Stevie. This is not something that should worry you. Please?' Nicole looks at me beseechingly.

It's astonishing that what was the source of so much stress to Nicole suddenly becomes no more than a simple lunch.

* * *

So it happens that the following day, I go with Nicole and Olivier to set up the lunch party. After packing everything into their van, forty minutes later we reach the venue. I gaze out of the window in horror. Firstly, it's less of a house and more of a chateau, with immaculately mown lawns, the garden bursting with spring flowers, suggesting that there is nothing at all simple about this lunch party.

Given the cost of their upkeep, in my limited experience, chateaux around here are usually event venues. But not this one.

'It has apparently been in their family for generations,' Nicole mutters under her breath as she leads me towards the back door, then along a panelled corridor into the biggest kitchen I've ever seen. 'Unpack this, will you?' She places the vast plastic box she's carrying on the side. 'I'll get the rest.'

After she's gone, I stand there for a moment taking in the vast refectory table that must seat at least twenty, the huge gas range; the antique dresser on which delicate china is arranged.

As I stand there, I wonder how many people have stood here over the centuries, taking in the huge arched windows, on the stone floor worn smooth by hundreds of thousands of footsteps.

I jump out of my skin as Nicole's voice calls out.

'Stevie? Can you open the door?'

As she comes in, I take some of the boxes she's carrying.

'Put them on the table. We have two hours before the guests start arriving,' Nicole says, glancing at her watch.

For the next two hours, we work together seemingly effortlessly, adding finishing touches to the multiple plates of delicious food, finishing just as some cars turn up.

'I need you front of house – to serve champagne.' Nicole hastily passes me a neatly pressed shirt. Seeing my face, she gets in first. 'I am sorry. I know how you feel about this. But it is an emergency.' She gives me a desperate look. 'Don't say you can't. I wouldn't ask if I were not desperate.'

My stomach churns with nerves as I put the shirt on. Coming over, Nicole smooths my hair back. 'It will be OK,' she says softly. 'I will be with you, Stevie. Come.'

We walk through the house together. Already, people are filtering through the front door – most of them carrying lavishly wrapped gifts – the majority of whom I'd guess to be in their early twenties.

In a vast reception room, I walk around with a tray of glasses, taking in the couture outfits and expensive jewellery, the beautifully styled hair.

As I circulate among them handing out glasses, my eyes are

drawn to a figure over by the window. There's something familiar about the set of his shoulders, the dark glasses pushed on top of his head. When he turns, I freeze.

It's the guy from the plane, the one with the headphones; the same guy I gave my book to.

Ned.

6

NED

As guests arrive for Persephone's birthday, for the billionth time I'm regretting committing to this. And lunch is just the first round of the celebrations. Tonight is a party for five hundred twenty-somethings and their partners in a vast marquee – and I'm dreading it.

In my current state of unemployment, and encountering the most uncertain of futures, I should be mingling, networking with potential clients. But so far, I've lurked by the window, doing my best to avoid Persephone and her friends.

I glance back towards the room, noticing one of the waiting staff, my eyes wandering to the tray of champagne glasses she's holding, wondering if I should have one before I start to play. Then as I see her face, I do a double take.

It's Stevie.

Her eyes widen with shock as I go over to her, a smile spreading across my face. 'What are you doing here?' For some reason, suddenly today feels less daunting. 'Um, stupid question.' I nod towards the tray she's holding. 'Mind if I have one?'

'Help yourself.' She watches as I take a glass. 'I work for Nicole

and Olivier – the caterers. In the kitchen. I don't usually do this.'
She shakes her head. 'But their waitress couldn't make it today.'

'Well, I'm really glad. It's nice to see you again.' I think about
how much has changed in my life, since that day I met her on the
plane.

'Are you a guest?' Suddenly she looks wary.

'Me? God. No.' Does she really imagine I'm one of Persephone's crowd? 'I'm the music. They want mellow over lunch –
then something a little livelier for tonight.'

'Wow.' Stevie's eyes grow round. 'What kind?'

'Today it's guitar – I also play the piano. I write music and
lyrics – and play at weddings and parties – such as this one.' I
shrug. 'Though so far, I'm not exactly the biggest of success
stories.' I'm about to make some quip about luck and timing, but
she gets in first.

'Maybe it just hasn't been your time yet.' She gives a couple of
glasses to a passing guest before turning back to me.

'I've been telling myself that for a while now,' I say honestly,
slightly mesmerised – as I was the last time we met – by the
intense blue of her eyes. 'But as more time passes, it gets harder to
keep the faith.'

'But you have to, don't you see?' she says earnestly. 'If you're
serious? I mean, you hear all these stories, don't you.' She stands
back as a gazelle-like teenager with inches-long eyelashes and
wearing ludicrous platform boots almost totters into her. 'The
books people write that languish forgotten in drawers, but they
keep writing, until years later, one of them becomes the next big
bestseller... Music's like that too, isn't it? I mean, one break could
make all the difference, couldn't it?'

She ends each sentence with a question, as though she's either
seeking concurrence or doubting herself. She's also the first

person in a long time who hasn't suggested I should think about re-examining my ambitions. But then again, she barely knows me.

At that moment, Geneviève sweeps towards us, a flurry of designer dress that looks like it's made of feathers, teamed with ornate high-heeled shoes and overpowering perfume.

'Ned, darling.' Ignoring Stevie, she kisses me on both cheeks. 'Can you be ready in ten? Everyone's about to sit down.'

'Of course.' As she walks away, she embraces a tall woman with fair hair, understatedly dressed in a way that stands out from the other guests. English or Dutch, I'm guessing. Definitely not French. 'Fay. Darling. How wonderful to see you. I'm so sorry Hugh couldn't make it...'

Clearly English, then. I turn to Stevie. 'Mother of the birthday girl. To tell you the truth, I've been dreading today,' I say under my breath, waiting until Geneviève's out of earshot. 'And that's an understatement. I got talked into it at my mother's birthday party – after too much red wine. Geneviève's a friend of my mother's. The wine was exceptional that day...' Shaking my head, I break off. I have only myself to blame. But it isn't just that. My mother's party marks the dividing line between blissful ignorance and the aftermath of her bombshell. My smile fades. 'You wouldn't believe how much has happened since then.'

Stevie gazes at me for a moment. 'I've been dreading this too.' Before she can elaborate, I notice Geneviève waving at me across the room.

'I think that's my cue to go.' If nothing else, I'm being paid well for this. 'Will I see you later?'

Stevie hesitates. 'Maybe.'

* * *

In what feels like no time, the first part of this gig is over. And I have to admit, in spite of everything else going on in my life, I enjoyed it. 'When do you play again?' Later that afternoon, taking a well-earned break, as we sit on a bench under a tree, Stevie's look of relief echoes mine that lunch is over.

'Not until tonight.' It was a relatively small crowd in performing terms, but I'm still buzzing.

She cups her hands around her mug of tea. 'You're very brave – I mean, playing in front of all those people. It would terrify me.'

'I love it,' I say expansively. 'It's what I was put on this earth to do.' Realising I sound a bit of a dick, I backtrack. 'At least, that's what I used to think. But now...'

'Now what?' She looks interested.

'Like I said, quite a lot's happened since then.' I sigh, just as some shrieking comes from across the garden before, through the mist, a bevy of bright young things stumble into view, clearly pissed.

'Having fun, aren't they?' Stevie says softly.

'They haven't a care in the world.' I watch them laughing, as one of them lights up a cigarette and passes it around, before they disappear back towards the house.

'You were about to say?' Stevie says lightly.

'You forget, don't you, how it is to feel like that?' I'm silent for a moment, still watching them, wondering where to start. 'Remember when we met on the flight? I think I told you I was coming back for my mother's birthday. At the time, I wasn't too thrilled about it. In my family, the lack of success of my music career is a subject of some controversy,' I explain. 'Anyway, as parties go, it turned out to be a good one.' I pause, aware of a lump in my throat as I think of my mother's speech. 'I remember noticing my mother seemed different. Only in small ways, but she said a few things that seemed out of character. As the party went on, I stopped thinking about it. Until the following day.' I pause, remembering. 'It turns out my mother is ill.' I look at Stevie. 'Like seriously ill.' I pause again. 'She has cancer.'

Shock registers in Stevie's eyes. 'I'm so, so sorry, Ned.' Her eyes are filled with sympathy. 'Has she started treatment?'

It's as though the afternoon light dims. I shake my head. 'She's having palliative care. There isn't really anything they can do.' I clasp my hands together. 'The thing is, the cancer's secondary.' I try to stop my voice shaking. 'She had breast cancer years ago. It was picked up early and she didn't even have chemo. But this...' I tail off. 'The cancer is advanced. None of us are sure how long she has.'

'I'm so sorry, Ned.' Stevie looks sad.

'Nina's devastated.' I gaze across the garden at a couple of geese rising into the sky. 'Nina's my sister. She lives with them. As it now seems I do.' I take in Stevie's look of surprise. 'We don't get in one another's way. The house is quite a big old place,' I explain. It's an understatement, I know. But having grown up there, I simply think of it as home. 'It's been passed down the generations on my mother's side. A labour of love, you could say – the upkeep is relentless. And you need to love it, because it's also a bit of a millstone if I'm honest.' I realise I'm doing a lot of talking about me. 'So that's my story.'

Stevie's silent for a moment. 'It's good you're in France, isn't it?'

I nod. 'Timing working in my favour for once – not that any of this is good.' Well, that's apart from seeing Stevie again. 'Anyway, enough of me. Where are your family from?'

The colour drains from Stevie's face. 'I don't really have one.'

Startled, I apologise. It's obvious from her reaction something's happened. 'You don't have to tell me,' I say quickly. 'I didn't mean to pry.'

'It's OK,' she says. 'You couldn't have known.'

Watching her, suddenly I forget about myself. 'What happened?'

'I used to think I was lucky being an only child.' She's silent for a moment. 'But now, I wish I weren't. You see, my parents died – in a plane crash.' She stares at her hands. 'A year ago.'

I look at her, shocked. 'God. That's awful.'

'It was.' Her voice wobbles. 'It took ages for it to sink in. After, I'd wake up every morning and, for the briefest moment, it was as though it had never happened, then it would hit me all over again. It happened in Africa – and for months after, it felt like any moment, they'd come walking back in with their suitcases and their stories...' She blinks away a tear. 'Then when I went out, I kept seeing them – in shops or across the street – only, of course, it wasn't them.' She pauses. 'It was like my mind was pretending everything was the same – like some kind of inbuilt defence mechanism, giving reality time to drip-feed through. It was still brutal, though.'

I stare at her, remembering how frightened she was in the plane. 'I'm so sorry.' Of course, it makes sense. 'It's hardly surprising you're scared of flying.'

She nods. 'Terrified would be a better word.'

As we sit in silence, nothing moves around us. 'So how come you moved to France?' I ask quietly.

'Well, after they died, I broke up with my boyfriend.' She shakes her head. 'It was hideous when it happened, but with hindsight, I suppose I should be grateful. He wasn't a nice man.' She pauses. 'He met someone else – he'd met her some time ago. He just hadn't got around to telling me. So I came in search of the place that held memories of happier times.'

Sitting there, I'm slightly in awe that she can pass off something so horrific as even remotely positive. 'My girlfriend just broke up with me, too,' I say.

'No way.' She stares at me. 'You mean, recently?'

I nod. 'Just after my mother's party – when I found out she was ill. She told me when I got back from France.' It's impossible to believe it was just last weekend, when it feels so much longer ago.

'Hard, isn't it?' Her voice is sympathetic. And as she looks at me, I realise she actually knows how I feel.

'Honestly?' I frown, wondering how it is that with my tendency to keep these things inside, with Stevie, I can't stop talking about them. 'Jessie and I were going through the motions – we had been for some time. The end was coming...' I say dramatically. 'It was just the timing that sucked.'

She looks thoughtful. 'I've often wondered if there's a reason so many things come at us at once. I mean, it knocks you sideways at the time, doesn't it? But maybe that's the point.' She pauses. 'When it happened, I could barely cope. But after, I got to thinking. What if the universe was sending me signs? Then when I didn't take any notice of them, the signs kept getting bigger – until I did.' She shrugs. 'Maybe it was some kind of cosmic wake-up call, or something.'

As far as I can see, there's nothing cosmic going on. It's sheer bad luck – and these things happen. 'You really think that?'

She shrugs. 'Who knows?' Her eyes are clear as she looks at me. 'I used to think I had things all worked out. You know – with my family, a relationship I thought was forever... Of course, none of it was. But I suppose nothing is – not really, when you stop and think about it.' As she glances at her wrist, I notice she's wearing what looks like a man's watch with a battered leather strap; wondering if it's her father's. 'I should probably go and find Nicole. She'll be wanting to start on the food for this evening.' Getting up, she pauses. 'It was nice to see you again. Hopefully, tonight, I'll hear you play!'

Getting to my feet, I stand there for a moment. 'It was good to see you too.'

She lingers briefly before turning and walking back to the house, leaving me kicking myself – for not asking for her mobile number. Or just asking if I could see her again. But I can catch her later this evening, I remind myself. Then I'm thinking about the timing of this. Bloody, brutal timing again. With my head all over the place, right now, I'm hardly the best company.

* * *

The following day, I awake early. After getting up, I walk the dogs along the familiar footpaths, pausing to watch the cherry blossom fall like snow, figuring out the landscape of this strange new world I find myself in.

Somewhere between the garden and the path that leads to the lake, I work out that if Jessie and I were still together, I wouldn't be here. It feels like the one good thing that's come out of our break-up. And after the gig going so well, there's a chance it will lead to others. Much to my surprise, I am glad to be back in France, especially right now with my mother ill – and after bumping into Stevie again.

It's a time of adjustment in many aspects of my life, including the one where I figure out what to do next, a conundrum on which, predictably, Nina voices her strong opinions.

'You need to get a job, little brother,' my know-it-all sister tells me with characteristic bluntness. 'It isn't good to have all this empty time on your hands.'

'It isn't empty,' I protest. 'It's creative. I'm mulling material for my music. Anyway, I want to spend some time with Mama.'

'As long as you're not wallowing.' Nina's silent for a moment. 'I know things are a bit odd at the moment – and it's good you're here for Mama, but can I say something? And it's only because I care, but whatever happens with your music – and I'm not suggesting you should give up on it – have you considered you might need a plan B?'

'No,' I say instantly, slightly nettled. 'You can't dip in and out of music. You have to immerse yourself.'

Nina sighs. 'What about the practicalities of life? Food, bills, running a car?'

I look at her startled. 'I've already done one gig. Hopefully it will lead to more.'

'Sooner or later you'll run out of twenty-first birthday parties,' she says dryly. 'Or you'll go out of fashion. Whatever comes first.'

'Ouch.' I wince. 'That was brutal.'

'Just giving you a reality check.' She pauses, then says more kindly, 'Someone has to. I'm sure you'll be busy, once word gets about.'

'Hopefully.' I sigh. 'Look, this has all happened rather fast – after breaking up with Jessie. I need a little time to get my head together.'

'Don't you think your music was part of the problem?' Nina looks at me. 'I mean, it couldn't have helped your relationship – Jessie covering everything.'

'We were a team.' I cling obstinately to my own version of things. 'Teams pick up the slack when the other is down. It's how it works – in theory, at least.' But I'm cringing at myself. I'm not sure I can remember a time when it was me who picked up any slack.

Nina's silent for a moment. 'If you didn't have this place, you'd be out on the streets,' she reminds me. 'If more gigs don't come along, get a job, Ned. It doesn't matter what. And I'll bet you an expensive dinner – at the restaurant of your choosing – it will help you feel better about yourself.'

'I feel fine about myself.' I fold my arms. It pains me to admit it, even to myself, but she has a point. 'There's just one snag,' I say. 'This is rural France. Absolutely nothing happens here. In fact, people leave in droves because it's so quiet.' It's why so many rural villages are half empty.

She shakes her head. 'Then maybe that's what you should do.' Coming over, she hugs me. 'I just want you to be OK, Ned.'

She smells of Chanel N° 5 – and French cigarettes. 'I will be.' For some reason, there's a lump in my throat.

Her arms drop. 'It's really good you're here – for all of us. But maybe where work is concerned, you should give yourself a deadline.'

'A *what*?' I frown at her stupidly.

'I don't know – something along the lines of a month – or maybe two. Why not see if you can make your music work around here? Summer isn't far away – there'll be the usual influx of expats and holidaymakers. Why don't you gig at some local bars? Just to get your name about?'

It's not a bad idea. 'I'll give it some thought.' It might get me through the summer, but I'll be in the same position next winter.

Nina reads my mind. 'If it doesn't work out...' She shrugs. 'Maybe that will be time to think about a plan B. It might not be as bad as you think.' She picks up her phone. 'Oh fuck. I have a call to make.' Nina runs an online fashion company.

'I could work for you,' I call after her as she walks away, half hopeful, half joking.

She glances back, raising one of her eyebrows. 'You and me work together? Thanks, but much as I love you, I don't think so.'

While I've hung on to our family's English connections, Nina is French to her bones. In the past, I could no more have imagined her living in London than I could see myself living here. But now... With no London life to go back to, more and more I'm seriously thinking that maybe the next chapter of my life lies in France – or even beyond. Slightly surprised at myself, I finish my coffee. It's a measure of how much has changed, I tell myself. And change isn't necessarily a bad thing.

There are times, too, when change can be agonising. No more so than when you're watching someone you love face a life-threatening illness that seems to be gathering speed at a terrifying rate. Typically, my mother is stoic, matter-of-fact.

'Ned!' Her voice is warm as she comes into the kitchen. 'I'm glad I've caught you.' She comes over and envelops me in a very English hug, and I realise how small she's become. 'I want to talk to you.' As she looks at me, there's the same ferocious strength in her eyes that there's always been.

'What about?' My heart starts to race, terrible scenarios flooding into my head – like she's about to tell me she has days rather than the months we're all counting on.

'Come and sit.' Pulling out a chair at the table before sitting down, she pats the one next to her.

Doing as I'm told, I wonder what it is she wants to say to me.

'Are you happy, Ned?' Her eyes are solemn, searching mine for answers.

'Me? Of course,' I bluster. 'You know me, Mama. Never one to be down for long.'

'No.' She pauses for a moment. 'You and Jessie… Can I be honest? I feel running out of time gives me the right to say things as they are.' She pauses again. 'She wasn't right for you, Ned. I liked Jessie but she is a driven woman. Her career is everything to her. I have known many women like her. Anything – or anyone – else will always take second place.'

'You had a career.' For some reason, I jump to Jessie's defence. 'So does Nina.'

'But the people we love will always come first.' My mother

looks wistful. 'I think Jessie is a cold woman. Her priorities... They are not right, Ned. Ambition has cost her a good man – and a good life.'

Not sure what she's saying, I frown at her.

'I'm talking about you,' she says softly, taking one of my hands. 'You need to believe in yourself, Ned. You are a good man.' Her voice wavers as she gazes into my eyes. 'And good men deserve the best.' She hesitates for a moment. 'I know I've always sided with your father about you getting what he calls a proper job...' She pauses again. 'But life is not about doing what other people think you should do – even what your parents think you should do.' She looks wistful. 'I have so many regrets that I haven't said this to you before, but if your heart lies in your music, you should follow it.'

As I take in the regret in her eyes, the love, I feel something inside me break free. I take a sharp breath. 'You mean that?'

She smiles, a little sadly. 'I do. I admire you for carrying on – in spite of us. I only wish it could have been with our support. But that's changed now. You have mine.' She pauses. 'I want you to have a comfortable life, Ned – so does your father. In so many ways, you're lucky. I don't think money will be a problem. But more than anything, I want you to know how proud I am of you. Not because of what you do, but because of the good, kind, honest person you are.'

I'm lost for words, my eyes suddenly blurring, as I realise just how much my parents' disapproval has weighed on me. 'Thank you,' I say huskily.

It seems that facing the end of her life is making my mother reassess not just her own choices, but those of her family, too.

'I'm working out a lot of things a little too late.' Her eyes glitter with unshed tears. 'Who am I to say what you should do with your life? I know your father and I have loaded our expectations on you... They're the same expectations our parents loaded onto us. But none of them matter. All they are are stupid conventions we should be questioning...' She shakes her head. 'There are many ways to live your life. And you are lucky, Ned. You have a talent. And you have this home, for as long as you need it.' She takes my hands. 'I suppose what I'm trying to say is you have all the time you need to find your own way.'

My mother is right. Of course, it helps that purely by accident of the family I was born into, money isn't an immediate issue, plus I have a roof over my head. I'm all too aware there are a lot of people in the world who don't have that. But I've wasted time, I'm realising. Pursuing a dying relationship, being half-arsed about my music.

But a new surge of energy races through me as I tell myself that ends here.

Needing a change of scene, and as part of my quest to find some kind of meaning in my life, I go to seek out Stevie. Well, by that I mean – not knowing where she lives – I locate the bar where I know she works.

The village is tiny, about a twenty-minute drive from my parents' house and after parking in a lay-by, I get out.

When I find the bar, there's a 'Closed' sign in the window. Noticing a woman inside painting one of the walls, I knock on the door, waiting until she opens it.

'Can I help you?'

'Um, sorry to bother you. But I'm looking for Stevie.'

'She is not here.' The woman has bright eyes and shoulder-length black hair untidily tied back. Still clasping her paintbrush, she frowns at me. 'Do I know you?'

'Er, I did the music for the party the other day, where you did the catering.'

'Ah.' Something registers in her eyes. 'You are English?' She frowns. 'You are the guy Stevie met on the plane?'

'That's me.' I'm oddly pleased that Stevie has been talking about me.

'I saw her talking to you. I asked her who you were,' she says dismissively. 'I would call her to say you are here, but there is no point. She never charges her phone.' She glances across the river. 'I probably shouldn't tell you. But if you want to find Stevie, she lives up there.'

I frown slightly. 'Why shouldn't you tell me?'

She looks exasperated. 'Those stupid rules people have about data protection. But this is Stevie we are talking about. And I don't give a shit about rules. Anyway, everyone knows everything in this village. Her house is halfway up the street – it has a green door.' She breaks off as her phone buzzes. 'I have to get that.'

Leaving her, I set off across the bridge, pausing on the other side when I see a bench. Stopping there a moment, I sit and watch the water sparkling where the sun catches it, thinking of England, imagining spring on hold there, the grey skies and cold that don't begin to compare with France, that are yet another reason to be grateful for being here.

But I didn't come to the village to while away an afternoon. I came to see Stevie. Getting up, I go in search of the little house with the green door. The hill is steep and as I walk, I pass no one apart from cats who scarper as soon as I look at them. I take in the other houses, each of them slightly different, yet united by a patina of age and the varying degrees of neglect that are typical in rural French villages; before halfway up, I reach the one with the green door.

Checking either side to make sure it's the only one, I'm only slightly apprehensive as I knock, then wait until it opens.

'Ned?' In jeans and a faded hoodie, Stevie looks slightly shocked. 'What are you doing here?'

I'd been prepared for surprise. But not for one instant had it occurred to me that Stevie would object to me turning up like this. 'Um… I was passing.' Then I think of the woman in the bar. 'Actually, I went to the bar where you work. I was hoping I might find you there. The woman I spoke to told me where you lived.'

'Nicole,' she mutters, looking less than pleased.

Standing there, I can't believe how badly I've misjudged this. 'I just thought it might be nice to talk – or have some wine. Some-time – it doesn't have to be now. But the thing was, I didn't have any way to contact you.'

'Oh.' She stands there looking slightly anxious, then glances behind her. 'You know, it isn't the best time.'

Guessing she's not alone, my heart sinks. 'No worries. Sorry to have bothered you. I'll, er, leave you to it.' Feeling like an idiot, I turn to walk away.

Then she seems to change her mind. 'Maybe we could go for a walk – if you like. Give me five minutes.'

She closes the door. Mollified, while I wait on the doorstep, an elderly woman walks past. '*Bon après-midi, Madame.*'

Before she can reply, Stevie reappears. Her face lights up as she sees the woman. '*Bonjour, Madame Picard.*'

'*Bonjour, chérie.*' The woman casts me a curious glance before carrying on. 'She lives further up the street.' Stevie looks at me. 'Shall we go?'

'Great,' I say, beaming at her.

In a cream-coloured fleece over her jeans and trainers, she wraps a scarf around her neck, then locks the door, checking it twice before pocketing her key.

'This way.' We start walking down the hill I've just come up, crossing the bridge where she waves to the woman at the bar. 'That's Nicole,' she says to me.

I nod. 'It was her who told me where you lived. Have you

worked there long?' The bar is so off the beaten track, it's hard to imagine how anyone finds it.

'I started there just before last Christmas.' She keeps walking. 'The bar only opens for six months – over the summer, when the tourists are here. The rest of the time, we do events and parties – like Persephone's.'

I'm curious about something. 'And you can stay indefinitely? I mean, doesn't Brexit make it almost impossible these days?'

'It does – but not if you have an Irish passport,' she says. 'My mother was from Cork – and I was born there. It makes it so much easier.'

'You don't need a visa?'

She shakes her head. 'Luckily.' She glances sideways at me. 'How is your mother?'

'On the surface, she's the same.' It isn't entirely true. Even seeing her each day, I notice how frail she's becoming. 'To be honest, I think she's getting her affairs in order – emotionally and parentally, at least.'

'Oh?' Stevie glances at me.

'It's funny,' I go on. 'Well, not so much funny as surprising. She's said a few things lately that have been unexpected.'

'I can't imagine how it must feel,' she says quietly. 'Knowing you don't have long. I mean, none of us know how long our lives are going to be, but that's kind of different to being told you have a finite amount of time.' Her voice sounds distant. 'I guess you'd probably be thinking about how it's going to be for everyone after you've gone. If there's any way of making it easier for them.' She lapses into silence. 'Except you can't, can you?'

I don't know what to say. Nothing about my mother's illness is easy. But I'm mindful also of what Stevie's been through. 'I'm sure you're right. I guess it's different for everyone,' I say.

'I'm so sorry, Ned.' Stevie threads her arm through mine. 'So sorry you're going through this.'

Feeling her arm on mine, suddenly I realise how much I like it there. 'It's just how it is.'

We walk in silence for a while, but it isn't an awkward kind of silence. It's one that's born out of empathy, of understanding. 'So, have you any more gigs coming up?' she asks.

'Not at the moment,' I say, 'My sister tells me I need to get a job, but as you've probably realised, there aren't too many of those around here.'

'Oh.' Stevie sounds surprised. 'I suppose there aren't. What kind of job does she think you should get?'

'Something to occupy the untapped and unexploited reaches of my mind,' I say a little cynically. 'Her theory is I spend too much time without a purpose.'

Stevie frowns. 'But you have your music, don't you?'

'That's what I've tried to explain to her. She still thinks I need a plan B, as she puts it.'

'What do you think?' Stevie sounds thoughtful.

'I hate to say it, but on the one hand, she has a point,' I admit, screwing my face up. 'But on the other, if I'm doing something else, it will take up time I could be using to write my big break-through song.'

Stevie's silent for a moment. 'But...' She shakes her head.

Stopping, I turn to look at her. 'But what?'

She looks slightly awkward. 'Well, if I'm being honest, and I don't normally ask things like this... but you said you have a big house... Does that mean that perhaps you don't have to worry about money – the way some of us do?'

I think about how to answer. She's right in thinking there's money in my family, but it's been engrained in me since childhood that unless the coffers are kept topped up, the money will run out – one day – though as I've found out accidentally and quite recently, that day is not yet. 'I suppose my family is relatively well off. But unfortunately, I'm less so.' My grandparents left me some money, but after years on a meagre income, most of it's gone.

'There's another way of looking at it.' There's silence as she pauses. 'What makes you really happy?'

'Happy?' Her directness takes me aback.

'Yes.' She pauses. 'You see, I have a theory that most of us don't think about it and we just go through life doing what we think we're supposed to do, or what everyone else thinks we should do. Then one day, before you know it, your life's nearly over and you're thinking of all these things you could have done but never found time for.'

It reminds me of what my mother said. I'm guessing Stevie's talking about her parents. How they couldn't have known that day they got on the plane that the end that had been out of sight was very rapidly drawing closer.

'Take your music,' she goes on. 'If that's what you love, and it makes you happy, it doesn't matter what other people say. OK, so it might be an unconventional life. But life shouldn't be about following convention – at least, I don't think so.'

I'm taken aback. 'That's almost exactly what my mother said. It was something she'd never said before. She said that if music is what I'm passionate about, I should follow my heart.'

'That's really lovely.' Stevie's arm tightens around mine. 'Doesn't that answer your questions? I mean, she's right, isn't she?'

I shrug. 'If it weren't for the simple fact that right now, it doesn't come near to generating an income I could live off. But it feels like what I should be doing with my life.'

A smile plays on her lips. 'You'll work it out.' She looks up. 'I can't believe we're here already. I really love this little church.'

I follow her gaze, uncomfortable all of a sudden, because I know it well. It's the church where the christenings and weddings in my family have taken place; where my grandparents are buried. A place where the veil between life and death is drawn sharply into focus. More sharply it seems since learning about my mother's illness.

But death is no longer a distant, far-flung thing. It's in our home, in my mother's frailty, the words she uses, her gradual withdrawal from life. The pain she hides, the love that shines from her as with each passing day, death moves imperceptibly closer to us.

7

FAY

With her arthritis playing up, at my neighbour's request, I take some flowers to place on her husband's grave. It's a gorgeous April afternoon, with barely a cloud in the sky.

As I park outside the church, I notice a couple in the lane. A young man who looks vaguely familiar, a woman with him, her red hair glinting in the sun. I watch as the light catches their face before, holding hands, they carry on walking up the lane.

I get out of my car and go through the gate. Holding my neighbour's posy of flowers, I make my way across the churchyard and lay it on her husband's grave. It's wonderfully peaceful here, the grass that's grown up around the graves dotted with tiny wild-flowers.

As I go back to my car, a voice interrupts my thoughts.

'*Excusez-moi, Madame.*'

Turning to see an elderly woman standing outside the church, I go over to her. '*Bonjour.*'

When I ask in French that is less than fluent if she'd like any help, she answers in English that is just as faltering.

'May I ask you for a lift to the village?'

'Of course.' I offer her my arm.

She takes it gratefully. 'I used to walk. I walked everywhere. But now, I am old.' She sounds resigned rather than bitter about it.

'It happens to us all, doesn't it?' On reaching my car, I help her into it.

'I am *quatre-vingt-deux*. I think in English that is eighty-two? It is my legs that feel old,' she says. 'But I do not. Do you live in this village?'

'I live in England. My husband and I have been coming on holiday here for twenty-five years.' I pause. 'I love it here.'

The woman looks surprised. 'So why do you not live here?'

It's a good question. One I ponder, along with what she said about getting older. If age does one thing to you, it makes you focus on time.

It's still on my mind a couple of days later. Finding myself driving past the church again, on impulse I pull over and get out.

Checking the church door and finding it open, I step inside for a moment. The interior is dark and cool, lavishly festooned with thousands of flowers in spring shades and branches of cherry blossom. It crosses my mind there's been a wedding in recent days. But as I notice an order of service, I realise they're funeral flowers.

Sitting down, I think how their transience seems symbolic, befitting the end of a life; their scent masking the mustiness that all churches seem to have.

My thoughts are interrupted by the sound of the door creaking open, followed by the lightest of footsteps.

'*Bonjour.*' The woman's voice is quiet as she glances at me, before taking a seat across the aisle.

'*Bonjour.*' I take in her sleek hair and loose-fitting jeans, her elegant ankle boots, wondering what brings her here, before berating myself. I may not be religious, but in rural France, traditional values haven't changed, the church still forming the centre of the community. But if it holds the answer to any of the great mysteries about life and death, I haven't found it yet. Nor it seems, has the woman.

After sitting there for a few minutes, she turns to me. 'Do you believe in God?'

Taken aback, I'm not sure what to say. 'Not really.' I decide honesty is the best policy. 'But each to their own.' I'm curious. 'Do you?'

She's silent for a moment. 'I suppose the question I ask myself is that if there is a God, why do so many people have to suffer?'

'The age-old question.' The one nobody has an answer for. 'It's probably an act of blasphemy to say such a thing in here, but I think God was invented to induce fear in people.'

'The wrath of God,' she quotes, shaking her head. 'All so that a few men can inhabit a position of prominence and power. And it has been mostly men, hasn't it?'

'Traditionally. But it's changing.' I look around. 'It's rather a lovely church, though.'

'It's pretty,' she says dispassionately. 'Filled with all these beautiful, dying flowers.' She glances around at them. 'And built, no doubt, by all those fearful worshippers, driven by the threat of going to hell.'

'Oh, I think churches are about a bit more than that,' I say gently. 'They're places people find comfort – some, at least.'

She sighs. 'I only wish I were one of them.' She looks at me. 'So what brings you here?'

'I'm not religious, but I suppose I rather like old churches. My neighbour happens to be a firm believer, but she has arthritis and her husband is buried in the churchyard. I come here now and then to put flowers on his grave for her. But it's the first time I've actually been inside.' I hesitate. 'So why are you here?'

She smiles distantly. 'Partly because of the unholy number of my ancestors lying out there.' She nods towards the churchyard. 'But I am just checking God out, I suppose. Giving him one last chance to prove himself. I mean, if he is going to show up at some point in your life, you would hope it would be in your hour of need.' She pauses. 'I apologise. I told myself I would not, but I am feeling wretchedly sorry for myself.'

Don't we all, sometimes, I can't help thinking. 'Maybe you're being a bit hard on yourself,' I say gently.

'Oh, I probably am.' She sighs. 'I suppose I do have good reason to feel quite angry with God – if he existed, that is. But at the end of the day, I am simply behaving like most people would. I am wasting what time I do have thinking about my death, rather than living.'

I look at her, shocked, suddenly noticing how pale her face is, how slight she is under her jacket.

She goes on. 'I should not be talking like this to you. I mean, I do not even know you.' There's a trace of humour in her eyes as they meet mine. 'And I've been lucky. I escaped one potentially terminal illness. It's meant I've had a lot of extra years. But this time...' She tails off.

'I'm sorry.' I don't know what else to say.

'So am I.' She pulls her jacket around her. 'Having cancer once changes your life. You never get over that sense of how fragile life is. But the second time...' She pulls herself up. 'Right now, I am having a moment. But it will pass.'

'You're very brave,' I say quietly.

She shakes her head. 'I really am not. But like most of us, I am addicted to suffering. You know how when you stub your toe, all you think about is that toe? It takes up more of our minds than the act of living does.' She shrugs. 'We become a victim of that too. I decided a long time ago, I did not want to be a victim. But here I am.'

'I'm sure that's easier said than done.' I'm thinking of the people I've met over the years, who don't know how to be anything else.

'All my life, I have never let myself become a victim,' she says fiercely. 'I have always made my own choices and achieved what was important to me. I'm trying to do the same – now, at the end.' She's silent for a moment. 'The thing is, I am not ready. And now that I'm running out of time, I'm questioning so many things.'

'It still isn't too late,' I say inadequately; inappropriately, too, given we've only just met. 'Do you mind me asking how long you've known about your illness?'

As her eyes meet mine, I realise she's about the same age as I am and my children come to mind, my heart twisting as I imagine how I'd feel in her shoes.

'A month.' She pauses. 'And I should not feel so bitter about it. At least I have time to talk to the people I love. But I still cannot bear the thought of leaving them.' Her voice wavers.

'I can't imagine how that feels,' I say humbly.

Her eyes are brimming with tears as she looks at me. 'Shit, isn't it?'

'It is.' I'm not sure what else to say to her. But even though it comes to all of us at some point, death is still taboo; we don't talk about it.

'You are so generously listening to me, and I haven't even introduced myself. I am Aimée.' Reaching into a pocket for a tissue, she wipes her face.

'I'm Fay.'

'An English name.' She smiles briefly. 'My husband is English. Do you live around here, Fay?'

'We have a house about ten minutes away. We've been coming here for the summer for years, since our children were young. They're grown up now.'

'Mine too.' A wistful look crosses her face. 'They take your life over while they are young, don't they? Then before you know it, they're off in the world, living their own lives. They don't need us any more.' She wipes away another tear. 'I always liked that they needed me. But in the circumstances, it's just as well.'

'You live near here?'

She nods. 'I was born here. After we married, we lived in London for a while. But when my parents died, we inherited the house that's been in my family for a long time.' She doesn't say how long. 'For someone who doesn't believe, you are spending quite a bit of time in a church.' There's humour in her eyes.

'I suppose I find churches a good place to think.' I decide to tell her the real reason. 'I'm at a bit of a crossroads, as it happens.' Going on, I tell her about Hugh and the allotment I've taken on. About the desire I have to forge something in this world that means something.

'Then you must do it,' she says quietly. 'I'm lucky. My husband has never held me back. If this allotment is important to you, you mustn't let your husband stop you. Life goes too fast.' She pauses. 'I am realising it is the saddest thing to have regrets.'

* * *

Leaving Aimée alone, I go outside. After the stillness of the church, the countryside seems brimming with life. Thinking of Aimée and her family, my mind turns to my own children.

If I weren't here, would they miss me? Telling myself *Of course they would*, I stop at my neighbour's husband's grave. Standing there, I ponder for a moment how, as Aimée just said, we are all of us here for such a short time.

But as I drive away, I'm unsettled. It happens, though, doesn't it? Sometimes we meet someone, or have a conversation, that makes us look at the world differently – in this case, Aimée. There is no guarantee about how long any of us will live. I might have years ahead of me. But I can't help thinking: *What would I do if I had months?*

It's not a subject I normally dwell on. But today, I can't shake the thought. And not in a macabre sense. It's as though I'm looking at time in a way most of us choose not to; at the duration of a life as finite – how at some unknown point, it will end.

What's happening to you, Fay? I know what Hugh would say. *Go to the doctor and get some pills...* But the truth is I couldn't talk to Hugh about anything like this. There's not the remotest chance he'd understand.

I think of the flowers in the church; transient things that grow from the tiniest seed, developing roots, then leaves, at some point blossoming into a beautiful, multi-petalled flower in all its glory, before the petals drop and leaves wilt before they die.

Rather like us, I can't help thinking. Where am I on that path? Still flowering? Or are my petals starting to fall? And I'm a realist. I know it's inevitable, but what's suddenly a burning issue is the time I've wasted – on trivia. The choosing of which washing detergent, or the perusing over packets of bread or cheese. The cleaning of a house that's already neat and tidy, the mundane television shows that pass an otherwise dull evening. The drawn-out coffees and lunches with people I have nothing in common with.

Most of my life, it's how I've filled my days. But it's no longer enough.

That evening, I pour myself a glass of wine and call Stu, my son, who moved to the US two years ago.

Stu answers straight away. 'Hey, Mum! How's it going?'

At the sound of his voice, suddenly I miss him terribly. 'Good, thanks. I'm still in France. But it isn't the same without you all.'

'I imagine it's a lot more peaceful.' He sounds amused. 'Is the weather nice?'

'Today has been lovely. Marcie came out for a few days, but it rained. How are you? How's LA?'

'Same as usual! A bit crazy! Mum, I'm always telling you, you should video-call.'

'And let you see what a mess I look?' My hair needs washing and I'm not wearing any make-up.

'All irrelevant,' my darling son says. 'Look, I'm sorry, but can I call you back later? I have a meeting about to start.'

'I'm so sorry. Of course. Call any time.' I always forget the time difference. 'Take care of yourself. Love you.'

'Love you too.'

Almost immediately, I try Julia, my daughter, but I get her voicemail.

'Hey, it's Julia, leave me a message.'

'Hi.' I pause. 'It's Mum. Just calling to see how you are! I'll catch you another time.'

Switching off my phone, I blink away tears. I miss the closeness of them, even though it's what I've always wanted – for my children to be independent, to have wonderful, busy lives. But it only reaffirms the emptiness, not just in my home but in my self, too.

For goodness' sake, Fay, I reprimand myself. *Stop wallowing. You're in this lovely house – and you have your health. It's a beautiful evening. The sun is warm, the birds are singing. If you're not happy, you're the only person who can do anything about it.*

I'm on my second glass of wine when my phone buzzes with a

call from Hugh. Knowing I can't go on putting off talking to him, I pick it up.

'Hello.'

'Fay? How are you?' He sounds slightly guarded.

'I'm fine.' My voice is overly bright. 'It's been lovely weather today.' I try to inject kindness into my voice. 'How are you?'

Ignoring my question, he cuts to the chase. 'Have you decided when you're coming home?'

'Not yet.' I hesitate. 'Is everything OK?'

'Of course it is,' he says crossly. 'What were you expecting? That my life would be falling apart without you?'

'Not at all, Hugh,' I say carefully.

'We'll talk about this once you're home.' He pauses. 'But until you are, I don't think there's anything else to say.' He hangs up before I can reply.

Sitting there in silence, I stare at my phone, guilt washing over me. This is all my fault. It's me, not Hugh, who's caused this distance between us. I should never have stayed on here. I should have done what I always do: gone home on the flight Hugh booked, then talked to him about how I'm feeling.

But then my guilt is replaced by frustration. How can I talk to someone who refuses to listen?

* * *

As a family, most of our visits to France have been in the summer months and the next morning, when I awake early and drive to the allotments, I take in the extraordinary beauty that spring brings. The trees coming into blossom, the lush green verges scattered with wild flowers. The soft warmth of the sun; the unutterable peacefulness.

Since yesterday, I've kept thinking of the conversation I had with Aimée, struck by how similar-minded we are in many ways; feeling it fuel something inside me, one thought overriding everything else. While Aimée doesn't know how long she has in this beautiful world, I still have time.

It feels like a light has been switched on. If only it were a feeling I could share with Hugh... If he could step back from his preconceived view of life, and recognise it's about more than work and his flaming golf club. But Hugh is Hugh. The man I married. And it's too lovely a morning to dwell on our problems. When I can't solve anything until I see him again, they can wait.

Meanwhile, I've come here to focus on the allotment. After a trip to our local market, in my impatience for visible results, I have seedlings to plant out – lettuces, onions, the first tomato plants. Smiling to myself, I imagine coming here in summer and picking the results of my labours; the simple earthly pleasure of eating sun-ripened tomatoes, fresh lettuces; the scent of basil leaves.

There's no sign of Zeke this morning. Ignoring my aching muscles, I lose myself in the routine of digging and planting, noticing the way the soil crumbles, pulling away what I think are weeds. But I'm not alone for long, and an hour later as I stand up to take a break, Zeke's voice comes from behind me.

'Looking good.'

I turn to find him gazing at the bed I've been digging. 'Do you think it's all right?'

'Can't go much wrong with digging.' His face breaks into a smile. 'You've got a thing or two to learn about weeds, though.'

'Oh no.' I'm mortified. 'You mean these?' I point to the pile of tiny stems I've pulled out.

He crouches down, separating some of them. 'These are

chives. See the little bulb on the end? And smell them.' He passes one to me. 'Onion, right?'

Slightly horrified, I sniff it, seeing immediately what he means. 'I can't believe I've done that.'

'Don't worry. Just plant them back in. Here. I'll show you.'

I watch him. 'What about the others?'

Standing up, he picks up the rest of the so-called weeds. 'I'm pretty sure these are rocket.' He passes them to me. 'This soil is mostly weed-free. If you find anything growing, I'd bet it's because Delilah planted it there.' He pauses. 'Fancy a cup of tea?'

* * *

Sitting on a rickety chair, I cup my hands around the mug of tea Zeke passes me.

'Lovely day,' I say, then realise how banal it sounds. 'You see, when I've come here with my family, it's always been during the summer. I've never been here at this time of year before.'

'Best time.' Zeke nods. 'But I say that every season. It's the change, you see. That's what we notice. If every day were summer, it wouldn't be the same.'

'I suppose not.' I sip my tea. 'This is very good.'

'Nothing like a good cup of English tea.' Zeke's silent for a moment. 'It's none of my business, but I guess you've just answered my question. You live in England?'

'Yes.' I frown slightly. 'But I'm planning to spend more time here – otherwise there'd be no point in me taking on one of the allotments.'

'You're retired?' Zeke watches me.

'Not exactly.' I sigh. 'Hugh – my husband – is old school. He's the breadwinner – I've spent my life looking after the house and children.'

'I guess that makes you old school too.' He grins, revealing a gap in his teeth.

I look up, slightly shocked. 'I suppose it does. I know it sounds like I haven't done very much, but to tell you the truth, I've always gone along with it. But now, of course, our children are grown up.' I shrug. 'I'm realising I need a sense of purpose in my life.'

He nods. 'I think we all have those moments. But bringing up children is important – don't underestimate it.'

'Yes.' And I know he's right. But that part of my life is over now.

'I get what you're saying, though,' Zeke says. 'It's like you know, don't you, when things have to change.'

'Exactly.' I'm deep in thought. 'It just seemed to come upon me rather suddenly.' I shake my head. 'I was at the church the other day. There'd just been a funeral there. I met someone who isn't well,' I explain. 'And after that, it got me thinking. None of us know, do we? When our days are about to run out?'

His expression is suddenly sober. 'You never said a truer word.'

I'm curious. 'Have you always lived around here?'

'Most of my life.' He pauses. 'I was born in Manhattan. My folks came over here when I was four. My mother was French. They made a pretty nice life here.' Cutting the conversation short, he glances up at the sky. 'It's warm for the time of year.' He gets up. 'Well, best get your seeds planted. After, water them, but only lightly. Same when they start to grow.'

A thought occurs to me. 'I'm going to have to go back to England at some point. Probably soon.' I hesitate – I should have thought about this before. 'Will they be OK – for a week – maybe two?'

'Most likely they'll be fine,' he reassures me. 'Tell you what, though. If it gets too dry, I'll water them for you.'

'Thank you.' But I'm frowning. 'What's that?' I point towards a patch of soil in one of his flower beds, where some dark shoots are coming through.

Studying them closely, he scratches his head. 'I'm not sure. And believe me, I've seen most things that grow around here.'

'There's an app you can get,' I say helpfully. 'It can identify most plants. I'll try and download…'

Shaking his head, he goes into his shed, coming out with a large, rather battered-looking book. 'If it's all the same to you, I prefer the old-fashioned way.'

* * *

That evening, I check the weather forecast. With a week of rain coming up, I decide it's time to fly home and face the music. Having sent Hugh a text to tell him my plans, I book a flight for the following day.

As I drive to the airport the next morning, the Corrèze countryside is verdant, miles of fields stretching in every direction, interrupted now and then by a historic town or village.

We are so lucky, I tell myself as reaching Limoges, I find a space in the car park. The house, running a French car, not worrying about parking costs… It's no more than luck that Hugh and I were born into caring families, which meant we went to good schools; but he's worked hard and his career has been successful. And I don't take any of it for granted. But I'm being pulled towards the next stage in my life – strongly enough to know that this time, I won't be in England for long.

It never ceases to amaze me how tiny the airport in Limoges is. It takes minutes to go through security, then walk the short distance out to the plane. My seat is in business class, the one next to me empty. But after take-off, we're almost immediately into cloud and as I drink the complimentary champagne I'm offered, thinking of Hugh in our house in Surrey, I have a physical sense of my wings being clipped.

8

ZEKE

Watching the plane fly overhead that morning, I think of Fay on her way back to England and her husband. The last couple of days, she's had things on her mind – get to my age, you have a feel for these things.

She's picked a good time to go, though. The rain starts later that afternoon, drizzle that slowly builds to a downpour. Retreating to my house, I stand at the open window upstairs, listening as it builds to a crescendo, breathing in the cool scent of it as a yowl reaches my ears.

Looking down, I see the cat looking up at me. Going downstairs, I let him in. He's in a sorry state. 'You need drying.' He follows me into the kitchen where I find a towel and dry him as he purrs gratefully.

Going to the fridge, I get the fish I bought the previous day. 'I must have known you were coming,' I tell him, cutting a piece of it into tiny squares, before feeding it to him.

There's no telling a cat what to do. And after that, he goes from being an occasional visitor to becoming a fixture in my life, even following me through the hedge into the garden five days later, when the rain eventually stops.

In just a few days, the landscape has changed, the buds on the trees opening in the warmer air, the wild flowers in bloom beneath the hedgerows, while the birds are in full song. But it isn't just nature that's been brought to life. The watery sun seems to bring out the gardeners, too. There's Jean, who's inherited the allotment his mother used to keep; Lily, who quietly comes and goes. Just two of the people who come here, for reasons known only to themselves; all of us revelling in the peace.

But there's nothing peaceful about Rémy this morning. When she sees me, she comes stomping over. 'I have been worrying,' she says crossly, her hands thrust in her pockets, her jeans mud-spattered. 'That the rain will wash everything away.'

I shake my head. 'You should know by now, nature's tougher than that.' I gesture towards the trees and hedgerows. 'How else would any of this have survived?'

'I am talking about seeds, Zeke.' She frowns at me like I'm stupid. 'They are like tiny babies. They are fragile.'

'You go and check. And babies are pretty tough, when it comes to it. Come back and tell me they're all OK,' I say to her, then watch her march off across the mud towards her flower beds, before turning my attention to my own.

The salad leaves I planted are healthy, the herbs revived by the rain. Even the tiny tomato plants are starting to shoot. Stopping, I feel myself frown. It isn't just the veg plants that have grown stronger. Those black shoots that Fay noticed, there are more of them.

Cursing myself for not finding out what they are, I get a trowel and dig until the soil loosens. As they come away, I notice the cat watching me. 'Fat lot of help you are,' I tell him. 'But OK. Seeing as you're here, how about lunch?'

Sitting down, as I unwrap my tuna sandwich, I suppose it's no surprise the cat doesn't leave my side.

'You will have ten if you are not careful,' Rémy tells me disapprovingly when she comes back. 'Cats have a grapevine – you do know that, don't you?'

'He's OK,' I say easily. 'How were your seeds?'

She looks down her nose at me. 'As you said. They are fine.'

'Told you.' I hold out a piece of my sandwich and the cat jumps onto my lap.

'They might not have been,' she retorts. 'And what about that English woman? Where is she?'

'You mean Fay?' I arch my eyebrows. 'She's gone back to England.'

'So you have given Delilah's garden to a woman who isn't here.' Rémy shakes her head. 'Seriously, Zeke. I do not understand why you do this.'

'She will be back,' I say sternly. I want to tell her to mind her own business, but I know she means well. 'Everything's just fine here. You go and worry about your own garden.'

* * *

I don't know what it is that's different about this year. Whether it's the air that smells different, or the sunlight seems brighter, the sound of the voices around me louder. But there's an intensity to everything. A sense of premonition, as though something unannounced is lying in wait.

Even at night, the sky seems wider, the stars closer in a way I've never seen before, that I can't un-see. I watch everyone else, wondering if they've felt it too. But as they carry on their routines of digging, planting and watering, if they feel any different, I wouldn't know.

It's probably the Universe at play; one of those transformational times some of us experience at some point, thrown at us to stop us in our tracks and make us question the way we see things. After all, if I believe what I've read, humanity is shifting. 'Evolving' is the word I've heard folks use – and I hope we are. Given the way we abuse this world, the alternative doesn't bear thinking about.

It's one of the reasons I set up the allotments. For people to respect this tiny corner of our planet; to work in harmony with nature. OK, so there's only a handful of us. But even the ways of a few can ripple out to others.

I sigh. The rigid thinking of the old ways has long had its day. Hopefully people are at last starting to see that.

As I gaze up at the sky, the first swallows have arrived. I watch them swoop and soar, marvelling at the incredible journey they make. And they're a sure sign that summer isn't far off, which means there's work to be done. I have beans and peas to plant around the frame in place for them to clamber up. But it doesn't take long and once it's done, I plant some aubergines and peppers, then pumpkins over by my compost heap. That's the trick with gardens. To utilise all of it; to stay a step ahead.

A voice startles me. 'Zeke?'

Turning, I see the figure of a girl making her way through the hedge. As she comes closer, her long red hair shimmers in the sunlight and I recognise her. 'Ah. Stevie! What can I do for you?'

I've forgotten how shy she is. In dungarees and a pristine white T-shirt, her cheeks are pink as she smiles. 'I went to your house. The lady next door told me you'd probably be here. I'm glad I've found you,' she says.

'It's nice to see you again. Did you get that car of yours fixed?'

'Billy mended it,' she says. 'He's been so helpful. While I think of it, I made you these.' Reaching into the bag she's carrying, she passes me a carefully wrapped packet. 'Emergency biscuits, just in case anyone else turns up on your doorstep!'

'Thank you. But you needn't have,' I say, taking them from her.

'You're welcome.' She looks at me. 'I suddenly realised I'd never properly thanked you for helping me that day. And for the vegetables you gave me. You were so kind. And I felt so terrible.'

'There's no need. I didn't do anything.' I'm touched, all the same, that she's come here.

'But you did,' she insists. 'More than you'll ever know. You see…' She hesitates. 'You know those days when everything goes wrong? When you wonder if they'll ever go right again? It was one of those.' She pauses. 'I wasn't sure what to do – about anything. The last thing I needed was my car breaking down. I was worried about how I was going to pay for it. But then I met you – and it felt like a turning point. After, everything started to change. You introduced me to Billy. He's so nice. And since… I suppose it's just things are looking up.' She stops suddenly. 'I'm sorry. I'm not sure why I'm telling you all this.'

I can see the difference in her. Her eyes are alive and there's a glow about her. 'Well, I'd say that deserves celebrating.' I pause. 'Cup of tea?'

'Thanks. I'd love one.'

'Good.' I point to an upturned wooden apple box. 'Sit yourself down on that, and I'll put the kettle on.'

I wait for the kettle to boil, amused by Stevie's unexpected appearance here. I'm not a bad judge of people, but I have to admit, she's surprised me. Shy as she is, I didn't expect to see her again, let alone for her to come back with a packet of biscuits. And I would have expected her to ask what everyone else does when they've seen where I live: *why do you have an allotment when you have that garden behind your house?*

But she doesn't. 'Here you are.' I pass her a mug, then reach for the biscuits. 'You'd better have some of these.'

'Oh no.' She shakes her head. 'Those are for you.'

I don't usually like biscuits – I keep them in the house for other people. But seeing as she's brought me some, I open the packet and take one. 'These are good,' I say through a mouthful.

'I know.' Holding her mug, she gazes around the allotments. 'How long have you been doing this?'

'Well...' I pretend to think. 'I'd say about thirty-nine years and ten months, give or take a couple of days.'

'Wow.' She raises her eyebrows, trying not to smile. 'What do you grow?'

'Anything seasonal,' I tell her. 'I'm not into all that forced stuff. Our bodies want food grown the natural way.' I remember what she said, about how she used to be a chef. 'You know, the kind of food you like.'

Her eyes light up. 'I couldn't agree more.' She pauses. 'Those things you gave me when my car broke down were amazing.' Her eyes wander across to the rows of radishes and chives. 'Do you ever have anything for sale?'

I study her. 'That's a very good question. The short answer is no. I don't do this to make money out of it. But maybe, if it would be of use to you, we could come to some kind of arrangement.'

She looks puzzled. 'I'm not sure what you mean.'

'Put it this way... Rather than money, I'm talking about an exchange of skills.'

She frowns. 'But I don't have anything to offer in return.'

I laugh, but not unkindly – it's how laughter should be, after all. 'Well, you know how to cook, for one thing. You reckon you could teach other people?'

A frown crinkles her brow. 'You want me to teach you?'

A smile spreads across my face. 'Not me. I'm done with

learning any fancy new stuff. I'm thinking more someone who needs teaching. I'm not sure who, just yet. But there'll be someone.'

Her look of confusion clears. 'You're talking about paying it forward, aren't you?'

I nod. 'Something like that.'

Frowning, she goes on. 'Billy told me about you believing in that. It's why he sorted out my car – for next to nothing,' She pauses. 'I still don't quite get it. You're saying you're going to let me have some veg you've grown – for nothing. Is that right?'

'Sounds good to me.' I shrug. 'Don't worry. There'll be someone to help out.' I sigh. 'Believe me. There's always some-one.' I get up. 'But for now... How about some salad leaves? And some new potatoes?'

The light is back in her eyes. 'That would be amazing.'

I chuckle to myself. There can't be that many people who'd find mud-covered potatoes and a random selection of salad leaves amazing. But I find myself liking the fact that Stevie does.

After she disappears back through the gap in the hedge, I start digging some compost into one of the beds I'm preparing. But as I rake the soil, I find a particularly persistent weed that refuses to be loosened. Bending down, I frown. It's the black one again. My plantsman's brain can identify most things, but this isn't like anything I've seen before. Nor is it in my book. Brushing the soil away from its dark shoot, I feel underneath for the roots, tugging at it before it comes away.

* * *

The changing of the seasons can be breathtaking. But here in the allotments, I'm aware of the magic a single day can hold, from the pure notes of the first bird's song as the sun rises.

Then there are the people who come and go throughout the day, with the stories they share, as well as those they choose to keep to themselves, but that's up to them. Even in this funny little village, like anywhere else, everyone has their own story. And all of it set against the constancy of the slow passage of the sun measuring the passing of each day. Days that speed up the older you get.

And today is another day that does just that. A day filled with the simple pleasure of tending a small piece of earth while the gentle pace of life goes on around me, until the light starts to fade and everyone drifts away, leaving me alone. Sitting there, I savour the peaceful hour as the sun sinks lower, taking in the dappled light and long shadows, a lone blackbird's sweet song. Forget all those highfalutin painters, I always say to people. Who needs them? Nature's paintbrush surpasses every one of them.

It's the time I live each day for, and as my eyes start to close, I see her through the trees, the last of the sunlight catching her soft hair, her feet bare, her eyes shining with love.

Imagining Marie sitting beside me, I dare not open my eyes, lest she disappears. As it always has and always will, this twilight hour belongs to memories of us.

* * *

The next morning, I'm up early making coffee in my kitchen when there's a knock on my door. Wondering who it could be at this hour, as I walk towards it, there's another knock.

'Hold your horses,' I call out. Unbolting it and opening the door, I find Stevie standing there. 'Hello again.'

Her face flushes. 'Sorry… It's early, isn't it? But I couldn't sleep – and I thought you'd be up. I mean, because you work with the seasons, I figured you'd be awake when the sun rises.'

I raise my eyebrows. 'Turns out you're right – well, usually.' I glance at my watch. It really is early. 'How can I help?'

She looks hesitant. 'It's about what you said the other day – about teaching people. To cook. Do you really think I could do that?'

I pause. 'I've just made some coffee. Like a cup?'

'Oh.' She looks flustered. 'Yes. I would.' She steps inside. 'Thank you.'

'You're welcome.' I close the door behind her.

In the kitchen, she looks thoughtful as she cups the mug of coffee in her hands. 'You see, I think I need to do something different. Since moving here, all I've really achieved is to decorate my kitchen. It isn't even that big.'

I frown slightly. 'What about work?'

'I work part-time,' she says hastily. 'It's a bit chaotic, to be honest. But it's how Nicole and Olivier are – a bit chaotic.'

'Nicole and Olivier in the bar?' I've been there once or twice.

She nods. 'I like it – don't get me wrong. But if I could teach people to cook, I'd really like that. I'd be helping them. Wouldn't I?' She looks at me as if seeking affirmation.

'I don't need persuading. So how are you going to find your students?'

'That's the bit I'm stuck on,' she confesses. 'I mean, people around here tend to eat traditionally, don't they?'

I can see where she's coming from. But then I have an idea. 'It's a bit of a deviation from teaching, but maybe the two would work together...' I take a deep breath, knowing this is a whole different ball game; hoping she doesn't run away. 'You could teach people the basics, but maybe offer to help – perhaps with small lunches or dinner parties – that way, you won't be in competition with Nicole and Olivier. Especially if you're serious about using seasonal ingredients...' I shrug. 'What do you think?'

Her mouth twitches slightly as she takes it in. As the cat appears out of nowhere, she leans down to stroke him. 'He's cute. Is he yours?'

'He seems to have decided he is,' I say ruefully. 'So what do you think? About the dinner party idea?'

'Maybe,' she says at last. Then she sighs. 'The thing is, I'm not good at talking to people. I'm fine in the kitchen, when I know what I'm doing and no one can see me. But anything else kind of freaks me out.'

I look at her sternly. 'You're going to let a thing like that hold you back?' I'm guessing she isn't particularly adventurous; that she probably prefers to stick with the familiar. But sometimes, it doesn't do any harm to push yourself.

She stares at me, anxious. 'You think it would work?'

'Why not?' I hold her gaze. 'You don't have a lot to lose by trying.' I pause. 'You feeling daunted?'

'A little,' she confesses.

'Why not try it? If it doesn't work out, you can think again.' I frown slightly. 'I know a few people. If you give me your mobile number, I'll put the word out – if you'd like me to?'

9

STEVIE

As I walk home, the sun is rising above the trees, the only sound the chorus of birdsong. Thinking of what Zeke suggested, the thought of trying something new is both exciting and terrifying. But what I notice most is the long-absent flicker of hope it triggers.

First, I need to talk to Nicole and Olivier and when I reach the village, my luck is in. Somewhat fortuitously, Olivier is up early too. Poised halfway up a ladder, he's fixing the lights outside the bar.

'Morning,' I call out.

'*Bonjour*.' He waves back.

Deciding there's no time like the present, I walk over. 'Need any help?'

'Almost done.' He comes down the ladder. 'This is very early, Stevie, even for you.'

'I know. I couldn't sleep – so I went for a walk. I've been talking to a friend. I have this idea – about work... and it's different to the bar, but I don't want to upset you and Nicole...'

'Slowly.' His eyes twinkle at me. 'Now tell me again. What exactly is it you are worrying about?'

When I tell him about my plan, he smiles. 'You couldn't have known, but this is perfect. Nicole is tired of all this outside cooking in other people's kitchens... And the summer is coming. We will be busy enough here.'

As I take in what he's saying, a weight lifts. 'You don't mind?' I say timidly. 'I was so worried I'd upset you. Which I wouldn't. I hope you know that.'

He laughs. 'I know you wouldn't. Of course, I will talk to Nicole, but I know what she will say. It will be fine – as long as you still have time to work here now and then. Otherwise, we will have a problem. But... that will be our problem – not yours.'

'Oh no.' I shake my head. 'I can't imagine I'll be doing many dinners. I'll have plenty of time to work here.'

Feeling lighter, I walk home, but I'm completely forgetting the saying about the best-laid of plans.

* * *

My new-found sense of optimism seems to fire up something inside me and back at home, I open the door into my little sitting room that, so far, has remained firmly closed.

Having stripped the walls and redecorated the kitchen, I've barely looked at the sitting room. This morning, as I go inside, I gaze at the dated wallpaper that's been here decades, the faded curtains that are gathering dust and, while studying the furniture, I try to work out what has to go and what can be upcycled.

For some reason, the pull of the past is powerfully nostalgic today, as sitting for a moment, I think about the people to whom this has been home over the years.

But time moves on – don't I know that better than anyone. It's why we should savour each moment of this precious life, and not squander it.

Quit philosophising, I tell myself. And I haven't squandered all of it. I've simply ground to a halt. Not any more, though. This morning, there's work to be done. After changing into my oldest dungarees and tying my hair on top of my head, I pull back the ancient curtains and push the windows open before making a start.

A few hours pass, during which I get as far as stripping two of the walls. Then as I start on the third, my phone buzzes. Usually I'd ignore it, but after talking to Zeke, however unlikely it is, there's the smallest chance it might be a potential client. To my utter astonishment, when I answer, that's exactly what it is.

Apparently she's heard of me through Olivier and wants to meet with me. So later that afternoon, I abandon my decorating, my stomach fluttering with nerves as I drive the half hour to the potential client's house. My intention had been to put some menus together before seeing anyone, but this has happened so fast, I haven't had time.

In my mind, I rehearse what I want to ask her, what I can suggest in terms of a menu, but it all goes out of my head when I turn into her drive, because this isn't just a house. It's a sprawling dream of a massive manor house.

In my mind I'm already rehearsing impossibly high standards, lavish place settings, the most elaborate of food. But that isn't what I do, I remind myself.

It doesn't stop me positively shaking with nerves as I park my car, sitting there for a moment, cursing Zeke as I consider what a terrible idea this was. But I pull myself together. I'm here now – and this is just an hour of my life. For better or worse, I'm going to do it. Then after, if I still feel like this, I can thank him and tell

him I've had second thoughts; that the bar is too busy; Nicole and
Olivier are going to need me.

Taking a deep breath, I open my car door and get out.

* * *

It turns out the party isn't until the summer, giving me time to
settle into my new role. And it went OK, I tell myself after, as I
drive home. I did a passable job of hiding the reality that underneath I was a quivering wreck. But people like my client have no
experience of how people like me feel. She also has a family – I
gleaned that much. She is not alone.

Nor am I, I tell myself firmly. So I may not have much in the
way of family who are blood. But there are people. People who
care enough to be there if I need them – Nicole, Olivier, Zeke.
Madame Picard, if I wanted some company and a cup of tea.
There's even Billy.

Slightly surprising myself as I think about them all, my
thoughts turn to Ned.

* * *

Largely thanks to Zeke, more, less intimidating bookings come in.
A small lunch party, a vegetarian buffet. A client who wants me to
teach her to prepare an afternoon tea. And I would have been
more than happy to keep things like that. Two or three evenings a
week, a Saturday afternoon, cooking a seasonal meal in someone's
kitchen.

In between, I try out new dishes and put together menus,
based on what's abundant in the market, and what Zeke can spare
from his garden. Needing to try them out, now and then, I call on

Madame Picard, offering her lunch in exchange for her honest feedback.

Today is one such day, and as I knock on her door with another experimental dish, it opens almost immediately.

'*Bonjour, Madame,*' I say brightly. 'I have brought lunch for you.' Limited by our knowledge, we've reverted to mostly talking in our native languages.

'Ah, *petite* Stevie.' Her face crinkles into a smile as she lets me in. 'Come.'

As always, her kitchen is cosy, the table scrupulously clean and already set for two with her finest cutlery. I put the casserole dish on the side.

'This one has been challenging me,' I confess as she takes two plates out of the oven. 'I want you to give me your honest opinion.'

'Of course.' Today she's dressed in a navy woollen dress and thick tights, the gold necklace she always wears over the top.

I serve up the food – a vegetable casserole in a rich sauce that to my mind, is lacking something. Putting a plate down in front of her, I'm keen to know what she thinks of it.

I sit down opposite, watching as she delicately tries a mouthful. Then silent, has another, before looking at me.

'It is good,' she says.

I know it's good. But. I'm sensing a *but*. 'It's missing something, isn't it?'

She frowns slightly. 'It is good as it is. But...' Getting up, she goes to her larder, coming back with a small, unlabelled jar of dried herbs. She passes it to me. 'Why don't you add just a little?'

Curious, I do as she says, then taste a mouthful, then another, eating in silence until the plate is empty. 'What was that?' I say, slightly dazed that the contents of that tiny jar have transformed my food into something magical.

She smiles. 'It is my secret. But don't worry, I have more.'

Getting up, she goes to the larder again, coming back with another little jar and passing it to me. 'For you.'

Two things happen after that. When I get home, I tip a spoonful of the contents of the jar onto a plate and try to analyse them. But I may as well be trying to capture a rainbow.

The second thing that happens is that next time I take her some food, I go in to find she isn't alone.

'Monsieur Valois is here. I didn't think you would mind,' she says quietly as she lets me in. 'He is very alone, *pauvre Monsieur*. Some of your beautiful food will make him smile again.'

'Of course.' After what's she's just said, I can hardly say no. Nor do I want to. '*Bonjour, Monsieur*,' I say cheerily as he nods from his seat at the table. '*Ça va?*'

'He is deaf,' Madame Picard mutters. 'Cannot hear a sausage.'

Trying not to smile at the increasing vocabulary which she doesn't always get quite right, I put the food down. 'Does he know this is experimental?'

She looks at me as though I'm mad. 'Your food is good. It is all that matters.'

A silence descends as they eat intently.

'You have used my herbs.' Madame Picard looks pleased.

'I have.' I pause. 'I've been trying to work out what they are. But I still don't know.'

Saying nothing, Madame Picard smiles to herself.

At the end, Monsieur Valois puts down his knife and fork. '*Bon*,' is all he says.

The next time I take some food to Madame Picard's, the two of them have been joined by Madame Bernard who lives on the edge of the village and is known for her strong opinions and lack of tolerance for the English.

'You stupid people who vote for Brexit should stay in your imbecilic little country,' is the first thing she says to me.

I stare at her, slightly shocked. 'I am sorry, Madame Bernard. I hope you enjoy your lunch.'

'Pah,' she says, sitting down in disgust.

'We're not all the same,' I say calmly. 'Are you hungry?'

She settles herself in the chair. 'I suppose so. I hope this is not English food you are serving.'

'Do not worry about her,' Madame Picard says quietly beside me. 'That woman is a lot of hot air. She is a pussycat, really. You will see.'

If Madame Bernard is a pussycat, as far as I can see she's a rather large ferocious one. Each time she's there for lunch, it's the same. Her air of disapproval, her obvious disdain of the English... so that it's with some trepidation I serve up the food. Today, it's a pie of flaked pastry, made with local spring vegetables from Zeke, in a delicate champagne sauce – and of course, Madame Picard's herbs which, these days, go into almost everything.

After placing the plates on the table, I raise my glass. '*Bon appétit.*' I watch apprehensively as Madame Bernard takes a mouthful, a look of disdain crossing her face. But she carries on eating, for the first time since I've met her seeming to lack an opinion.

'Did you enjoy your food, *Madame*?' I say politely as I take her plate away.

She sniffs. 'It was OK, as you English like to say.'

Madame Picard stares at her, outraged. 'It was sublime, Madame Bernard. And you know it was. Can you not, just for once, admit that?'

* * *

Since our walk, I've met up with Ned a couple of times, as slowly, I find myself letting my guard down, enjoying the easiness between us; that there's comfort in knowing you're not alone.

'It's always the same – like she can't bring herself to say anything nice,' I explain to Ned as we walk along the river one afternoon. 'I don't understand why some people are like that.'

'Me neither.' He pauses. 'Unless genuinely, it wasn't her kind of food.'

I've thought of that. 'But it's been three times, Ned. Three times she's sat there and looked as though...' I shake my head. 'Honestly? She looks as though she'd like to hurl the food at my head. But I can't believe she'd go on turning up if she didn't like it.'

'What about the herbs?' he says.

I've told him how Madame Picard's herbs are a mystery to me. 'What about them?'

'Just that they seem to have a magical effect on people.' He smirks. 'Like they're hallucinogenic, or something.'

'It isn't funny.' I nudge him with my elbow. 'I've tried them.' I remember the meal being mood-enhancing, which I put down solely to my food.

'Can I try them?' Ned asks.

I shrug. 'If you like. But none of this helps me deal with Madame Bernard.'

'If I were you, I'd stop cooking for her,' Ned says easily.

'I could.' I'm silent. 'But I like Madame Picard, and Monsieur Valois. Neither of them cook. It's something I can do for them.'

'That's all very well,' Ned says. 'But what's in it for you? I mean, they have a delicious lunch – for free. You get nothing, as far as I can see.'

I've thought about this a lot. 'Well, I get to test my recipes on them. But also...' I think about Zeke's philosophy, of paying it forward, but I seem to have got into a bit of a muddle with it. 'I don't think it's as simple as getting something instant in return. Nor should it be. Zeke has this idea that we should pay it forward, without expectation. I happen to think he's right.'

Ned grins. 'You mean, I should go off doing gigs for free, and something will come of that?'

'That wasn't what I meant. But you won't know unless you give it a try,' I can't help smiling. 'I suppose to me it makes sense, because Zeke gives me all these vegetables from the garden. And I don't pay him. But I use them in the meals I cook for the people in the village.'

'I guess there's some kind of logic in that.' Ned doesn't sound convinced. 'Maybe you should start teaching them.'

'You could be on to something.' Ned doesn't say anything. But as I know, he has other things on his mind. 'How is your mum?' I ask quietly.

Beside me, he tenses. 'Fading.'

Instinctively my hand reaches for his. 'I'm so sorry.'

'I keep thinking...' He pauses.

'What?' I encourage him.

'About what happens. When someone dies,' he mumbles. 'How one minute someone can be here, and the next, they're not. How can it be so instant?'

I shake my head. 'I don't know.' I've thought about it many times, in relation to my parents; about the split-second their lives were suddenly gone; whether it was as immediate as a light being switched off. 'We don't talk about it enough, do we?' I say carefully. 'What happens, and what happens after.'

'I think about it too much.' Ned's grip on my hand tightens. 'And when I try to imagine life without her, which is what is going to happen, it's like my mind shuts down.' His eyes are desperate as he turns to look at me. 'Jessie used to say I hide my feelings. That I never cry. She was right.' He shakes his head. 'Take now, talking to you about my mother. There are no tears in my eyes, no lump in my throat.' He pauses, staring at me. 'It's like I'm talking about a stranger, Stevie – like I'm dead inside.'

I look at him anxiously. 'We all deal with things differently. This is just your way.'

'What if it isn't? To be honest, I'm starting to wonder whether there is something wrong with me.' A look of anguish crosses his face. 'What if I'm one of these people who can't feel?'

10

NED

May

Taking in the worried look on Stevie's face, I'm mortified. I'm not used to blurting my feelings out – and we all have our worries in life. Who am I to think she wants to hear about mine?

'Sorry.' I try to backtrack. 'Just my somewhat inept way of expressing how I'm feeling.' I try to make light of it. 'Thank you for listening. You've done me a huge favour. I'll shut up now!'

Stevie's silent for a moment. 'It's OK, Ned. There is no right way when you're going through something like this. However you feel, whatever you say, it's OK.'

Silent, I'm aware of the unfamiliar beginnings of a lump in my throat.

* * *

It's still there when I get home. Hearing my mother talking to Nina, I avoid them both, slipping through to the back of the house, to the room we've always called the den.

It's a room that Nina and I used to claim as our own, with a large fireplace and an enormous sash window that we and our friends used to clamber out of. It isn't a big room, with only just enough space for the two vast battered sofas scattered with cushions that dominate it.

In the corner is one of my old amps; next to it, my first guitar. I go over to it and pick it up. Then, as I hold it against me, I'm enveloped in the past, remembering the expression on my mother's face when she gave it to me as though it were yesterday; my feeling of disbelief, that this guitar was actually mine. The ghost of Nina is here, her long hair windswept, her skinny legs dangling off the arm of the sofa she's sprawled on; so are the impromptu bands that formed, then parted ways. All of it set amidst the joy of being a teenager, of not having a care in the world.

Sitting down, I play a chord, the lump in my throat back big time. As I play another, the door swings open and Nina comes in – the flesh and blood one this time, rather than the ghost.

'Thought it must be you.' As she looks at me, she frowns. 'You OK, Ned?'

'Me?' I come close to telling her I'm not. That I have all these feelings I don't know what to do with. But I stop myself. 'Of course I am.' Getting up, I put the guitar carefully back. Then taking a deep breath, get a grip of myself. 'Let's get a drink.' I hold my hand out towards her. 'Come on. I'll open a bottle of red.'

When Nina asks if I have any more gigs coming up, I change the subject. I do the same when she mentions our parents. And though the wine helps, I'm aware of this undercurrent of something, a kind of turbulence, gathering force as it swirls inside me.

I hold it together through dinner that evening, through my mother's poignant attempts at humour, my father's apparent obliviousness to it all. Life going on as usual; all of us, as we sit together, apparently denying that the day is fast approaching when my mother isn't going to be around anymore.

It isn't until I'm alone again that I pinpoint exactly what it is. First off, I feel older. Not in years, but it's the legacy of my mother's illness that simplicity and carefreeness have been swept away; my childhood no more than a distant memory.

You need to stop banging on about your childhood, Ned. For fuck's sake. You're a grown-up, I tell myself, as a choked sound comes from me. Rather than let it out, I turn it into a cough. Like I said to Stevie, I'm beginning to think there's something wrong with me.

Or maybe this is grief's quiet shadow.

But I can't grieve. Not while she's still alive.

Needing to get out, I go to the kitchen. Whistling to the dogs, I call out to anyone who's listening. 'Going for a walk. Won't be long.'

Before anyone can reply, I pull on my boots and jacket, then go outside. It's warm, but then this is France; it's May, the beginning of summer. Fields that not so long ago were bare earth are now covered in green. I cast my mind back to this time last year in London – to intermittent blue skies broken by unpredictable rain showers; to cold air and people perpetually in a hurry.

As I walk, I turn my mind to the other looming issue in my life, the seeming impossibility of my career – the resolution of which seems equally insurmountable right now.

As the dogs disappear at full speed, I whistle after them. My mother has them well trained and in a few seconds, they come tearing back. For a moment I envy the simplicity of their lives; their joyous enthusiasm.

But back to my career... When other people make some kind of living from music, why can't I? It's another light bulb moment as I realise I've never actually believed I'm good enough. I have no doubt a therapist would say I've always needed my parents' approval. That I've misconstrued their lack of support as my lack of talent.

But people do actually like my music. I think of the parties and weddings where I've played; of the people who've made a point of telling me. Until now, I'm not sure I've actually believed them. But maybe I should.

* * *

When I get back to the house, I go to find Nina in the wing she's taken over as hers. 'Do you have a moment?'

'A moment, yes.' Looking up from painting her nails, she glances at the large metal clock hung above the fireplace. 'Henri is on his way.' Henri's her boyfriend. 'So what is it?'

'I want to ask you something.' I hold her gaze. 'And I want you to suspend belief while I do.'

She gives me a what-the-fuck look. 'OK.' She glances behind her. 'Can you get me a drink while you talk?'

'Sure.'

I go to the back of her open-plan kitchen diner and get out a glass for her, then one for myself, pouring us both some wine before taking one over to her.

'OK. Sit down, little brother.' She nods towards her oversized sofa. 'Now, tell me what this is about.'

I have a sip of the wine. 'Well, seeing as you seem to be good at getting fledgling enterprises to fly, I want to pick your brains – about my music.'

'Oh.' She looks surprised.

'Before you say anything, I've decided I need a mindset change. I need to approach this differently.'

'I'm not going to argue with that.' Nina frowns at me. 'And you want me to suggest how?'

I nod. 'Any ideas gratefully received.'

'Well...' She waves her hands to dry her nail polish. 'You need as many people as possible to know about you, don't you? That means playing for people with connections. Party planners,' she says suddenly. 'That's the obvious starting point. Come the summer, you know how many weddings there are going to be around here.'

Excitement stirs inside me at the thought of some big-budget weddings. How come I haven't thought of this before? The downside is, they're one-offs, which is also the upside, because if it doesn't go well, there was never going to be a repeat booking. Shocked, suddenly I realise I have to stop thinking like this.

'It's a good idea. Don't happen to know one, do you?'

Nina rolls her eyes. 'As a matter of fact, you're in luck. I know not just one, but two.' She pauses. 'Do you have a website – or something online they can look at?'

My heart sinks. 'No. I haven't got around to it.'

I wait for her justifiably scathing critique of how useless I am. 'Come here tomorrow – at half past eight,' is all she says.

'In the morning?' I say, just to be sure.

'Of course in the morning.' She sounds exasperated. 'I'll help you put something together. In the meantime, gather any video clips of you performing, or any audio clips of your songs. And write something about yourself – what inspires you, what you like to do in your spare time, that sort of stuff.' As she stops talking, a car pulls up outside. 'That's probably Henri. He's early.'

'I'll get out of your way.' Getting up, I linger a moment. 'Thanks, Nina. You're the best.'

'I haven't done anything yet.' The doorbell clangs. 'I'd better finish getting ready.'

'Want me to get that?'

She smiles. 'Thanks.'

After letting Henri in, we have a brief and entirely superficial exchange about his vintage Bugatti and the weather. I then go to the kitchen to look for a pen and some paper, before making my way to the den to start writing some notes.

* * *

'You really think this is good?' Nina says bluntly the next morning, going on before I can reply. 'Let me read this to you – and tell me honestly what you think. *Local musician who knows all the old hits. Available in Corrèze for discos and parties.*'

'What's wrong with that?' I frown slightly.

'No one has discos, Ned. And if they did, they'd hire a DJ, not a guitarist. I can't believe you didn't think of that.' She slams the paper on the table – if you can slam a piece of paper. 'You are supposed to be selling yourself. Something along the lines of…' She pauses. '*Talented musician available for weddings and events. Writer and performer of original music, but will personalise content to your taste for your special day. Available throughout south-west France.*' She pauses. 'Not perfect, but better. We should speak to Susie and Carin – they're the wedding planners I was talking about. See what they say. You should also think about using social media.' She types on her laptop. 'Do you have any images?'

'I have these.' Getting out my phone, I scroll down and show them to her.

'Not bad. Send them to me. I'll edit them.' Not for nothing does my sister run a successful company. 'I have a meeting to go to. Can you come back this evening? Hopefully I'll have put something together. You can check it through before I send it to Susie and Carin.'

I'm inordinately grateful for my sister's superlative organisational skills. But I can't help feeling slightly emasculated. Everything she's proposed is bang on, leaving me questioning why I'm not capable of doing this for myself.

As I reach the kitchen, my mother calls out, 'Ned... Is that you?'

Going in, I find her sitting at the table. 'I was just with Nina. She's helping me put a website together, for my music. And she has some contacts.' After relying on word of mouth and the band I used to play with, for the first time, I'll have a plausible online presence of my own.

'Things are looking up?' my mother says softly.

I pause. 'Hopefully they will be. Thanks to Nina.'

'Come and sit down.' She pats the chair next to her. 'You know, you don't need your sister. I know you think you do...' she says more sternly. 'But it's all here, Ned.' Reaching out, she touches where my heart is. 'All you have to do is believe in yourself.'

I breathe in sharply. Whether it's her words, the touch of her hand on my heart; the way she's homed in on exactly what I'm already thinking, but the lump in my throat is back. 'I'm trying to.' My voice is husky.

'You are not like most people I know.' Love shines from her eyes. 'You are not fussed about houses and clothes and cars and all that stuff.'

'Ah, you mean like Henri?' I quip, desperate to lighten the mood.

'Henri...' She raises her eyebrows. 'I am sure Nina will work that out. But we are not talking about Nina. We are talking about you.' She pauses. 'Don't be afraid, Ned, to be who you really are.' She touches my hand. 'Just be you.'

My vision blurs. There's so much I want to say to her. To tell her how wonderful she is, that her support means the world. How much I love her. But as always seems to happen, the words stick in my throat. An utterly and completely inadequate, 'Thank you,' is all I can manage.

* * *

The strangest day follows, as I struggle to attach meaning to the unfamiliar feelings I'm experiencing. Elusive words seem to float ethereally around me, remaining out of my reach, while it feels like a hitherto unknown part of me is trying to burst through its shell. And it hurts. Eventually, in desperation, I go for another walk, this time without the dogs, driven by a need to be alone.

It's a typical early summer day, bouts of warm sunshine broken by heavy downpours. One of them catches me out in the middle of a field, sweeping in before I can run for shelter. Abandoning any hope of staying dry, I stand there, surrendering to the elements. In every direction the sky has lowered, torrential rain pouring from the clouds, puddles forming under my feet, seeping into my trainers.

Soaked to the skin, the strangest feeling comes over me. It's being this close to nature, to its uncontrollable power. In what's a slightly ego-shattering but long overdue reality check, I'm suddenly realising what I should have worked out years ago. And it's oddly liberating that in the middle of this sodden field, in this vast, beautiful country that's just one corner of an even more incredible world, I am just one relatively insignificant human being.

I am small.

11

FAY

I land at Gatwick to grey skies and pouring rain, but then it's May. I should expect no more. But after getting an Uber, I'm fast realising these are less showers than more prolonged downpours.

On my way home, I gaze out of the window as an unexpected pang of homesickness hits me. Not for Surrey, but for France.

As predicted, I walk into an untidy house where the floor is in need of hoovering and unwashed plates are piled on the side, even though we have a perfectly functional dishwasher. Out of habit, I clean it all up, throwing a window open to let some air in, before taking my bag and going upstairs.

Already, the freedom I felt in France feels no more than a distant memory. Reaching our bedroom, I stand in the doorway for a moment. Hugh and I have shared this room since we moved here over thirty years ago. I know each detail, each creaking floorboard, each mark on the walls. Apart from a fresh coat of paint every few years, little has changed.

Like the house itself, it represents security, familiarity. It's also a small piece of our family's history, with memories of our children curling up in bed with us when storms kept them awake; of hushed moments of intimacy that have grown rarer over the years, until they dwindled completely.

But we are older, Fay, I tell myself sternly. *You and Hugh, you've had your moments. You're forgetting, aren't you? Passion is the territory of youth.*

Going in and sitting on the bed, I sigh. The fact is, we are not that old. I'm sixty-one, Hugh sixty-four. We have decades ahead of us – with luck. And I'd like to think that I'm not entirely done with passion in my life.

The thing is, I have a choice, I realise as I sit there. Just as Hugh has a choice. I can go on being dull, middle-aged Fay, resigned to the fact that her best years are behind her; that from here on, it's a downhill slope to old age. That it's my lot to keep house for Hugh, to be here when our children rarely visit... To fulfil the expectations of everyone else in my life. To not rock any boats.

This is nonsense, Fay, I tell myself. *Just listen to yourself. Sixty-one, for goodness' sake. You have so much life left. And there's nothing wrong with rocking a few boats. After all, this is your life. What about you?*

Getting up, I stare at myself in the mirror, at my clothes, chosen for being generic, just as the colour of my hair is. Both of them safe. But safe can be boring, can't it? Change never did anyone any harm – and I have a burning desire for it.

When it comes to getting started, there's no time like the present.

* * *

That evening, by the time I hear Hugh's car pull up in the drive, I've been through my wardrobe and chest of drawers. Looking around at the plastic bags I've filled with stuffy, uninspiring clothes ready to be taken to the charity shop, I carry them along to Julia's bedroom. Closing the door, I go back to mine and Hugh's. Inside, I glance in the mirror for a moment.

Already, my eyes are brighter, while with my hair pinned up in a messy kind of up-do, I look younger. The old me would have redone my hair – nice and tidily, not a strand out of place, but somewhat defiantly, I leave it as it is. In any case, it kind of goes with what I'm wearing – a pair of yoga pants I'd forgotten I had, and a baggy, loose-knit sweater.

Turning off our bedroom light, I go downstairs. Already I feel lighter in myself, but as I reach the kitchen, a sense of trepidation fills me. Telling myself how ridiculous this is, I take a deep breath and banish it.

Or at least, I try to. 'Hello, Hugh.' *Noticed anything different about me? But if I walked in with purple hair, you wouldn't notice, would you?*

'Evening, Fay.' He glances briefly at me before taking off his jacket.

When did this start? This polite reserve between us. I've been away for just over a month, yet it's almost as if we don't know each other. But maybe that's it. That underneath the roles we've always played, maybe we don't. I go to the fridge. 'I'm having a glass of wine. Would you like one?'

'I think I'll change first.' Without looking at me, he goes upstairs.

When confrontation presents itself, I have a personal philosophy that unless you can find the right moment, it's wiser to walk on eggshells. But this is the problem, I tell myself. I'm as bad as he is, allowing myself to feel intimidated, or anxious about upsetting him, when I've done absolutely nothing wrong. Quite the contrary, in fact, I remind myself as I wait for him to come downstairs.

'Your wine. Come and sit down, Hugh.' I feel oddly calm as I walk over to the table and put his glass down. I pull out a chair and sit down opposite. 'There's something I want to tell you about. Something rather good, actually.' I watch him sip his wine, still avoiding eye contact with me. 'You see, while I was in France, after you told me you didn't want me to change our garden, I went to enquire about an allotment. There was a piece in the local paper about a garden for the community. I hadn't realised there would be a waiting list – and, of course, after it was in the paper, flocks of people wanted one. Anyway, it just so happened I was in the right place at the right time when one came up...'

At last, Hugh looks at me. 'What on earth are you talking about?'

As he says *earth*, a nervous giggle comes from me. 'That's quite fitting, isn't it?' My smile vanishes as I take in his face. It's like thunder. 'Hugh, what I'm trying to say is I've taken on an allotment.'

He looks incredulous. 'You've done what?'

'I have an allotment,' I say patiently. 'It's a couple of miles from our village – in this huge walled garden. It means you get what *you* want – the garden staying the same. While I get a chance to try out something I really want to do. Because I do, Hugh. More than anything.' But as I look at him, I know he won't understand.

He stares at me. 'You've done this without discussing it with me?'

'I know I should have...' My voice grows smaller. 'But when I told you I wanted to grow things, you tried to put me off.' I pause. 'The thing is, Hugh, you simply don't understand. I want to dig the ground myself, get my hands dirty – and yes, get mud on my jeans.' I watch his mouth fall open. 'I want to plant vegetables I want to eat, and pick flowers I've grown from seed. It's real, Hugh. And I'm not going to give it up. You see, I've found I rather love it.'

'And who pays for this allotment?' His voice is cold.

It's a low blow, but in his ordered little world, it's his way or the highway. 'I would, if I had a job,' I say quietly. 'But if you remember, you've never liked me working.' It's sounds ridiculous – and archaic. But it's true.

Scratching his head, he sighs. 'Look, I know how much you miss the children being at home. That's what this is about, isn't it? A midlife crisis of some sort... Maybe you should talk to someone.'

I gaze at him, flabbergasted. I can't believe he actually said that. That he thinks a few extra hormones will bring back the predictable, wifely behaviour he's always taken for granted. I think of Aimée coming to the end of her life, but how she's followed her heart; she's lived; how she's running out of time, yet she's still living.

Time isn't something any of us can take for granted. I stifle the urge to slap him. 'This is not about having an empty nest, Hugh,' I say icily. 'This is about me.'

Clearly out of his comfort zone, he shifts uncomfortably in his chair. 'Don't you think this is a little odd? A woman of your age and means, spending her days digging a garden she doesn't even own?' He pauses. 'I take it you've looked into the legalities,' he says coldly. 'Because you're going to run into problems with staying longer than ninety days – assuming that's what you're planning.'

I look at him, suddenly sad that he and I have come to this. That even at this point in life, he hasn't a shred of empathy. Instead, everything that comes out of his mouth is negative. He's also an utter snob.

Suddenly, I've had enough. 'It's the perfect time to take up gardening. And I've been reading up on visas. I have enough of what my mother left me to meet the financial requirements.' I pause. 'Just for the record, there is nothing wrong with digging. It's also far more worthwhile than anything I'd be doing here.' Looking at him, I take a deep breath, wishing he could apologise. Be supportive. After all, it's the first time in our marriage I've wanted to do something without him. But he won't. More to the point, he can't. Sadness fills me again. 'Maybe it would do us good to spend some time apart.'

He looks startled for all of about a minute. 'Don't expect any help from me,' he says curtly.

'I wouldn't dream of it.' Suddenly I feel claustrophobic. 'Don't worry, Hugh. I'm not going to ask you for anything. By the way, I'm going out,' I say quietly. 'You can cook yourself some supper.'

He frowns. 'You can't go out now. You've only just got back.'

'I can do what I like.' I pick up my keys. 'Especially after the way you've just spoken to me.' Getting up, I finish my wine and pick up my jacket.

He looks shocked. 'Where are you going?'

Reaching the back door, I hesitate. 'I'm not sure.'

As I walk outside, he calls after me. 'When will you be back? Dammit, Fay. You can't behave like this.'

But it isn't up to Hugh what I can and can't do, I remind myself. I am not beholden to him or anyone else. Getting into my car, I glance towards the house, half expecting him to come out after me. But much to my relief, he doesn't.

I start my car and pull out of the drive. But there is no euphoria to this latest desperate grasp at freedom. Just the feeling of deepest sadness at the ever-increasing void in my marriage; that it's reached a point where I can't be in the same room as Hugh without feeling I'm losing myself.

With no idea of where I'm going, for the next hour I drive, aimlessly, until I find myself where I started from this afternoon. At Gatwick airport.

How was that only this morning? Parked near the end of the runway, I watch an aircraft take off, as a few minutes later it's followed by another. Sitting there, I sigh. What happened tonight with Hugh has been a long time in the making. Thirty years of marriage kind of long. And I shouldn't be too hard on him. It isn't because he's changed. It's because I have.

I listen to the patter of rain on the roof of the car, the sound drowned out as another plane takes off. *Oh, to be on it…* I think wistfully. But running away isn't going to solve anything.

Leaning my head against the window, a sigh comes from me. What would I say to someone else in my position? In the past I would probably have got all high-and-mighty – *Marriage is for keeps; you ride these things out, make allowances.* And other similarly patronising platitudes.

But as I think about us, there's a single, more fundamental question in my mind. One I've never asked myself before. Are we done? Or are Hugh and I worth fighting for?

What I wouldn't give right now to speak to my mother. Closing my eyes, I imagine her smile, the sound of her voice. But I know what she'd say. *After all these years of looking after everyone else, isn't it time you did something for yourself?*

And the thing is, you can't unsay things, just like you can't go back. Only forwards. Whatever happens from now on, things aren't going to be the same between us, as I realise that without planning to, I've crossed a line.

It's a couple of hours later by the time I get home. Parking on the drive, I gaze at the house, taking in the light in the kitchen, the curtains Hugh hasn't got around to closing – probably hasn't the whole time I've been in France.

In many ways, I have so much, but it doesn't make up for the absence of happiness in my life. Having poured heart and soul into being a wife and mother, I haven't left anything for myself. And it's no one's fault – I've let that happen.

I sigh quietly, trying to put into words why the allotment is so important to me. The untapped need I have to surround myself with nature. To discover the simple pleasure of being in the elements; of planting a seed and watching it grow.

I think of Hugh sitting inside, pouring himself another glass of wine. Predictable, but Hugh likes predictable. His Monday to Friday routine, with golf on Saturdays and Sunday mornings. He likes to know what's for lunch, that I'll be there when he comes in from work. That he never has to worry that I'll do anything unpredictable. I mean, heaven forbid. This is Fay we're talking about. Sensible, middle-aged Fay with her unadventurous highlights and sensible shoes. So frigging sensible it's utterly tedious. But again, it's what Hugh likes. He's a simple soul, the provider and decision-maker, his authority unquestioned; with everything he needs to sustain him comfortably within reach, and that's the point. It's too comfortable. Too safe. But it wouldn't enter his head that life's about more.

* * *

After an evening during which Hugh stonewalls me, I go to bed early, feigning sleep when he joins me. Awaking early the following day, I leave him sleeping as I go downstairs and put the kettle on.

A bit later, I listen to the familiar sounds of Hugh getting out of bed, then showering and dressing, before coming downstairs as he always does, at precisely twenty minutes past seven.

When I pass him a mug of coffee and plate of toast, he looks surprised. 'Perhaps we can talk tonight,' I say gently. But I should have known it isn't going to be that easy.

He starts. 'I'm going to be late tonight, Fay,' he says curtly. 'Don't wait up.' Picking up his brief-case, he's out of the door. Seconds later, he's in his car and driving away.

His pride is hurt, I tell myself. His ego, wounded. He'll be fine once he enters the office, begins the familiar routines of work. Meanwhile, I spend a fruitful morning exploring the complex and long-winded reality of the French visa system, working out that I can apply for one that will give me six months in France. The thought lifts my spirits. And in these days of remote working, there's no reason why Hugh can't come too – if he wants to. But I have a feeling that even if I suggest it, he won't want to.

After an early lunch, I go shopping. Since losing my mother, I haven't touched my inheritance. When it comes to money, I'm frugal – I'd also sooner spend it on our children than on myself. But today, for the first time in months, I'm looking for clothes.

And to my delight, I find them. Shorts that I can garden in; clothes with a bit of sass and swing, that I can imagine seeing me through a long, hot French summer, as well as splashing out on an emerald-green maxi dress.

A couple of hours later, I find myself outside a hair salon I've often passed, writing it off as far too glamorous for middle-aged housewives such as I am. Looking through the window, I pause. Hugh isn't going to be home until late. And even if he were coming home early, why shouldn't I?

Nervously, I push the door open. A stylist beams at me.

'I don't suppose you have an appointment available, do you?' I'm already backtracking. 'I'm sure you don't. I should have booked.'

'Actually...' The stylist studies the diary. 'As it happens, someone cancelled. I still haven't filled it. It's in twenty minutes. Would you like it?'

'Oh.' Slightly shocked, I gaze at her. 'Yes. Please – I would.'

Twenty minutes later, I'm sitting begowned on a chair while Stella, as her name is, asks me what I want her to do.

'I'm not sure,' I say hesitantly. 'Other than wanting a change...' I decide to say it like it is. 'I'm afraid I've come to look rather middle-aged – and frumpy. I suppose I'm open to ideas...'

After flicking through some suggestions in one of the books she shows me, Stella gets to work. Much to my relief, she seems to understand that I prefer not to chit-chat. Sitting there, I watch her wrap strands of my hair in foils until about half an hour later, she's done.

'I'll bring you some magazines,' she says, coming back with glossies like *Vogue* and *Vanity Fair*, followed by a latte.

It's a far cry from the old-fashioned salon I usually go to. But being here feels a little rebellious somehow. Fits with how I'm feeling. Affirms how good it feels to be doing something different.

Sometime later, I watch Stella blow-dry my hair. Instead of pale grey-blonde, there are depths of brown in there, with chunky layers giving it body. When she's finished, I stare at myself.

'God.' My eyes grow round. It's like she's taken years off me. Unable to stop looking at myself, I can't believe the trans-formation.

Stella looks worried. 'Don't you like it?'

'Oh no,' I say, dazed. 'You are a genius. I love it.'

* * *

That evening, while Hugh is out, I assemble my paperwork to take to the Visa Processing Centre. By the time he comes in, I'm drifting off to sleep as I hear him come into our bedroom, his foot-steps stopping in the doorway for a minute. If he'd come over, or climbed in and cuddled against me... Maybe it would have thawed the ice between us.

But he doesn't.

* * *

The following morning, a thirty-minute train ride takes me into London, where a short Tube ride later, I reach the visa centre. After the palaver of assembling the paperwork, the process is relatively straightforward, and half an hour later, I'm on my way out again. Crossing my fingers I've done enough to grant myself a summer in France, all I can do now is wait.

That night, when Hugh comes in from work, I've made his favourite – pork in a white wine and cream sauce – and opened a bottle of red wine.

After changing out of his suit, he looks tired as he comes into the kitchen. 'How was your day?' I ask gently.

'The same as most of my days,' he says shortly. Then he pauses. 'But I don't suppose you're interested in what I actually did.'

I'm taken aback. Or maybe I should see this as progress. 'But I am, Hugh.' I pass him a glass of wine. 'Why don't you sit down and tell me?'

Taking it, he sits at the kitchen table. 'Well, first I had to check the account summaries for our biggest client – and just as well, because there were several mistakes. After sorting that out, I had a meeting with a Chinese client. Managed to persuade them that we were the company they need. Straight after that was over, I went to meet another client for lunch, for more of the same. Then this afternoon, I had to fire someone – a junior who, quite simply, isn't delivering.'

'Oh. That must have been hard,' I say sympathetically.

'Not really. She's unreliable and indiscreet. It couldn't go on,' he says brusquely. 'And you're probably thinking it sounds harsh.

But people have to deliver – and if they're not up to it, there's no place for them.'

I look at him sadly, realising that this is what fills his mind. Office politics; with all the accompanying posturing and ego-strutting, kowtowing to associates; in between, delivering the kind of news that can devastate someone's life. It's no wonder he looks so tired and pale. It must be exhausting. 'I went to the visa centre today.' I hold his gaze. 'Why don't you come to France with me? You could work from there, and fly back for urgent meetings when you need to.' I pause. 'Don't you think it would be good for us?'

'It's out of the question.' Looking away, he doesn't say why. 'So you're really going then?'

I nod slowly. 'I am.'

He looks at me properly, for the first time in days. 'You've had your hair done.' He doesn't say if he thinks it's nice or not. Instead, a wary look crosses his face. 'I can't think why I haven't asked you this before – but have you met someone?' He says it emotionlessly, as if establishing facts at one of his business meetings.

I stare at him, shocked. 'Of course not.' I'm speechless for a moment. 'You honestly thought that just because I've had my hair done and I'm wearing some different clothes, I'm doing it for another man? I can't believe you'd think that of me.' Incredulous, I shake my head.

'I didn't mean…' he starts.

'It's exactly what you meant, Hugh.' I get up. 'I'm doing this for myself – just as I've done this for you.' I'm talking about the meal I've cooked. But as I go to the oven and take out his pork, it resembles something like shoe leather.

* * *

After a fractious and controversial weekend, it feels like a miracle when far sooner than anticipated, I find out my visa application has been accepted. With my passport safely back, I pack a couple of cases with what I'm going to need this summer. Hauling them downstairs, I think of Hugh briefly.

I'm sad that he doesn't understand; that he doesn't want to do this with me. That he's filled with resentment and feels so wronged. That he's incapable of seeing this from my point of view. Because when it comes to his, believe me, I've tried.

After booking a flight, I do an online food shop for my husband, timed to arrive on Thursday evening when, as far as I know, he'll be home. I make a last attempt to speak to him that evening; to call a truce between us.

But he's as obstinate as ever. 'If you think I'm going to make this easy for you, you're wrong.'

'I think that's sad, Hugh.' I look at him regretfully. 'Sad that you feel so stubborn and bitter. That you can't embrace even the idea of a few months of living differently. That everything has to be set in concrete... To stay exactly as it's always been.' Aware of my voice getting more high-pitched, I tail off. 'I suppose I'm just sorry... that you feel like this.' That for the first time, we don't want the same thing.

But as I stand there, I know with certainty.

I'm not sorry enough to stay.

12

ZEKE

As the sun grows warmer, two weeks on, I'm beginning to regret my promise to Fay about keeping an eye on her allotment. This time of year, there's a never-ending list of garden chores, meaning there's never enough time.

'You should give it to someone else. Someone who is here,' Rémy remonstrates. 'You are running yourself into this earth you love so much.' She pauses. 'I will make you a cup of this horrible English tea you like.'

I stare at her. '*You*, make me tea? I don't think so.' It's typical of the banter between us, but today, she doesn't respond.

Ignoring me, she goes into my shed and switches the kettle on, before turning to look at me again. 'I am serious.' The laughter has gone out of her eyes. 'You look tired, Zeke. I am worried about you. And it isn't just me.'

'You should be ashamed of yourselves.' I wag a finger in her direction. 'Gossiping behind my back.'

'Not gossip, Zeke. Here.' She passes me the mug of tea she's made. Then standing there, she studies me. 'You work as if you were a young man when you are not. You should be slowing down. It is too much.'

'Try telling nature that.' I shake my head. 'There is too much to do. And it is what it is – you know as well as I do.'

'So when is she back – this Fay?' Rémy makes no attempt to keep the contempt out of her voice.

I frown. 'Can I ask you something? Only what is it that you have against her?'

'First, she is English,' Rémy retorts. 'She is not part of our village, Zeke.'

'People come and go,' I remind her. 'She loves being in France. She and her husband have a house here.'

Rémy looks mutinous. 'I know. They are these English expats who come here like it is one long holiday. They do not know how it is to live and work here.'

'I think if you asked her, Fay would tell you she'd love to spend more time here.' Glimpsing movement across the garden, I look up. 'Well, you're not going to have to bend my ear any more. She's back.'

Coming towards us, Fay looks different, somehow. Studying her, trying to work out why, I decide it's her eyes. They're brighter. Happier. 'Welcome back,' I say. 'And not a moment too soon. Everything is growing like crazy.'

'So I see.' She turns to Rémy. '*Bonjour.*'

'*Bonjour*, Fay.' Rémy gets up. 'I have been telling this old man he needs to stop overdoing it. Maybe now you are back, you can do the same.'

'Oh?' Fay looks at me quizzically. Then she looks guilty. 'But you've been looking after my allotment, too. I am so sorry – I have been away so long. I had to apply for a visa.'

'You are staying?' Rémy looks taken aback.

'For as long as I can,' Fay says. 'I'd stay forever if it weren't for

Brexit and all this stupid bureaucracy.'

Rémy stands there, a look I can't read on her face. 'I like your hair,' she says abruptly, before turning and stomping off towards her own allotment.

'I'd say that's a compliment.' I can't help smiling. 'So you've got a visa, then?'

She nods. 'There was an unbelievable amount of paperwork. But apart from that, it wasn't too bad. But I have it now. It means I can stay for six months.'

I can't help wondering how that's gone down at home. 'And your husband?'

'I asked him to consider coming with me for the summer. But he wouldn't,' she says, a little sadly. 'And knowing I could be here, I couldn't have stayed there.'

I change the subject. 'Well, I'm not sure you'll recognise your allotment. Since all that rain around the time you left, we've had unbroken sun. I've never known things to grow so fast.'

'Including the weeds?' She arches an eyebrow towards me.

'You're learning fast,' I say, a little proudly. 'Come. I'll show you.' But as I get up, she points towards something.

'Have you found out what that is?'

I'd kind of forgotten about them while she was away. But as I follow her gaze to the patch of dark leaves that's now colonising an empty corner, I shake my head. 'Not as yet.' I stare at them for a moment. 'The thing is, fast as I dig them up, they grow back.'

Those dark leaves niggle at me. To my mind, a garden is a metaphor for life. Which is why a few days later, still perplexed, I go to see my doctor.

'You are here because you have a weed in your garden?' She looks at me as though I'm certifiable.

'Yes – and no,' I say carefully. Sitting there, I try to explain. 'You see, the way I look at it, all things are connected. And here is this thing I can't explain.'

She shakes her head. 'This connection you talk about... it is not within my remit, Zeke. You should maybe seek out a shaman – or a witch doctor.' She's silent, frowning. 'Anyway, what were you going to say?'

'I guess I see our impact on a garden as more than just digging the ground and cutting down trees. I think there's some kind of exchange that goes on.' I pause, thinking. 'Wasn't there some prince who banged on about talking to plants and the difference it makes – to them? Well, as it happens, I buy into that. Some folks say that if you listen, trees have a heartbeat. It's quieter and slower than ours. But if you stand among them, you can feel it. It's kind of calming.' I pause, to see if she's following. 'In the same way, I believe we impact the environment we spend time in – not just physically, but energetically.'

'So this weed you're talking about is related to something that's happening to you – is that what you're saying?'

I nod. 'I suppose I am.' Nothing ever comes of not questioning what folks believe, however far-out it may sound.

She tilts her head on one side. 'I suppose it would do no harm to have a blood test.'

As I drive home, I'm not sure whether she's booked me in for a blood test just to keep me quiet, or whether she considers there's something in what I was saying. Too late, it crosses my mind I should have asked her.

* * *

When I get home, there's a note wedged into the door-frame.

Bonjour Zeke,

    I made a pie earlier. I brought a piece of it for you. It's watercress and spring herbs. And the pastry's made using one of the eggs from your neighbour. I hope you like it.
    Stevie

I glance down to the small parcel wrapped in paper that's been left on the doorstep. Touched that she's thought of me, I pick it up and take it inside.

I've never been to Stevie's house. But I know the bar where she works in the village, and the following morning I take a walk there. It's a fine summer day, the leaves unfurled, festooning the trees in the brightest of green, the birds in full song. As I walk along the lanes, that strange sense I've had before is back, as though I'm waiting for something; unless it's the results of the blood test, I'm not sure what.

Following the road around the corner, suddenly I find myself whisked back to the past, to when Marie and I first met.

I remember walking along a lane just like this one. I was going to her house, my heart full to bursting as I reached it, even before I saw her. It was enough to know that she was there, that in a few minutes, I'd be gazing into her eyes. But Marie was special.

I'd have waited an eternity, all for a few seconds of knowing her. And I'd do it again. A sigh comes from me. The important things in life aren't what most folks think they are. It's about the people we love, this life going on around us. The sun that rises every morning. The endless miracles that go on happening; that will go on, long after all of us have gone.

Talking of miracles... I stop to look at what used to be the ruins of a fine old manor house, that someone has bought and is breathing new life into. The crumbling walls have been rebuilt, the old shutters rehung, the avenue of overgrown plane trees pruned back. But this is the strange dichotomy of life in rural France – these houses that have been long-abandoned becoming someone else's dream.

The village comes into view, and as I walk down the lane, the slope steepens. Then across the river, I see the bar. While in winter it's deserted here, at this time of year, it comes to life, as it is right now. Suddenly this village has a beating heart: it never ceases to astonish me the difference a few tables and chairs make, with some excellent food and some of the wine grown around here.

As I get closer, I take in the couple sharing breakfast together, the group of hikers drinking coffee. Reaching the bar, I wait for one of the staff to come outside.

'Can I help you, *Monsieur*?' In an immaculate white shirt and an apron, it's almost certainly the owner whom Stevie has told me is called Olivier.

'Well, thank you, I'm hoping you can. I'm looking for—' Before I can finish, I'm interrupted.

'Zeke?' I turn to see Stevie's face at one of the windows. 'Just a minute.'

Her face disappears, then she reappears through the doorway. 'Did you get my pie?'

'As a matter of fact, I did. I brought your plate back.' I pass her the bag I'm carrying.

'Oh. Did you like it?' She suddenly sounds uncertain.

'I did. It was very good,' I say gently, then glance at the man who's still standing there.

'Oh!' Stevie blushes. 'Olivier, this is Zeke. He grows the vegetables I told you about. It's Olivier's bar,' she explains to me.

'I thought as much. A pleasure to meet you.'

'You also.' He glances at Stevie. 'Take a break. I will bring coffee for you both.'

'Oh.' She looks surprised. 'Thank you.' She gestures towards a table. 'Shall we sit there?' Sitting down, she frowns at me. 'You have walked all the way here?'

'I have indeed.' Though I hate to admit it, it's farther than I remembered.

'I should give you a lift home. It's hot today.' Stevie sounds concerned.

'Nonsense,' I say firmly. 'The walking does me good. So...' I study her. 'How's it going, with your new project?'

'Not exactly as I planned,' she confesses. 'In fact, I've got myself in a bit of a muddle. I asked one of my neighbours if she'd mind tasting some of my recipes... I thought it would be best if someone French gave me their opinion. Anyway... after a couple of meals, the next time, she had a friend of hers there, Monsieur Valois. Then Madame Bernard joined them. Last time I took some food round, there were six of them.'

'Oh my.' I try not to smile. 'I can see your problem.'

'It really is a problem.' Stevie's words are heartfelt. 'They are all so kind – except maybe not Madame Bernard – but they look forward to eating together. And they are all alone.'

'That's what they say to you?' I'm outraged. 'Well, I can tell you for a fact that Monsieur Valois has a son in the next village. I heard he asked his father to move in with him and his wife – the stubborn old so-and-so refused. As for Madame Bernard... Her family used to come and see her every couple of days. But she was so rude to them all she drove them away.'

'Madame Picard is nice.' Stevie's voice is small. 'I like her. And I know she doesn't have anyone else nearby.'

I nod. 'I believe that's true. But I see your problem.' I pause. 'You're going to have to say something to them, aren't you?' An idea occurs to me. 'I might be able to help. Want to come round to my place later, when you've finished here?'

* * *

Despite Stevie's opposition, I walk back to the allotments, though halfway back I have to admit I'm beginning to wish I'd taken her up on her offer. But as it turns out, it doesn't matter. No sooner has the thought entered my head, when I hear a car slow down behind me before a voice calls out, 'Zeke? Would you like a lift?'

Turning, I see Fay leaning out of the window of her Citroën. Relief fills me that it's her and not Rémy, who'd have undoubtedly given me another of her lectures. 'If you're sure it isn't any trouble, that would be most kind of you.'

When I've always prided myself on my fitness, as I climb into her car, I'm shocked at how out of breath I am. 'Think the heat's getting to me,' I say lightly.

She hesitates. 'None of us are getting any younger.'

As she drives, I bask in the cool of the air conditioning, pondering her words. Age isn't something I pay much attention to; I see it more as an attitude of mind, though this morning my body's feeling every day of its seventy-eight years, no question.

'Were you going anywhere in particular?' Fay asks.

'I went to the bar in the village – to see someone. Young English girl who works there,' I explain. 'Nice lass. One of those people who's rather alone in the world.'

'Oh.' Fay glances at me. 'Have you known her long?'

Thinking how my serendipitous meeting with Stevie is similar to the way I met Fay, I smile. 'A couple of months. Her car broke down. I asked this chap I know to help her.' Talking of which, I haven't seen Billy in a while. 'It's good having some young folk around here.'

'I hope you don't mind me asking.' Fay sounds hesitant. 'But are you OK, Zeke?'

Taking in the concern in her voice, there's a lump in my throat I turn into a cough. 'Bright as a button,' I say. 'Or at least, I will be once I get my blood results back.'

She's silent for a moment. 'So there is something?'

'I doubt it very much,' I say firmly. Thinking of that darned black weed again, I change the subject. 'You should meet Stevie. I have a feeling the two of you would get on.'

'I'd like that.' Reaching the garden, Fay's about to pull up in a lay-by.

'Keep going,' I say to her. 'There's another way in – and it's easier to park.' I direct her along the lane, then the cut-through that comes out close to my house. 'You can park anywhere here.'

'What about the people who live there? Won't they mind if I leave my car here?' She stares at my house for a moment. 'Rather lovely, isn't it?'

'Oh, I wouldn't go worrying about them too much,' I say firmly. 'Come on. The garden's this way.' After locking her car, she's still glancing over her shoulder at the house as she follows me along the path through the gap in the hedge.

* * *

The walk to see Stevie has sapped my energy and while Fay goes off to work on her allotment, untypically for me, I drag out a chair and sit in the shade. I think about my comment to Fay on the way here, about how the village needs more young people. But there's the age-old problem. In the small, rural communities around here, there simply isn't enough life for them.

Closing my eyes, I take a moment to feel the softness of the air on my face. Nature, a piece of earth to grow things, they've always been enough for me.

'Zeke?' The voice comes from far away. *'Zeke?'*

Blinking, I open my eyes to see Fay standing there, concern on her face. 'You were asleep. I thought I'd better wake you – looks like rain's on the way.'

Glancing up, I see the band of heavy cloud she's alluding to, slowly moving in and obscuring the blue. 'That's a shame,' I say cheerfully. 'I've haven't even started yet.'

Fay frowns. 'Zeke, it's gone five.' She pauses. 'Maybe I can give you a lift home?'

Astonished at how much time has passed, suddenly I remember Stevie. 'Could you spare a few minutes to give me a hand?'

Between us, we gather some chard and beetroots, as well as a basket of salad leaves and herbs. 'I promised her some potatoes.' As I finish digging, the rain starts to fall.

Fay helps me carry everything back through the gap in the hedge. As I walk towards my house, she calls out, 'Zeke? The car's this way.'

'I know it is. Come and have a cuppa with me.' Walking towards my gate, I push it open and wait for her, enjoying the look of incredulity on her face.

'Why didn't you tell me this was your house?'

I shrug. 'Because then I have to explain why I spend most of my time in the allotments – and most folks fail to understand.'

She follows me around the side of the house, then just stands there. 'This is yours too?'

I nod proudly. 'It mostly takes care of itself.' My back garden is mostly canes of raspberries and loganberries, with a small orchard of fruit trees, and banks of herbs and flowers. I cut it back in winter, then mulch it, but that's about all.

Oblivious to the rain, she gazes around. 'It's beautiful.' She turns to me. 'So why the other garden for the community?'

I nod. 'That's a good question.' I look at her. 'You'll be soaked to the skin if you stand there much longer.'

'I don't care.' Her eyes are mesmerised as she looks around, taking it all in. 'There's a bit of magic here, isn't there?'

'I like to think so.' My eyes are suddenly misty, my heart filled with warmth that someone else has noticed it, too.

Following me inside, Fay says little. While I make a pot of tea, she washes the potatoes I dug, then the salad. 'How is it being back?' I ask her.

'Oh, it's good.' She pauses. 'To be honest, if feels more like home than England does at the moment, which is strange given I've lived there all my life.' She sounds surprised. 'Doesn't make sense, does it?'

The older I get, the less makes any sense to my mind. 'I guess there are some places we just feel we belong.'

'You're right.' She looks perplexed. 'I hadn't thought of it like that before.'

As I'm pouring the tea, the doorbell rings. 'That will be Stevie.'

Fay picks up her jacket. 'I should leave you. I'd forgotten you have plans.'

'Put your jacket down,' I say, because this meeting is overdue. 'If you're not in a hurry to be anywhere, why don't you stay?'

I open the door to find Stevie standing there, dwarfed by the enormous hood of the coat she's wearing. 'You look like you're dressed for a monsoon,' I tell her. 'Come in. There's someone I want you to meet.'

Stevie looks wary. 'I could come back another time if you're busy.'

'I'm not.' I start walking towards the kitchen.

'Stevie's a chef,' I say to Fay, by way of explanation. 'Rather a good one, it seems. The problem is, she's too good and she's ended up cooking for half the village, which is all very well. But I rather think they're taking her for granted.'

Stevie's ears flush pink. 'It isn't quite like that,' she says timidly. 'You see, I asked my neighbour, Madame Picard, for her opinion on some of my recipes. Then she started inviting some of her friends around to share them...'

'Sounds like they must be rather good,' Fay says kindly. 'I hope they're paying you?'

'They're not. And they should be. Now...' I turn to Stevie. 'That pie you brought me was mighty good.' I glance at Fay. 'It was watercress and herbs. Isn't that right?' I ask Stevie.

She nods. 'I used ethical cheese – from a small farm near the village.'

'Ethical?' Fay looks mystified. 'What's unethical about cheese-making?'

'The goats only produce milk to feed their babies,' Stevie says. 'So if we use it, it means the babies are taken away and given a supplement. Except at this farm, they only take a little. The babies get most of it.' She turns her blue eyes to meet Fay's. 'It's one of those things, that once you know about it, you can't pretend it doesn't go on.'

It clearly isn't something Fay's thought about before. 'So what are you going to do about your neighbour's friends?' She frowns. 'Is it costing you money?'

'A little,' she confesses. 'Mostly, I use the veg Zeke gives me – and what Madame Picard has in her larder. And their feedback has been helpful,' she adds quickly. 'I suppose it's like what Zeke said when he told me I could use his vegetables: there would be something I can do for someone else – and I kind of got to thinking this is that something.'

'The principle is admirable.' Fay shoots me a look. 'But it shouldn't be costing you money. Don't get me wrong. It's a noble thing you are doing, feeding them such wonderful food. But I agree with Zeke. I think they're taking advantage of you.' She pauses. 'Next time, I could come with you, if you like?'

'I was going to suggest the same,' I say. 'I wouldn't mind betting Madame Picard will understand.'

Stevie looks anxious. 'That's very kind of you, but there's no need. I'll think of something.'

* * *

The following day, I get a call from my doctor's secretary, asking me to make an appointment to see her. Far from being surprised, it feels like an inevitable next step. Though towards what exactly, I still don't know.

When I reach the medical practice later that afternoon, I'm the only person in the waiting room. It's a pleasant enough room, white painted, the tall windows letting the light pour in, with an ornate fireplace in which there's an artificial flower arrangement. Yet none of it counteracts the feeling of foreboding that hangs over me.

It grows stronger as the doctor's door opens and another patient comes out. Frail, she takes the arm of the young man with her. His face is strained, his sunglasses pushed up on his head, while her face is gaunt, her expression one I recognise as that of someone who doesn't have long for this world. My heart goes out to her, and to the young man with her. Presumably her son, I'm guessing.

As they step outside, it's my turn.

13

NED

June

'You OK, Mama?' Outside, I try to take her weight as she eases herself into the passenger seat, making a note to myself that next time, the doctor will be coming to her, not the other way around.

Closing her door, I go to the driver's side and get in. Starting the engine, I pause, aware that as more time passes, each outing takes more from her. 'Is there anywhere you want to go on the way home?' I say gently.

She's silent for a moment. 'Actually, there is.'

* * *

It's a hot day, a kind of taste of the midsummer to come. Even so, I get a cold feeling as I park as close as I can to the church. Unless a miracle happens, it's a summer my mother won't see. And right now, miracles seem in short supply. Maybe that's why she wanted to come here. Maybe she's made some pact with a God that doesn't exist for a few more weeks on this earth.

'Take my arm.' I feel how little weight there is of her as she takes hold of me. Slowly we make our way towards the door. It's a short distance that most of us would think nothing of. But at this stage in my mother's life, it's a marathon.

Opening the church door, as I help her inside, I shiver. It's the cold; the mustiness of the air, as I have a sense that for her the veil is thinning between this world and whatever comes next.

Or maybe there's nothing after this, I'm thinking, as I sit beside her on one of the pews. Maybe when you close your eyes that last time, there is no afterlife. No drifting somewhere else. Just an ending of everything you were, like a light going out.

I stop myself. It's depressing enough without dwelling on it. I should be focusing on each minute of the remaining days we have.

On the pew beside me, my mother has barely moved. 'Do you think there is a God?' I ask quietly.

'No.' She says it calmly.

I'm puzzled. 'Then why did you want to come here?'

'I've asked myself the same,' she murmurs. 'At first, I must admit I sent some very angry rants out there – just in case anyone was listening. But then I got to thinking. A church isn't just about some mythical God. It's where people come at pivotal times in their lives, to celebrate births, weddings...' She tails off. 'And the lives of those we've lost.' Her voice wavers. 'I suppose now and then, when I've come here, I think I've glimpsed a sense of connection – with my ancestors, that is. Not God.' She turns to me. 'Does that shock you?'

I shake my head. 'Not in the least. I think if there were a God, he'd put a stop to things like...' I stop suddenly.

'Like my illness?' she says softly.

My hand finds hers as suddenly I don't know what to say.

'I've had a wonderful life, Ned.' She gazes towards the front of the church. 'What makes me so incredibly sad is the thought of leaving you and Nina. And your father, of course. But mostly...' She pauses. 'It's you two. Being your mother has brought me the greatest joy. I would have loved to be around to see you both happy and settled with someone. Maybe even be a grandmother... But mostly, I can't bear the thought of leaving you two.'

As she speaks, I feel a lump lodge in my throat while as she leans her head against me, tears roll down her face. It's another of those moments in which there is so much I want to say to her. But I can't find the words, except perhaps the most important ones that, at times like this, are the only ones that matter. 'I love you, Mama.' Swallowing, I lean my head against hers.

We stay like that for some time. A mother and son finding what little comfort there is in the only way they can, until eventually she tries to get up.

After helping her to her feet, I take her hand, as it hits me; it's probably the last time she'll see this place, and I'm aware of a sense of finality as we make our way to the back of the church, then through the door where outside, after the cool of the church, the heat is welcome.

My mother's hand grips mine more tightly. 'Can we go home?'

'Of course.'

Our progress is slow, my mother taking in the peace around us, the green of the trees; the flowers as we walk. Just as we reach the car, a Citroën pulls up beside us and a woman gets out.

'Aimée?' Her eyes rest on my mother.

A look of surprise crosses my mother's face. 'Fay? How are you?'

'I'm well. I got back a couple of days ago...' She tails off. 'How are you?' There is incredible gentleness in her voice, an understanding; empathy, for my mother.

My mother glances at me. 'This is my son. Ned.'

'Hi.' There's something vaguely familiar about her.

'Nice to meet you, Ned.' Fay's eyes are filled with kindness as she glances at my mother again. 'I won't hold you up.' She pauses. 'But I'm glad we met again.'

'How do you know her?' I ask as we drive away.

My mother is silent for a moment. 'I met her in the church – a while ago now. We had one of those *do you believe in God* kind of conversations, a bit like you and I just did.' She pauses. 'I liked her. So English, of course... But she is nice.'

It's a long-standing joke that she feels she has the right to be disparaging about the English given she married one of them. 'I think I'm quite English,' I say humbly. 'Sorry about that.'

'Never be sorry.' She shakes her head. 'Just don't forget your French roots.'

'*Moi*?' I say overdramatically. 'Anyway, actions speak louder than words, Mama. I live in France, now. Remember?'

* * *

In between the most poignant, heart-searing, heartbreaking moments with my mother, I try to establish some contacts that will bring me work this summer. Thanks to Nina, I meet her friends Susie and Carin who add me to the databases of some Dordogne wedding venues, and it isn't long before a handful of bookings start coming in.

'It isn't enough, though, is it?' I say glumly.

'It's a start.' Nina sounds matter-of-fact. 'For fuck's sake, Ned, what were you expecting? Things take time to get off the ground.'

'Time is one thing I don't have,' I say miserably.

She ignores me. 'I'm having some friends to dinner tonight,' Nina says matter-of-factly. 'Come. You need to talk to people. Six thirty. Don't be late.'

But I can't shift this feeling that hangs over me. 'Not sure I'm in the mood.'

'Little brother...' She comes over and sits next to me. 'I know things are tough. Right now, they are tough for all of us. And you are allowed to feel sad. But you have to pull yourself together – at least, for some of the time. You need a plan, and you need to grasp every opportunity. I know you're worried about Mama. We all are. I don't stop thinking about her...' Nina's eyes glisten with tears. 'But there is work to do. The future to protect. And while it's fine to take time out now and then, life has to go on.'

* * *

She's right – Nina usually is. That evening, I realise I haven't accepted her invitation. But nor have I turned it down. Still in two minds, and half an hour later than she told me to turn up, I head for her kitchen.

I'd assumed Nina would be cooking one of her slightly random dinners. But when I go in, there's a girl with red hair stirring something on the stove. When she turns around, I stare at her, stunned.

'Stevie?' I say incredulously.

'Ned?' She looks shocked. 'What are you doing here?' She shakes her head. 'Stupid question. You're one of the guests. Nina's through there.' She gestures through the open doors towards the terrace.

'I'm not one of the guests,' I say. 'Actually, I live here.'

Stevie looks stunned.

'Nina's my sister.' I watch Stevie take it in.

'I hadn't worked it out.' She shakes her head in disbelief.

'I thought Nina was cooking tonight. This is our parents' house – this wing is Nina's. There isn't any part that's mine – in case you're wondering. Which you probably aren't,' I add, realising I'm giving her a whole load of information she doesn't need. 'But actually, now you know where I live – for now, at least,' I joke, taking in her look of confusion, berating myself for using the word 'actually' twice in close succession; swearing I'll never use it again.

'I didn't know Nina was your sister,' she says at last. 'Or that you lived somewhere like this.'

'How could you have? Anyway, it's just another enormous great French house.' I try to play it down. 'It's not as though there aren't plenty of them!'

'True.' But Stevie doesn't smile. 'How is your mother?'

I sigh. 'Not good,' I say quietly.

'I'm so sorry.' Her eyes are sad as she looks at me. 'It must be a hard time – for you and Nina.'

'It doesn't get much harder.' My voice wavers.

'Do you like Bellinis? Sorry, I forgot for a moment you're a guest!' She passes me a champagne flute of something fizzy and coloured. 'Funny, isn't it? I mean, me not realising Nina's your sister?'

I nod. 'You could say.' My heart warms as I look at her. 'I wasn't sure I was going to come tonight. But I'm glad I have.' I pause, gazing at her. 'It's great you're here.'

She flushes slightly. 'It's nice to see you too,' she says.

Taking the Bellini from her, I drink half of it without pausing for breath.

I watch her, fascinated, as she adds a spoonful of herbs from an unlabelled jar before stirring them into the food she's cooking. 'Smells great.'

'I hope it tastes OK.' She sounds anxious. 'Promise you'll tell me what you think – if you're staying, that is?'

* * *

Belying her shy exterior, when it comes to food, Stevie is a domestic goddess, I discover. Perfectly organised, the canapés are ready at the exact split-second Nina comes into the kitchen, in a bit of a flap.

'I don't know why I do this,' she says, pouring herself a glass of wine and taking a gulp. 'It's so stressful making sure everyone is OK.'

For someone so sorted, Nina can't half be a diva. 'Can I remind you,' I say to her, 'that firstly, you are not doing a thing. Stevie is doing it all, and secondly, it is all perfectly under control.'

'Canapés are here.' Right on cue, Stevie points to the plates on the table. 'Would you like me to take them outside?'

'I can manage. They look amazing.' Nina looks relieved.

'Thank you. Maybe Ned will help you?' Stevie suggests.

Nina frowns slightly. 'Do you two know each other?'

I take one of the plates. 'We met in Gatwick airport – when I came home for Mama's birthday. We've seen each other a few times since.' It's my turn to frown. 'But I'd no idea Stevie was cooking for you today.'

'Wow.' She glances from me to Stevie. 'Some coincidence, wouldn't you say?' She picks up the second plate of canapés. 'We better take these out to the others.'

'You should go and party,' Stevie says as Nina disappears onto the terrace.

'I probably should,' I say reluctantly. 'I'm supposed to be mingling. Nina's idea,' I say when Stevie looks confused. 'All in the name of helping my music career.' Slightly disappointed at the thought of leaving her alone, I go outside.

* * *

Even for one of Nina's parties, the evening goes with a swing, but though she gives the impression of a slightly ditzy-but-charming hostess, she never leaves anything to chance. Conversation is lively and witty, the wine perfectly chilled, the canapés mouth-wateringly delicious. Even the weather is on her side and it's one of the hottest evenings so far this summer, the air filled with the sweet scent of roses in full bloom, the terrace lit with hundreds of fairy lights.

When it comes to serving the first course, I go to the kitchen where Stevie is flustered. 'Can I help at all?'

'Yes. No.' She spins balletically around one way, then the other, before grabbing a bottle of olive oil. 'You're a guest, Ned.'

'It's only Nina. She's hardly going to mind if I help.'

But Stevie shakes her head. 'It isn't the point. *I* mind. It's important to do this the way I always do.'

'Well, if you need an extra pair of hands, you know where I am.' I go back outside, making myself useful by topping up wine glasses before sitting next to one of Nina's friends, a guy who as it turns out is called Axl. He's in a band that plays in Bergerac every week throughout the summer. And as luck would have it, they're looking for a guitarist.

After that, immersed in conversation with Axl, the evening flies by. Stevie is indeed a sublime cook and each plate of food is delicious. After the last course, slightly pissed, I stand up and tap my spoon against my glass.

'Everyone...' I wait for them all to stop talking. 'I'd just like to raise a glass to our hostess, my very lovely sister, Nina.' There's a round of quite rowdy cheering and clinking of glasses before I go on. 'But also, to the best-kept secret around here, the talented Stevie who has cooked this superb meal that we have all enjoyed so much. Stevie? Could you come out here a minute?'

Her cheeks are pink – endearingly so, I can't help noticing –

as she steps out onto the terrace, standing there for a few seconds to more rapturous, slightly pissed applause, before turning and disappearing inside, catching my eye for a split-second.

'She is very good,' Axl says beside me. 'If more people knew about her, she would be in demand.'

'That is the general idea,' I say magnanimously, forgetting it isn't my place to say that and that I really should have asked Stevie first. But, carried away in the moment, I'm already envisaging Stevie's food gracing the tables of the Dordogne's rich and famous. It doesn't occur to me that she might not want that.

Axl is one of the last to leave, after a large brandy and extracting a promise from me to be at the next band practice, weaving his way back towards his ancient 2CV. Shortly after, the others drift away.

Leaving Nina and Henri, her boyfriend, on the terrace, making a serious dent in a bottle of Louis XIII cognac, I go inside. With everything tidied away, Stevie is wiping down the work surfaces.

'It was a truly amazing meal,' I say, watching her. 'Seriously. Now that the word is out, you're going to have clients flocking to your door.'

A look of horror crosses Stevie's face. 'That isn't why I did this.'

'Oh.' I'm taken aback, but not for long. 'Seriously, though...' I lean my elbows on the worktop. 'Would it be so bad? You could pick and choose your work.'

'I could.' Pausing, she looks at me. 'It probably sounds silly. I mean, you're used to performing – in front of hundreds of people – on a stage. It's your world. Don't get me wrong. I love to cook and I don't mean to sound ungrateful. But in an ideal world, I wouldn't set foot out of the kitchen.'

Suddenly I'm realising what I've done; how difficult my

speech, such as it was, must have been for her. 'I'm so sorry.' My face feels hot. 'Earlier... I didn't mean...'

She looks confused. 'I'm not sure what you're talking about.'

'My speech – if you can call it that.' My sense of mortification is growing as I look at her. 'It's probably your worst nightmare.'

She hesitates. 'Not quite my worst... But it was up there.'

'Will you forgive me?' I say humbly. 'If I promise never to do it again?' Then I have a flash of inspiration, which I should probably have ignored. But after a little too much wine, I have no sense of self-moderation. 'To make it up, next time you cook, why don't I come along as the waiter?'

She looks at me, speechless.

But I'm on a roll. 'I'm personable enough, wouldn't you say? I'm good at pouring wine. And that way, you wouldn't have to talk to any of the guests...' An inspired line, though I say so myself. 'Think about it,' I advise her. 'In the meantime, how about a drink?'

* * *

After helping her load her equipment into her car, I take a couple of champagne flutes and a bottle from the fridge, then lead Stevie away from the house towards the lake. The air is balmy, the cicadas in full voice, now and then interspersed with a raucous croaking sound.

Beside me, Stevie stiffens. 'What was that?'

'Just the frogs.' It's always astonished me that such tiny creatures can create such a racket. 'Shall we sit on the grass?'

After the heat of the day, the grass is dry and sitting down, I open the bottle of champagne. Pouring us both a glass, I pass one to Stevie. 'To you.' I raise mine. 'And to your divine food.'

She smiles. 'Thank you.' She sips her champagne. 'I'm glad it's over though.'

'That bad?' I look at her, curious.

She sighs. 'No. Like I said, I love cooking. And I love that other people are eating my food. I'm just not good with people I don't know. It's... I guess I find it daunting.'

'Actually, it will probably get easier,' I say with a wisdom I don't have. *Actually* – that word again. I thump a fist against my head.

'Are you all right?' Stevie's frowning at me.

I sigh. 'I'm tired – it's been a long day. It's probably best to take anything I say with a pinch of salt.'

Stevie glances back towards the house. 'Beautiful, isn't it? Do you know how old it is?'

'It dates back to the fifteen hundreds, though the main part is sixteen hundred and something.'

'I bet it's haunted.' She pauses. 'It must be like living in another world.'

'I wouldn't describe it quite like that.' I frown. 'It's a big old house that costs a fortune to maintain, according to my father. It's cold and very draughty in winter – and we get through tons of firewood, quite literally. But our lives are like anyone else's. We're an ordinary family – just like I'm an ordinary guy.' It's what I believe, even when I'm sober.

She's silent. Then something comes from her that sounds like, 'For frick's sake, Ned. You think any of this is ordinary? Your family owns all this. You're pursuing a music career. These are things most people only dream of.'

Her words bring me up short. 'You're right,' I say hastily. 'Of course you are. And that wasn't what I meant. I suppose what I should have said was that living in a big house doesn't make you different to anyone else. And money doesn't solve everything.

That...' I nod towards the house. 'It's my parents' place. Without them, I have nothing in the world. And I haven't a clue what to do about it.'

'I can't imagine you'll ever be destitute,' she says more gently. 'I mean, here we are, sitting on your beautifully mown lawn, beside your private lake, sharing what looks like an incredibly expensive bottle of champagne.' Her lips twitch into a smile. 'But I kind of like what you just said.'

'Which bit?' I say.

'About money. How it doesn't solve everything. Because it doesn't.'

Topping up her champagne glass, my mind turns to my mother. 'I wish it did – but all the money in the world can't make my mother better.'

'No,' she says quietly.

Lying back, I take in the clarity of the night sky, the myriad stars that are so clearly defined in the darkness. Beside me, Stevie does the same.

'Peaceful, isn't it,' she says.

The silence is broken by the frogs starting up again. 'Mostly.' Smiling, my hand edges closer to hers until our fingers are touching. I wait for her to move hers away, but she doesn't.

'You were lucky to grow up here,' she says wistfully.

'I know.' I'm silent, thinking. 'But actually, I probably don't know, do I? Not really. I mean, I've never known anything else.'

'No.' She pauses. 'I was lucky, too. We never had a lot of money. But I always felt safe. And I was loved.' She pauses again. 'That's the most important thing, I always think. To feel loved.'

'Yes.' Thinking of my mother, of how it felt within her arms, of her endless, unconditional love for me and Nina, the lump in my throat is back. Edging my fingers slightly closer, I take Stevie's hand.

* * *

When I open my eyes, for a moment I'm wondering where I am. Beside me, Stevie is still sleeping, her copper hair catching the first rays of sun as it creeps above the horizon. Turning, she yawns sleepily, then opens her eyes.

Seeing me, they widen.

'It's OK,' I say gently. 'We both fell asleep. But you're just in time to see the sun come up.'

Sitting up, she shakes her hair over one of her shoulders. 'I'm so sorry. I can't believe I'm still here.' She starts to get up. 'I should leave.'

Grabbing her hand, I pull her down. 'Just a few more minutes. I promise, it will be worth it.'

The dawn chorus echoes around us as we sit there together, watching the sun chase the night away.

'I've never done this,' Stevie says in wonder. 'I mean, just sit on the ground and watch the sunrise.'

'Well, it's time you started,' I say, nonchalantly putting one of my arms around her shoulders; as I do, watching her cheeks flush slightly. 'It's one of nature's wonders.'

'It really is,' she says, fiddling with the oversized watch she wears.

'Can I see?' I take her hand in mine, studying the watch.

'It was my father's. It's really old.' Her voice shakes, just slightly.

We sit there together watching the sky lighten, until the first rays of sunlight edge above the horizon. I get to my feet. 'Come on. I'll make you a cup of coffee.'

Stevie looks anxious. 'What about your sister?'

'Don't worry about her.' Instead of going to Nina's part of the house, I take Stevie to our family kitchen. Still in their beds, the dogs noisily thump their tails when they see us, but it's too early for them to budge. 'You are lazy creatures,' I admonish them, gently scruffing their heads before getting some cups out. 'Have a seat,' I say to Stevie. 'It won't take long.'

After making a couple of cups, I take them over to the table where Stevie is gazing around the room.

'You do know that this single room is bigger than most people's houses,' she says.

'I do,' I say humbly. 'It's an incredible room.' It's one of my favourite parts of the house, but not for its grandeur. I sit down next to her. 'I have all these memories in here, of family meals, of friends stopping by. Of love.' As I speak, I surprise even myself, but every word of it's true. 'So what are you doing today?'

'Good question,' she says. 'I'll probably take Madame Picard lunch. I don't think I told you – they're going to start paying me. Fay – a kind of friend – came up with the idea that they should contribute what they can towards the costs.'

The name Fay rings a bell somewhere, but I can't place her. 'Well, don't forget, if you're ever in need of a waiter...' I say, remembering my rather drunken promise to her.

She raises one of her eyebrows. 'I thought that maybe that was the wine talking.' She smiles. 'But I might just take you up on that.'

'Please do.' Our eyes meet. Just as I'm trying to think of something to say, the door opens and my father walks in. His face is lined and there are dark circles under his eyes.

Looking at him, I'm suddenly anxious. 'Hey, Dad.'

'You're up early. I didn't expect to find anyone in here.' His eyes turn to Stevie.

'This is Stevie. She cooked for Nina last night.'

'Ah. Yes, Nina did mention something about a dinner.' He

starts opening and closing cupboards. 'There's a bottle of morphine here somewhere. Your mother needs it.'

My mother's illness is never far from my mind, but as he speaks, it's centre stage again. 'I think it might be in this one.' Opening another cupboard, I find the bottle and pass it to him.

As he goes back upstairs, Stevie gets up. 'I really must go.'

I nod. 'I'll walk out with you.'

I like this girl, I'm thinking as we walk out to her car. *I like her a lot.* As she opens the door, I stand there, watching her. Then awkwardly, I lean towards her and my lips brush against her cheek.

14

As I drive home, I can still feel Ned's lips against my cheek, unable to work out if it was the kind of kiss you give a friend, or if it was more than that. I try to decide how that makes me feel, as suddenly I'm remembering Ned's face as he passed the bottle of morphine to his father; his eyes emblazoned with sadness, the oddness of the unemotional exchange between them; the shared experience of losing someone they both love seeming to emphasise a distance between them.

It's still early, the street quiet as I unload my car then go to park it. I should be tired, but my mind is restless, the reality of Ned's kiss, of his mum slipping away from this life making me strangely aware of the world around me.

Standing at my kitchen window, I take in the sun as it rises higher through the trees, the sound of the river's gentle flow; I think of the way our lives come and go, but none of this changes.

Putting on my painting clothes, I open the windows in my little lounge and carry on decorating the last remaining wall. When it's done, I stand back and study the blank canvas in front of me. But I can't help thinking of Ned's family kitchen; how it isn't the walls that make it home. It's the decades' worth of memories, photographs and paintings; of furniture that's been in his family for as long as he can remember.

I have a sudden yearning for the familiarity of my parents' house; for the old sofa, the china my mother had collected, the framed photographs, the faded cushions. None of it worth anything to anyone else, but to me, it was home.

A tear rolls down my cheek before I wipe it away. Their house was never about the stuff inside. It was about them. And life moves on, I remind myself. But it doesn't stop me missing the past.

It gets me thinking. So far, I haven't been able to open my parents' box of photos, and going to the cupboard where it's been since I moved here, I decide it's time. I take it out and for the next hour, nostalgia takes over me as I study photos of my childhood. Of the house I grew up in; of birthdays and Christmases; of holidays in this village, here in France.

As well as of my parents, there are bundles of old photos of the grandparents who doted on me; of my mother's sister, my only aunt. I pick out a few with the intention of framing them, to hang later in this room. It's only when the box is almost empty that I find the letters.

* * *

I'm still sitting on the floor when hours later, there's a knock on the door.

'Stevie? *Coucou*, are you there, *ma chérie*?'

Recognising Madame Picard's voice, suddenly I realise I've forgotten her lunch. I get up and open the door. '*Bonjour, Madame.*' To my horror, a tear rolls down my face.

She looks worried. 'What is wrong?'

'I've had a bit of a shock,' I say, wiping my eyes. 'And I'm afraid I lost track of time. I haven't got around to making lunch yet.'

Coming inside, she closes the door. 'Then it is my turn to cook for you,' she says firmly.

'But you don't cook,' I protest.

'Whoever told you that?' She rolls up her sleeves. For someone so small, she is suddenly formidable. 'We will eat first. Then we will talk. What is all this?' She shakes her head towards the boxes I brought back after cooking for Nina last night, tutting to herself as she puts them to one side. 'You have *fromage*?'

I nod. 'In the fridge.'

'*Bon.*' Turning her back on me, she sets about making lunch.

I watch, astonished. I could have sworn she told me she didn't cook. Or maybe it got lost in translation. At any rate, she conjures up a tasty-looking croque-monsieur. When she passes me a plate, I realise how hungry I am.

'The thing is, all my life I thought they were wonderful. Perfect, even.' Only after, as Madame Picard washes up, do I try to explain how I'm feeling. 'My parents had these incredible, selfless careers working for charities that looked after orphans in war zones. They helped so many people. One of them was usually around when I was growing up, but when I got older, I remember them flying off to all these war-stricken places. I used to worry about them – all the time. Then today, I found these letters.' I pause. 'It turns out my mother was in love with someone else.' Gazing at my empty plate, instead of the love I used to feel whenever I thought about my parents, there's this alien feeling in its place, of emptiness.

'She was still your mother. And no one is perfect, *ma petite*,' she says gently.

'I realise that. But I thought they were going to help all these children who had no one.' I can still remember how much I hated them going away; how when my friends' parents stayed at home, mine didn't. But I'd always told myself that other children needed them as much as I did. And if one of them went alone, I never questioned it. 'Until now, I'd forgotten that sometimes, only one of them would go away. I thought it was because my grandparents were getting older. But I realise now, there was obviously another reason.'

'But they were happy. You would have known if they were not.' Madame Picard studies me. 'And you were loved.'

My eyes are hot with tears again. 'Yes.' I swallow. 'I was. And they seemed happy.' There was never any hint of animosity between them.

'Maybe they had an agreement.' She shrugs. 'I think you call it an open marriage? In France, it is common to have affairs,' she says. 'People do not get so upset about it. Sex is one of life's pleasures. I think it is that simple.'

My eyes widen. 'Is that what you did?' Mortified I've asked her, I backtrack. 'I'm so sorry. It's none of my business.'

'I do not mind that you asked. This is the difference in our cultures.' She smiles. 'You are embarrassed for asking, while for me... it is less important. And since you have asked, there was another man. I also had a long and happy marriage. My husband... he had several affairs. But I let him get on with it. I knew he loved me.' She pauses. 'Your parents spent a lot of time away, didn't they? But they loved each other – and they loved you. All these things people say about marriage and fidelity... We have expectations that sometimes I think are unrealistic. The point is, I think, to be happy.'

I sigh. 'Thank you, Madame Picard.' I'm still thinking about what she said. 'I suppose I've always thought of them as amazing and selfless. And it's the thought that the two people I loved most in the world weren't enough for each other.' Imagining how my father must have felt, my eyes fill with tears.

'It doesn't mean they weren't everything you believed of them. And sometimes it happens that relationships change,' she says gently. 'But you know they loved you. That is what matters, is it not?'

Suddenly I'm frowning at her. 'Madame Picard. Your English is very good today.'

She looks at me. 'I will tell you something, *ma petite* Stevie. My English is not so bad. But if I do not speak it, the stupid English will not bore me with their stories of their big houses and fancy holidays... *Terrible*,' she adds, in French. 'But you are not like them. You are one of us.' Patting my hand, she gets up, reaches into her pocket and takes out an envelope. 'I will leave you now. But before I go, you must know that I have had strong words with that Madame Bernard. When it comes to your beautiful food, she is a mean woman, so I told her of this. She did not like to hear it. And Monsieur Valois has been most generous; the others, too. This is from all of us.'

I take it and open it to find a bundle of euros. I stare at it, dumbfounded. 'This is too much.'

'It is not enough,' she says firmly. 'You see... It is so much more than about the food you cook for us.' Going on, she tells me that as well as eating better than they have in years, they have routine in their day, and companionship; that though sparks fly between them, they've rekindled their somewhat questionable friendships. It hasn't been without its moments, of course, but all in all, it's for the good.

'Madame Picard?' I have to ask. 'Those herbs you give me... What's in them?'

She shakes her head. 'You do not need to know, *ma petite*. You like them, do you not? *Bon.* So that is all you need to know.'

* * *

After she's gone, I make a cup of tea, then sit down, still thinking about what she's said. Even if my parents' relationship wasn't the monogamous bliss I'd believed it to be, for them, it must have worked. And Madame Picard's right. I still have every reason to be proud of them.

Suddenly I'm thinking about my ex. Before my parents died, I'd assumed he and I would get married and live happily ever after – just like I believed my parents had. I'd have lived a small, modest, unchallenging life. I wouldn't have questioned my decision. And maybe my small life would have been enough – though now, I can't help thinking that one day, something would have happened to wake me up.

But life isn't neat and tidy. And we are shaped by what happens to us – in my case, by losing my parents. And I like this life I'm building here, I'm realising, however uncertain it is, but I'm OK with that because when you stop and think about it, not much is certain in life.

* * *

It's a defining moment that leads to more defining moments, that, as they settle in my mind, slowly shift the way I remember my parents, but not in a bad way.

'It's just that I'd always thought of them as being perfect,' I say to Ned a few days later. 'But Madame Picard was right. No one is perfect. We're all just human.' I shrug. 'We all make mistakes.' I watch the slightly baffled look on his face.

'Perfection is much overrated,' he says at last. 'It's far too much to live up to, for one thing.' A humorous look crosses his face. 'And there's no chance anyone is ever going to find me perfect.'

'Ha. You don't know that,' I tease. 'When you're rich and famous and being stalked by all these groupies...'

'Never,' he declares, but he pauses just long enough to show he's thinking about it. 'The only person I know who comes anywhere near to perfect is my mother.'

He says it with such love I feel my heart twist. 'How is she?'

He's silent for a moment. 'Getting weaker. When she gets up, she's in a wheelchair now. Nurses come in most days – to make sure she's comfortable.'

A cold feeling comes over me. Compared to what Ned's mother is going through, everything else seems irrelevant.

He clasps his hands together. 'I just wish there were something I could do for her. I'd do anything.' There's anguish in his eyes as he looks at me. 'But there isn't. All we can do is be there.'

'Oh Ned.' I reach for one of his hands and squeeze it. 'You mustn't forget how important it is, just being there,' I say gently.

* * *

Since Nina's dinner party, I have been approached by several potential clients. I discover that Ned is right – that it does get easier. Tentatively, I book in four more dinners, while in between, I carry on working at the bar.

In just a couple of weeks summer is suddenly in full swing, the holidaymakers arriving in droves. Couples, families, hikers and cyclists, making the most of the endless hot days and beautiful countryside. It makes it easier to manage that Nicole observes strict and typically French mealtimes – lunch between twelve and two, dinner from seven thirty, meaning in between, we serve only drinks.

One morning when I arrive there, Nicole is beaming from ear to ear. 'We have such exciting news, Stevie darling! Don't we, *chéri*?' She glances at Olivier. 'We have a licence to hold our first music festival! Right here! Or out there, I should say.' She nods towards the grass along the river. 'Imagine, people coming from miles around. It is what this little village needs – some life in it.'

My eyes widen. 'Here?' As she mentions music, my immediate thought is that Ned should be involved.

She nods. 'Is there anywhere better?'

I follow her gaze towards the river, imagining a stage set among trees strung with lights, crowds of milling people.

'Stevie?' Nicole sounds impatient. 'What do you think?'

I smile at her. 'I really like the idea.'

'*Merde*.' Nicole looks impatient. 'This is very exciting news, and all you can say is you *like* it.'

'I love it, Nicole,' I say hastily. 'Also, I know someone. A musician.' But I've already told her about Ned. 'Remember Ned? He plays the guitar, and he sings. He grew up around here – he must know loads of people.'

'Perfect.' Her eyes gleam. 'Give me his mobile number. Right now. I must call him.'

* * *

'Do you think there's enough space out there?' Standing outside the bar several hours later, Ned looks doubtful.

'We're not exactly talking Glastonbury, Ned.' I'd hoped he'd be more enthusiastic. 'But even that had to start with a few musicians in a muddy field.'

'I guess. I'll do what I can.' But he looks distracted.

I look at him. 'It could be really great, you know. For getting your music known around here.' I pause. 'You're miles away, Ned.'

'Sorry,' he mumbles.

'It's OK,' I say gently. I know he's thinking about his mother. How could he not be? But he should be thinking about his music career, too. 'Your mum will love you doing this – and that you're involved in the community.'

His face clears. 'You're right. She will. If she's up to it, we could bring her down here in her wheelchair.'

'It won't be a problem. We need it to be accessible to everyone,' I say. 'Got any ideas who else might be interested in playing?'

He looks thoughtful. 'Actually, yes.'

I raise an eyebrow. It isn't the first time I've noticed he says *actually* quite a lot.

'There was this guy at Nina's party where you cooked. His name is Axl. We've become friends – I've been practising with his band in Bergerac since the party. It's a mix of jazzy and chilled. I guess it depends what Nicole wants, but I reckon they'd be great.'

'Fantastic! I'll tell her.' Nicole's excitement has rubbed off on me and I'm loving the idea of being a part of this. 'We have all these plans for food and drink...' Breaking off, I notice Ned smiling at me. 'What is it?'

'Nothing.' But he holds my gaze. 'OK! I guess it's just good to see you happy.'

* * *

Out of the blue, I get a call from Zeke's friend, Fay.

'I was hoping you might be able to help me out,' she says. 'You see, my family are coming out for a couple of weeks. I thought it would be rather nice to welcome them with one of your lovely dinners.'

Swallowing the trepidation I still feel, I take a deep breath. 'Of course,' I say brightly. 'How many will you be? And when is this?'

Taking down the date, I breathe a sigh of relief. It's two days before the music festival, but given it's a small gathering, it won't be a problem. 'I'll put it in my diary.'

'Thank you, Stevie.' She sounds grateful. 'Perhaps we can talk more about it nearer the time.' She hesitates. 'Have you seen Zeke lately?'

My ears prick up. 'Not for a while, as it happens. Why?'

She hesitates. 'I'm not sure. I have this feeling that something isn't quite right. He hasn't said anything – and I don't want to pry. But don't worry. I'm sure it's nothing.'

But she isn't sure, I'm thinking, as she ends the call. If she were, she wouldn't have said anything.

Too late, I realise I've forgotten to tell her about the music festival. Resolving to do it next time we speak, with a few hours free, I decide to drive up to Zeke's, parking outside his house before making my way to the allotments. And when I get there, I can't stop staring. In every direction, they're filled with colour; burgeoning, with beans, tomatoes, peas, peppers. With richly coloured purple aubergines and the wide faces of sunflowers; the whole alive with insects and birdsong.

My imagination starts to explode with ideas for salads in vibrant colours, with freshly made baba ganoush, delicious sauces for pasta dishes.

'Can I help you?' I turn to see a woman in a faded T-shirt and grubby dungarees frowning at me.

'I was hoping to see Zeke.'

'Oh.' She studies me. 'You are that girl he gives his vegetables to, right?'

'That's me.' I pause. 'Do you know where he is?'

She shrugs. 'I haven't seen him. But you could try the house.'

I make my way back through the hedge. At the front door, the cat wraps himself around my legs. I bend down. 'Where is he, boy?' Miaowing, the cat just watches as I knock on Zeke's door, waiting a moment before trying again. But there is no answer.

15

FAY

Speaking to Stevie, I sound like any other mother, planning for the arrival of her loved ones, wanting everything to be perfect for them. But a sigh comes from me. I may have booked Stevie to cook, but the truth is I'm not sure they're going to come.

I sigh again. I wasn't exactly truthful with her – not just about my family, but about Zeke. Thinking of Zeke, suddenly I'm worried about him again. The thought galvanises me into action, and closing up the house, I go over to see him.

The endless hot days show no sign of abating and the rich greens of early summer are turning to parched shades. Reaching Zeke's, as I get out of the car, the heat hits me. I make my way towards the path to the allotments, but when I reach the other side, there's no sign of him.

Going back to the house, I knock on his door and wait for him to open it. But he doesn't. It's possible he's out. But it's too hot for walking and I have a niggling feeling he isn't. Going around to the side of the house, I open the gate that leads to the back. 'Zeke?' I call out.

Standing there for a moment, through the fruit trees I see a movement. Making my way towards it, Zeke comes into view. Sitting on a bench, he seems lost in thought.

'Zeke?' I say again, more quietly.

He starts, then turns to look towards me. 'Fay!' But his voice lacks its usual brightness. 'What are you doing here?'

Seeing him get up, I hurry towards him. 'Please don't get up, Zeke. I just came over because...' I falter. 'I don't mean to interfere. It's just that you weren't in the allotments... and you didn't answer your door. I suppose, to be honest, I'm rather worried about you.'

I stand there, waiting for him to throw his head back with his typical laugh; tell me there's no need to worry.

'Why don't you come and sit down?' As he pats the bench next to him, I know something's terribly wrong.

'You've no need to worry about me,' he says at last. 'But seeing as you've asked...' He breaks off, rubbing his brow. 'The thing is, I'm not sure where to start.'

'With what's going on?' I try not to sound anxious. 'Whatever that is? Of course, only if you want to. I just thought...' Feeling his hand lightly touch my arm, I stop talking.

'Everything's just fine,' he answers. 'As for what's going on now, it goes back, Fay. Way back. But doesn't everything, once you start thinking about it?' He pauses. 'You know that black weed in the garden? How long ago was it that we noticed the leaves?'

'A few weeks?' I stare at him, wondering why he's talking about a weed.

'That's what I reckon. But the fact is the part of it we can't see has been there a whole hell of a lot longer.'

A cold feeling comes over me. 'What are you saying?'

'I have cancer,' he says calmly. 'And before you say anything, there's no reason to get upset about it. Something's going to get all of us, one day. Anyway, it's too late. Like that danged black weed that's taking over my garden, it's spread.'

Shock hits me. 'How long have you known?'

'Since I got those blood test results back.'

'You've had scans?' I say quickly.

'I went for one.' He shakes his head. 'That doctor of mine was most insistent. She's a nice young lass. She understands.'

'When do you start treatment?' I'm still trying to take it in.

He shakes his head. 'No point. Not when it's gone as far as it has.'

'But you can't know that.' I'm frowning. 'Not unless you've had more tests.'

He's silent for a moment. 'I've had tests, Fay. The doctor insisted.' He pauses. 'You see, it's like that weed. There's no stopping it – you've seen it for yourself. You know how many times I've pulled those roots out, but it just grows back.'

I look at him, horrified. 'Zeke, you must have treatment. You can't base your decision on that weed.'

'I don't have to do anything.' There's stubbornness in his voice. 'I'm seventy-eight, Fay. It feels like it's time.' Turning to me, his eyes meet mine. 'There is one problem I do have, though. And that's over there, the other side of that wall.' He glances in the direction of the allotments I've come to love. 'Bit of a double-edged sword, all that is. You see, over there, I don't get a chance to think, what with all them people coming and going... That's the reason I'm sitting here, trying to figure everything out.'

As I watch him, I realise he's a long way towards working everything out. It isn't a matter of being resigned to what the future holds. He's made peace with it; and now he's starting a process of signing out, is the only way I can describe it.

'If there's anything I can do,' I say quietly, 'please ask.'

'It's kind of you, Fay. But I can't burden anyone else with what I've chosen to take on. No.' He frowns slightly. 'There has to be a better way.'

* * *

Back at home, I can't stop thinking about Zeke; how in spite of his gregarious ways, the time he has for everyone else, he has no one close in his life. There's obviously a story – I've seen photos of a woman and a little girl on the wall in his house, whom I assumed were family. But given he never talks about them, it seems I'm wrong.

In the short time I've known him, he's never been anything but upbeat and strong. And the following morning, when I go to the garden, that's what he is again. If I didn't know, I wouldn't guess anything was any different.

'Morning, Fay.' Winking, he lifts his invisible hat to me. 'Now, I've been looking at that garden of yours. If I were you, I'd get on top of those weeds. And your first tomatoes are not far off ready.'

Overnight my optimism has returned, and a thrill of excitement ripples through me as I think of my family arriving; of cooking for them with everything I've grown here; it isn't the day to dwell on doubts. The sun is high in a cloudless sky. And, best of all, Zeke is here, where he belongs. 'I better get to those weeds.' I pause. 'You look well this morning.'

He nods, the faintest movement. 'Thank you,' he says.

* * *

As I work on my garden that day, I think how it's the first time in my life that I have months stretching ahead here. It's time I can fill however I wish to. I've given little thought to the life in England

I've left – far from it. The more I'm drawn into French village life, the harder it gets to imagine leaving.

I'm already sinking into the slowness to the pace of the days, the genuine sense of community that's long been lost where I live in England; while there's a gentleness to the people – with the exception of Rémy's abrasive tongue. But underneath even that lies a good heart, as I discover when she comes to find me that afternoon.

'You have spoken to him?' She nods in the direction of Zeke's distant figure. 'Only, I am worried about him.'

I'm silent. It isn't my place to tell her what's really going on. 'I think there is something on his mind,' I say carefully. 'I'm sure he'll tell us – if he wants to, that is.'

After a day of gardening, I drive home through the heart of the village. The bar is busy, the car park filled with cars, holiday-makers mooching lazily beside the river, one or two dogs splashing noisily through the water.

That evening, I sit outside with a glass of wine. The air is warm and still, alive with the buzz of insects. I watch little butter-flies of china blue, larger ones with wings of filigree lace. I've noticed them in Zeke's garden, hovering above wild flowers and unmown grasses, each one of them a tiny miracle of nature in a world that increasingly bears the imprint of man.

Staring out across our lawn that's always been neatly mown, I see it for what it is: convenient for me and Hugh, but inhospitable to insect life. When none of us really use it any more, the decision is easy. The following morning, after cancelling the gardener, I'm wondering why I haven't done it before.

What the lawn needs now is a day of rain. But there's no sign of it.

'Beautiful, isn't it?' I say to Zeke, when I arrive at the allotment the following morning.

He shakes his head. 'We need rain. But I reckon we're going to have to wait.'

'I hope not.' I glance at the sky. Gardening has given me a new appreciation of what rain means and this morning, there isn't a cloud in sight. Then as I look at his garden, taking in the ever-present black weed that seems to thrive no matter what, I feel myself shiver. 'How are you today?' I ask quietly.

'I'm just getting on, same as usual.' His eyes meet mine. 'I kind of figure I might as well.'

'I should help you dig up that black weed,' I say firmly.

But he shakes his head. 'Like I said, there's not a lot of point.' He pauses. 'In any case, I've tried. The thing just grows back stronger.'

Standing there, I'm frowning. None of this seems right – Zeke being ill, being alone in the world, while he's the most generous-spirited man I've ever known. 'Are you doing anything this evening?'

He looks surprised. 'Are you asking me out, Fay?' he quips.

It's a relief to see his sense of humour back. 'I thought perhaps you might like to have dinner with me.'

He pauses for a moment. 'In that case, it would be rude of me not to accept. Thank you.'

'Good,' I say briskly. Glancing at my watch, I can't believe it's already four thirty. 'How about we leave here in about an hour?'

* * *

An hour and a half later, I pull into the gravel driveway in front of our house. Zeke stares at it for a moment. 'How long ago did you buy this place?'

'It must be twenty years ago.' I try to think. 'My daughter was five. We celebrated her birthday here. Which means Stu, my son, must have been seven.' I remember it as though it were yesterday: their excitement as they explored the garden for the first time; their shrieks growing louder when they saw the pool. 'Why do you ask?'

'Believe it or not, I came to a party here once – though it was a lot longer ago than that.' He opens the car door and gets out. 'It's looking good.'

'Hugh's always paid a gardener,' I say hastily. 'But actually, I've just cancelled him.' I pause. 'I'd like your opinion on something.' I lead the way around the back of the house. 'All this...' I gesture towards the lawn. 'We've always mown it. But I want it to be a place where wildlife can live.'

Zeke's face creases into a smile. 'I like your thinking.'

But as I survey the lawn, it's almost barren. 'The only thing is, it isn't going to grow until it rains.'

'Even if it does, it's going to take longer than the rest of this summer for the wildness to come back,' Zeke says. 'Reckon you're going to have a right stubbly lawn this year. But as for next, as long as you stick with it... Let it grow from early spring. It'll look a treat.'

'I don't mind stubbly,' I say hastily, trying to hide my disappointment.

'Maybe you won't have to wait so long.' Zeke gazes up at the sky. 'Need the rain, don't we?'

I haven't noticed the clouds gathering. As I watch, the garden is cast in shadow as they blot out the sun. I turn to Zeke. 'Let's go inside.'

In the kitchen, I pour him a beer, then a glass of wine for me, and wash the veg I picked earlier. 'Do you like fish?' I ask.

'I surely do – I eat most things.' He looks around. 'This is a fine house, Fay. I like what you've done with it.'

'Thank you.' For some reason, I'm inordinately pleased. 'It was a lot of work in the beginning. But it was fun.' In the early days, it was a highlight of our family's year, packing up the car in England before making the journey here. Arriving late at night, throwing the shutters open the following morning to the magic of a world so far from the one we'd left behind. 'Our children loved it.' So did Hugh and I. Things were different then; so much has changed. I turn to Zeke. 'Do you have children?'

He's silent for a moment. 'A little girl.' He changes the subject. 'So what are we feasting on tonight?'

'Sea bass with my very own vegetables,' I tell him. 'There might be a sauce. You'll have to wait and see.'

It doesn't take long to grill the sea bass and steam the vegetables I've picked. But his reluctance to talk about his daughter hasn't gone unnoticed. Nor has the way he described her as a little girl. I'm about to ask more, but instinct tells me not to.

Zeke watches me serve up the food. 'So, Fay, are your family coming out here to join you at all?'

'I'm hoping so.' I carry two plates of food to the table. 'We've talked about August – if they have time.'

'They don't have time for family?' Zeke looks surprised.

'It isn't like that,' I explain. 'Stu, my son, lives in the States. And Julia, my daughter, works so hard.'

'All the more reason to take a holiday,' he says.

I sigh. 'Yes. But it isn't that simple. When she isn't working, Julia always has a long list of friends to catch up with. As for Hugh...'

'Your husband?' Zeke looks at me. 'How does he feel about you being here?'

'He isn't happy about it.' My voice is suddenly tight. 'I asked him to come with me. I would have liked that. But he wouldn't.'

'And I guess that leaves you feeling guilty.' He shakes his head. 'Well, I'll tell you now – get that thought right out of your head, because you shouldn't.'

I look at him, surprised. 'Not even when it was me who wanted to spend more time here?'

'I imagine there's a good reason for that.' Zeke takes a forkful of fish. 'You're a fine cook, Fay.'

'Thank you. I suppose...' I'm not sure where to start. 'In England, my life doesn't mean anything.' But that's only a part of it. 'Here, I feel I'm someone.' Awkward all of a sudden, I try to laugh it off. 'If that doesn't sound like a full-blown midlife crisis...'

'It sounds like someone who's lost her way a little,' he says gently. 'It wouldn't be right not to try to find herself again.' He pauses. 'Whatever that takes.'

My eyes fill with tears. He's summed it up so perfectly. It's exactly how I feel. 'It isn't Hugh's fault I feel like this.'

'No. But that's not the point. And if you don't mind me saying, it sounds like he doesn't understand.'

'He doesn't.' I get up, fetch the wine bottle from the fridge and top my glass up. 'He honestly thinks life should unfold in this locked-down, predictable, very traditional way. There is no spontaneity or adventure in his life. All he thinks about is work.' I shake my head at Zeke. 'I don't even know what to say to him any more.'

'Give it time. Time's a great thing,' he says. 'You can't fix everything overnight. And sometimes you shouldn't try. Wait and see what happens this summer. Life has a way of surprising us.'

'I'll drink to that.' I raise my glass. He makes it sound so simple. 'To life.' Chinking my glass against his, I catch the look in his eyes.

'To life,' he says quietly.

Emboldened by the wine, I ask what I've been holding back from. 'How are you, Zeke? Really?'

'I get tired,' he admits. 'Some mornings, I have to force myself out of bed. And before you say it, I know maybe I should ease up, but once I give in...' He tails off. 'I'm what you'd call a classic case of denial.'

'You're not, though,' I say gently. 'Not really.'

'No. Don't miss a thing, do you?' He looks thoughtful. 'I saw my doctor again the other day. We talked it all through – again. But it doesn't change anything. The thing is, for all kinds of reasons, I suppose I'm ready,' he says simply. 'I've been ready for years.'

I frown. 'What do you mean?'

'I'm an old man. And I guess there are folks I've lost I hope I'll get to see again.' He's silent for a moment. 'I've often wondered why some of us get to live a long life – and others don't.'

'Maybe it's random,' I say doubtfully.

'I don't know about random. I mean, here we are on a spinning lump of rock – if that's not a miracle, I don't know what is. But most of us forget that, don't we? I mean, it's home for millions of species, yet we treat it as though it's ours for the taking – and we're making a right old mess of it.' He shakes his head. 'Makes you wonder what the point is.'

I sip my wine. 'I'm not sure what to say. I do think about these things – but not very often.' Though since spending so much time alone here, I'm starting to, more and more.

'You're not alone, Fay. I reckon most of us don't. When we're young...' He shrugs. 'We all think we'll live forever! But then we get older... We start asking questions. Now, I guess the simple truth is, I'm tired, Fay, like I said. Seventy-eight years will do me just fine.'

* * *

As I drive him home, the atmosphere is sober. 'You're a good listener,' I say as he gets out of the car. 'Thank you.'

He looks surprised. 'The same goes for you.'

I get out and walk him to the door. Opening it, he turns to me. 'It's been a good evening.'

'It has.' I linger a moment.

Standing there, Zeke gazes around him. 'You know, on the way back here, I was thinking. It's a pretty good life here. Nice people, beautiful countryside... I reckon the best we can do is seize the moment, as they say these days.' After taking my hand, in an exaggerated gesture, he kisses it. '*Bonsoir*, Fay.'

I go back to my car, glancing back to see him watching me, before he goes inside and closes the door; waiting a little longer as the kitchen light is switched on, before getting in my car and driving away.

Back at home, I stand in front of our house. As I gaze upward, the darkness of the sky only magnifies the clarity of the stars. The magnificence of it takes my breath away, as does the thought that this spinning rock we live on, as Zeke described it, amongst everything else out there, as well as being miraculous, seems so small.

* * *

The following day, I pay an overdue visit to my neighbour – I call her my neighbour, but in reality she lives halfway between here and the village.

'I have not seen you in weeks.' Madame Bernard is less than forgiving about my absence.

'I did tell you I was going away, Madame Bernard. And I've been back a while. I've just been rather busy.' I look at her more closely. 'You're looking very well.'

'I am old.' Getting up, she limps exaggeratedly towards the fireplace. 'Where did you go?'

'I had to go back to England to apply for a visa.'

A look of disdain crosses her face. 'A visa?' She makes a spitting sound as though it is an evil thing. 'Well, now you are here, I want you to take this.' She takes a wilting posy off the mantelpiece, presumably destined for her husband's grave. 'It has been here for days. It is almost as dead as he is.'

I stop on the way to the church and pick a few blooms from a hedgerow to revive the dying posy, before paying one of my rare visits to the church. When I reach it, to my surprise, I see Stevie standing outside.

'*Bonjour*,' I call out.

'Oh. Hello.' Her blue eyes are anxious. But then almost every time I see her, there's an anxiousness about her.

Reaching her, I stop. 'How are you?'

'Good.' She looks hesitant. 'I'm here with a friend. He's inside. That's why I'm waiting here.' She glances towards the door. 'I thought it was best he was alone.' She hesitates again. 'His mother is very sick.'

Last time I saw Aimée, she was with her son. 'Is that Ned?'

Stevie looks surprised. 'You know him?'

'I met him very briefly – with his mother. I'm so sorry,' I say. 'It must be so hard for him.' I hear the church door clunk open. 'I'll leave you alone.'

I make my way across the churchyard. Placing the flowers on

Monsieur Bernard's grave, I glance across to where Stevie has her arms around Ned, feeling my heart go out to them.

I wait until they've walked away before heading back to my car. It's hot again, the sun needle-sharp against my skin, the air still, soporific, but as I drive, all I can think of is the boy who's about to lose his mother.

Out of nowhere, I feel a fire burn inside me, as I realise how lucky I am. That my children are happy and healthy; that right now, we have absolutely nothing to worry about, as at last I think I'm working it out.

The secret of a good life is to live it.

16

ZEKE

July

It's true what I said to Fay. For all kinds of reasons, I'm weary, deep in my bones. In more ways than one, I've done my time.

Life moves too fast for folks like me, these days. And I'm not frightened of dying. But there's this fear I have for everyone that's left behind, that all folk who live and breathe on this planet should share. And that's for the future of this world and for everything that lives on it, from the smallest insect to the mightiest tree.

One man alone might not be able to change the world.

But I've always believed that if enough of us care, together, just maybe, we can make a difference.

Whether I've done my part or not, who can say? But at least I've tried.

17

NED

As we walk away from the church, Stevie glances at me worriedly. 'Are you OK?'

'Ace,' I say brightly. 'Absolutely fine. What shall we do now?'

From the way her eyes hold mine, I can tell she's not convinced. 'We could go to the bar,' she says.

Out of the corner of my eye, I glimpse a woman driving away, vaguely recognising her. 'Great idea.' Desperate to get away from the church, from all the symbolism it embodies, I grab Stevie's hand and walk faster.

The thing is, it isn't just the church I'm trying to get away from, it's the emotions welling up inside me. Swallowing hard, I try to get rid of the lump in my throat.

'Slow down, Ned. It's too hot!' Beside me, Stevie jogs to keep up.

Reluctantly, I slow down. 'It's just that I don't like churches.'

'But you were the one who wanted to go inside.' Stevie sounds puzzled.

'I know.' I don't understand it myself. 'Anyway. Box ticked. Done, never to be repeated.' But as I speak, I know it isn't true.

That there will be times that no matter how I'm feeling, I will have to steel myself to endure another religious ceremony of some kind, while I'm trying not to think how it's more likely to be sooner rather than later. 'Let's talk about something else.'

There must be something in my voice because Stevie stops. 'Ned?'

Turning, my eyes meet hers. 'Can it wait till we reach the bar?'

'It's OK, Ned,' she says ever so gently, her hand resting on my arm.

Standing there, my vision blurs. 'I don't know what you mean,' I mumble.

She hesitates. 'What I mean is, it's OK if you feel over-whelmed, or emotional. You don't have to hide it – especially not from me.'

'I'm not hiding anything,' I lie.

'I know how it feels,' she says in the same gentle voice. 'Well, not to know I'm about to lose someone. But I know how it feels to be alone.'

'But I'm not alone, am I?' Rallying, I force a smile. 'I have you, and my parents...' At least for a little longer. Feeling my levels of discomfort rising, I gaze down the lane. 'And I have Nina. Stevie, can we get going? Please?'

'OK.' Giving in, she starts walking again.

After that, the afternoon takes a bit of a nosedive. OK, so I'm the typical guy who isn't in touch with his emotions – except that isn't quite right. It's more that I have a problem when it comes to expressing them.

At the bar, under the shade of an enormous umbrella, other than a brief exchange with Nicole and Olivier, Stevie seems to retreat into herself.

After my second espresso, I broach the elephant in the room.

'I've upset you, haven't I?' I say humbly. 'If I have, I'm truly, and terribly, sorry.'

She looks troubled. 'I just think it might help you if you stopped bottling everything inside and let yourself talk about it.'

A sigh comes from me. 'I get that.' I look at her. 'But when I try, I can't.' It's the nearest I get to telling her how I feel. And it's true. The words are there. I just can't say them.

She shakes her head at me, before a small smile plays on her lips. 'I forgive you.' The smile fades. 'I know that things are tough for you right now. I suppose I just wish I could help you.'

As she looks at me, two things happen. The first is that I'm struck by a powerful recognition of how lucky I am to have Stevie in my life. The second is that she genuinely cares – about me. 'You do,' I say, reaching across the table to take her hand. 'I'm not sure why, but it helps to know you understand, and that you don't think I'm weird, or something,' I add, trying to make her smile again.

'Be careful, Ned,' she says quietly. 'That it doesn't catch you up. These things you're feeling... they don't go away.'

'At the moment, it helps me cope.' Staring at my coffee cup, the lump in my throat is back.

Across the table, Stevie's face lights up suddenly. 'Billy!'

'Hey.' This guy stops at our table. Tall and tanned, he smiles at her. 'How are you doing? How's that car of yours?'

'It's great, thank you. Have a drink with us. This is Ned. Have you two met?'

'Hi, Billy.' I hold out a hand, slightly taken aback by Stevie's animated reaction; if maybe she likes him, as in *likes him*.

He hesitates. 'I only called in to drop something off for Olivier. But why not?'

Billy seems like a nice guy, but as he tells Stevie about his travels across Asia, her eyes lighting up as she listens, suddenly

I'm not in the mood. I get up. 'I should get home,' I say. 'I'll leave you two to it.'

Stevie looks disappointed. 'It's a pity you can't stay,' she says.

As I head back to my car, I feel like I've made a fool of myself. I could have stayed. Chatted to Billy, even talked to Stevie a bit more. Thinking of those beautiful eyes, the feel of her hand on my skin, I'm already wishing I had. But I'm not great company just now. And wherever I am, there's a restlessness that seems to follow me.

Nothing that can't be cured by music, I tell myself. Until now, it's been my cure-all – for almost everything. But as I drive, even with my latest playlist on bone-shakingly loud, I can't cut through the feeling of numbness I have.

Back at my parents' house, I sit outside in the car. Staring at the front door, I'm wondering how it will feel once my mother is no longer here.

I get out and go inside. After making a cup of tea, I take it through to the sitting room where my father's watching television, a glass of wine on the table beside him.

For a minute, I imagine nothing has changed. That our family is as it's always been; that any minute, my mother will walk in, carrying a bunch of flowers she's cut from the garden; chattering about some charity dinner for one of the many and deserving noble causes she supports.

'All right, Ned?' Ensconced in some horribly English programme about Tory politicians, my father barely looks up.

'Yeah.' I sit on the sofa, trying to focus on what the interviewer is saying. But for all the sense it makes to me, she could be talking a foreign language.

In the bosom of our home, as I think of it, there's no sense that our worlds are imploding; that we are about to lose the woman the three of us love most in the world. Instead, in that moment, it would be easy to believe that everything is as it's always been.

'Quite interesting,' my father says, still staring at the screen. 'Ever thought about going into politics, Ned?'

I'm speechless. Me and politics are like oil and water. Shake us together as much as you like, we just don't mix.

'I had the chance, once,' he says unexpectedly. 'A chap I knew said he could introduce me. I thought about it. I even discussed it with your mother. She said the chances were it would change me – and not in a good way. She was probably right, I realised. So that was that.'

He sounds unbelievably matter-of-fact as he talks about her. It's also the first time he's mentioned anything like this and I can't help wondering, *What else don't I know about him*?

'Have you eaten?' I get up.

'Too early, isn't it?' Checking his watch, he looks surprised. 'Goodness. I'd no idea how late it had got. I suppose something to eat would be a good idea. Your mother was sleeping earlier. I'll go and check on her.'

'I'll go.'

In the unfamiliar silence as I walk towards the stairs, I'm thinking how when someone's ill, no matter what their diagnosis is, it's human nature to hang onto hope – that things aren't as bad as they seem; that the person who's ill will get better. Until the day comes when you know there is no hope, because you know in your heart they're not going to.

As I make my way upstairs, it's as though the house itself is holding its breath. Outside my mother's bedroom, I knock quietly before pushing the door open. As soon as I see her, I know that day I knew was coming is already here.

Determined to hide the emotion bubbling up inside me, I go over to her bed. As she lies there, her face is colourless, her skin stretched over her delicate cheekbones. But there's the faintest of light in her eyes as she tries to smile.

'Ned,' she whispers.

Crouching down, I take her hand, stroking it gently. 'Hey, Mama.'

'How was your day?' Each word carefully pronounced, yet at the same time drawn out, giving away the effort it takes her.

Swallowing the lump in my throat, I try to smile. 'Good. I went for a walk.' Staring at her hands, I'm thinking how they soothed me as a child. The way they held me close and kept me safe. The same hands that cooked our meals and held the books she read to me and Nina. 'Is there anything I can get you?'

She sighs, only it comes out as a whisper of a breath. 'Time.' With what seems like a supreme effort, she reaches up to stroke my face. 'Dear Ned.' Her eyes glisten with tears.

My own eyes fill with tears. Then I feel my heart twist. In that moment, it's as though I can feel her pain, her sorrow, her regret that she won't be here in our lives, to see us married. To hold her grandchildren in those beautiful hands. To grow old alongside my father.

'I love you, my dearest Ned.' Her eyelashes flutter. 'Never forget that,' she whispers.

'I love you too, Mama.' It's too much. Overwhelmed, my eyes brim with tears as I gently lift her hand and kiss it.

I leave her bedroom before she can see me cry. Then head for the nearest room which happens to be the bathroom. And as I close the door behind me, I slump onto the floor as for the first time I cry properly, tears and snot pouring out of me in an uncontrollable expression of premature grief, for my mother, for the future we'll never share.

I stay there for some time until, spent, I drag myself to my feet and gaze at my reflection. A puffy face and bloodshot eyes stare back at me. Turning on the cold tap, I splash them with water to little effect. Then drying my face, I go downstairs.

The house seems filled with an odd silence, our lives seeming to have become condensed in some way; the line between life and death, between what's important and what isn't, never more sharply demarcated.

On autopilot, I make a pot of coffee and take a cup to my father. 'Where's Nina?'

'At the vineyard. There's a party tonight. Your mother and I were invited…' His voice suddenly husky, he breaks off, the first outward sign of the emotion he's hiding; the underlying message, life goes on.

The strangest feeling stays with me that evening. Sitting with my mother as she sleeps, as I fend off the millions of memories that come flooding back; watching my father's unexpected gentleness with her. As I'm forced to accept the inevitable that in a matter of days, or at best, a few weeks, the four of us will be no more; we will become three.

Life is the most paradoxical of realities, I can't help thinking as I watch the slightest movement of my mother's chest. A succession of beginnings and endings, in the midst of which, for the short while we're here, we go about our ordinary lives, forgetting how fragile life really is; forgetting that one day, just like my mother's, our lives will come to an end.

It's as though the past is hounding me, as suddenly I'm thinking about the time I've lost; how before I moved back, while I was partying and playing music in England, she knew she was dying.

Music's what you do, I tell myself. *It's your job.* But when I think of all the time spent with people who mean nothing to me, the guilt I feel is crushing.

* * *

That night, as I glance around my bedroom, the past tightens its hold. I think of the different incarnations it's had, morphing from a small child's room to a teenager's pit, to what it is now, tastefully decorated in shades of green, with my mother's trademark touches – the metallic lamp, the modern artwork, the woodcarvings from a trip she took to India. All of it done with love and until now, utterly taken for granted.

But all my life, I've never questioned that my parents wouldn't be here.

Reaching under the bed, I pull out the bottle of whisky I put there, opening it and taking a swig. I follow it with another, feeling the familiar heat in my throat. For now, it helps. But it isn't the answer. The trouble is, I don't know what is.

18

STEVIE

When I get to the bar before lunchtime, Nicole is even more stressed than usual.

'We have this booking,' she says. 'Twenty people, Stevie. In the middle of a fully booked restaurant.'

I frown. 'But that's OK, isn't it? I mean, we're always busy at this time of year.'

'It is that Dutch family,' she says. 'You know that tall man who is very rude?'

'His wife is lovely,' I remind her.

Nicole's eyes flash. 'You are too nice, Stevie. I do not like them. And it is not her who has booked us.'

'I'm sure it will be fine,' I try to reassure her.

* * *

As well as being the hottest day of the year, it's the busiest to date, with cyclists and hikers ordering drinks right up until lunch begins at midday. It doesn't help that the Dutch family are late. Not that Nicole notices. She's too distracted by the group of teenagers with a dog as one of them picks it up, dangling it by a back leg before dropping it over the wall into the river.

As the dog submerges then comes to the surface, Nicole looks furious. 'I cannot watch this. It is the third time they do this.' She passes me the tea towel she's holding. 'I will be back in a minute.'

'Hey,' I hear her call out. 'Stop this. *Right now.* Or I call the police.'

As the teenagers erupt into laughter, one of them makes an obscene gesture at her while, sensing an ally, the dog changes course and swims towards her. Crouching down, Nicole calls the dog. Cowering, it makes its way over to her. Taking it by the collar, she coaxes it back to the bar as a round of applause breaks out amongst our customers.

Reaching me, her face is thunderous. 'You know who that was, don't you?'

I look at her, mystified. 'Who?'

'He is the son of this vile Dutchman who has booked *that* table.' She nods towards the still-empty reserved table. 'And this is his way of amusing himself while he waits for his father. You see how arrogant – to book on a busy day, and to be late.' She glances at her watch. 'Forty-five minutes late. We could have used the table in this time.'

'What about the dog?'

Bending down, she gently strokes it. 'I will put him in the back. He will be safe there.' As she leads him away, a car pulls up. It seems Nicole is right and as the occupants get out, one of the teenagers comes running over. After a brief exchange, all of them head towards the bar.

Slightly wrong-footed by Nicole's outburst, and realising that this is the Dutch booking, my face flushes. '*Bonjour, Monsieur.*' But before I can show him to his table, Nicole reappears. Seeing the teenager, a look of rage crosses her face.

She comes over and stands in front of them. 'You are not welcome in my restaurant.' She glares at the Dutchman. 'This is your son?'

'I believe you have our dog,' he says curtly. 'Kindly return it to us.'

'No.' She shakes her head. 'I would like you to leave. I will not have animal abusers in my bar. You and your family are not welcome here.'

Behind her, the customers are silent as all eyes are on the Dutchman.

'First you will give us our dog.' His eyes bore into her.

'So you can abuse him again?' Nicole stands her ground. 'No way. I will contact the police and I will tell them what your son has been doing. As you can see, we have a great many witnesses.' Turning, she gestures towards our customers.

He's silent for a moment. 'This is theft, you do realise this?' He stares at her. 'It is I who will be calling the police.'

Nicole folds her arms. 'This is private property. You are trespassing, *Monsieur*.'

'You have not heard the last of this,' he mutters, before turning and walking back to his car.

'Asshole,' Nicole says under her breath as she watches him drive away. 'Come, Stevie. We have work to do.'

Several of our customers go out of their way to applaud her, and I take down some names and contact details, in the event that we need witnesses. For the duration of lunch, Nicole says nothing, just works at lightning speed, stopping now and then to acknowledge what seems like unanimous support for her actions.

If that weren't surprising enough, that afternoon, after lunch is over, as the bar empties, a fair-haired woman walks over to us.

'I am so sorry,' she says to me.

I look at her curiously. 'What for?'

'My husband.' Glancing behind her, she looks anxious all of a sudden. 'Your colleague saved our dog?'

'Oh.' My cheeks flame red as I recognise the horrible Dutchman's wife. 'Perhaps you should talk to Nicole.' I hesitate, then gesture to one of the empty tables. 'I'll go and find her. Why don't you take a seat?'

When I go to the kitchen, there's no sign of Nicole.

'She's out the back – with that dog.' Olivier sighs, but it's obvious he doesn't mind.

Going through to the little garden behind the bar, I find Nicole sitting in the shade stroking the dog.

She looks up briefly when she sees me. 'He is so scared.' Her voice is small. 'How can people be so horrible?'

'Not all of them,' I say. 'The Dutchman's wife is in the bar. I told you she was nice. She's come to apologise.'

I don't overhear the conversation that takes place, but half an hour later, Nicole and Olivier are the new owners of a very relieved-looking dog.

'She has signed him over to us.' Nicole looks dazed. 'She says it wasn't the first time, but her husband is as bad as her son. Neither of them will listen to her, and she can't bear for it to go on. I gave her some money – not because she asked, but so that I have now officially bought him. She said she is going to give it to an animal sanctuary.'

'Wow.' I'm taken aback at how quickly it's happened. 'What about her husband? He isn't going to like it, is he?'

'I don't care what he thinks.' Nicole shrugs. 'The dog belongs to us now.'

For such a tiny, peaceful place, it's unusual for anything like this to happen around here. But the day isn't over yet, and thanks to the village grapevine, minutes after I get home, Madame Picard knocks on my door.

Her eyes are troubled, her usually neat pinned-back hair all over the place. 'I heard, Stevie... That poor dog. It is good that Nicole has it now.'

'It is.' Frowning, I'm about to ask her how she knows when I notice she isn't alone, that Madame Bernard is just behind her.

'You see what happens when all these people come here?' Madame Bernard sounds disgusted. 'We used to be a quiet, peaceful little village. Now with all these migrants... nothing but trouble.'

'I think that's a bit of an exaggeration, Madame Bernard,' I say tentatively. 'It was just one boy – and his father.'

'That is what you think.' She makes a guttural sound. 'I can tell you one thing. It won't be the last of it.'

I look at her uneasily. 'But Nicole has paid for the dog. It's a done deal.'

'That man...' Madame Bernard wags a finger at me. 'I have seen him around. And I know his type. He is arrogant. He is not a man to be thwarted.'

My stomach turns over. 'I hope you're wrong.'

* * *

'How is the dog?' I ask when I see Nicole the following day.

'It is like when a baby is small.' Her eyes are tired. 'He cried. So he and I curled up on the sofa. He slept in my arms. He is fine now.'

I decide not to tell her what Madame Bernard said, but it seems Nicole is thinking the same. 'If that Dutchman turns up here, call the police,' she tells me. 'Do not wait for even one second, Stevie. Understand?'

I nod. 'Of course.'

'And do not under any circumstances tell him where Merlot is,' she adds. 'Now, we have work. We must start.'

'Merlot?' I say, as I follow her into the kitchen.

'The dog – he is called Merlot now,' she says impatiently. 'And in all this, I am forgetting about the festival. I must get in touch with all of the acts. And you must tell Ned, tickets are selling fast! We must organise glasses – and beer.' She rolls her eyes. 'You English love your beer.'

'I think wine will be more popular,' I point out. 'We should speak to one of the local vineyards about selling it here.'

'Good idea.' She stops. 'Put it on the list. We are looking at five hundred people, Stevie. Five hundred! So much to do... But it will be fun!'

Suddenly I'm thinking of Ned. The festival is only a month away. The timing isn't good for him. Then I remember Fay. Her family are arriving a few days before the festival. I make a note to self to tell her about it, before the tickets are gone. Zeke, too. Thinking about him, I realise how long it is since I've seen him.

* * *

'You're looking good,' he says approvingly when I go to find him in the garden that evening. 'The French summer suits you. I'm guessing you've come for some vegetables?'

'Thank you. But not today.' I hesitate. 'I've been too busy at the bar for any private dining. And we have this festival coming up. Here.' I pass him one of the posters we're pinning up around the village.

He looks impressed. 'There's nothing like a bit of music to bring folks together. I'll pin it up, if you like.'

'Would you?' I say gratefully. Standing there, I take a deep breath, feeling the tension leave me.

'Tough week?' Zeke sounds sympathetic.

'Yes and no.' Noticing an unused wooden box, I turn it over and sit on it. 'The bar's been super busy. In the middle of it, Nicole rescued a dog that was being abused by its owner.' I sigh.

'That's a heavy sigh, young lady.' Zeke looks at me curiously.

'It's not just that.' I'm thinking of Ned. 'It's a friend of mine. His mother is dying.'

'That's too bad.' Zeke's silent for a moment, before shaking his head. 'But at least this way, there's a little time – to say the things they want to say to each other.'

'I know.' I hesitate, frowning. 'He's one of those people who finds it hard to talk – and I'm worried about him.'

Zeke looks at me. 'I know it's tough, but at times like this, there isn't anything you or anyone else can do. It's his journey. He has to find his own way.'

As I head back to my car, my phone buzzes. 'Hey, Ned.'

'I've just experienced a miracle,' he declares. 'Sorry?' I frown at my phone. 'I'm not sure what you're talking about.'

'You've actually got your phone with you – and it's charged,' he teases. 'Sorry. Only it doesn't happen very often.'

'That's not true,' I object. 'I always have it with me.' Though I have a memory of Nicole saying the same to me. 'How are you?'

'OK.' His voice is suddenly sober. 'Are you doing anything? Or can I come over?'

'Of course,' I say brightly. 'I've just been to see Zeke. I'm on my way home.'

Minutes after I get back, Ned knocks on the door. In a thin grey T-shirt and faded jeans, his hair is typically scruffy. Not for the first time, I fight the urge to run my fingers through it.

'Like a drink?' I ask, trying to ignore the way my heart is racing the way it always does when Ned is near.

'I'd love one.' Pushing his sunglasses on top of his head, he gazes around the kitchen. 'Shame you don't have a garden.'

'I have better than that.' Taking a bottle from the fridge, I pick up two glasses. 'Follow me.'

It's the first time anyone else has stepped beyond my kitchen as I lead the way through my sitting room. 'This is really nice.' He sounds surprised.

'Thanks. Bit of a work in progress,' I tell him. 'Judging from the wallpaper I stripped, it's the first time it's been decorated in about sixty years.'

He goes over to look at the photos I've hung on one of the walls. 'This is you?'

I nod. 'With my parents.' I let him stand there a moment. 'This way.' I lead him up the stairs. At the top, a door leads to my bedroom and bathroom, while another leads outside. Opening it, I step onto the terrace.

Following me out, Ned looks impressed. 'This is really cool.'

I smile. 'It's very tiny – compared to your place. I mean, you could fit the entire house into your hallway.'

He grimaces. 'That's probably true of a lot of houses around here.' He pauses. 'But I really like yours. It's homely.'

For some reason, I'm inordinately pleased he likes it. And it's exactly as I wanted it out here. Decorated with pots of brick-red geraniums, it's a big enough space for the small table and couple of bistro chairs I've carried up here. 'Well, I really like it. Have a seat.' I place the glasses on the table and pour some wine.

Sitting down, Ned takes a glass. '*Santé.*' He chinks it against mine.

'Cheers.' I stick to the familiar. The wine is wonderfully cool and I watch the tension slowly leave Ned's face.

'This is the greatest view,' he says. 'You can spy on your neighbours, too.'

'I'd never do that,' I say hastily. Though I have listened to Madame Picard singing to herself, and I know Monsieur Valois likes to sit outside for hours staring across the river, completely alone.

'Actually, one of the things I wanted to talk to you about is the festival,' Ned says. 'Axl and I have put a set together. I've recorded it.' Suddenly he looks uncertain. 'I, um, wondered if you might like to hear it.'

'I'd love to.' My cheeks flush pink as I watch him get his phone out. 'You have it with you?'

'Indeed I do.' He glances around. 'Don't happen to have a speaker, do you?'

'A tiny one.' I hesitate. 'I'll go and get it.'

After retrieving the speaker from my sitting room, I pass it to Ned. Then sitting there, I listen as the music starts. As it plays, looking out across the rooftops towards the countryside beyond, it feels like the perfect place to listen to it.

'What do you think?' he asks when the first track finishes. 'There's more, by the way.'

'I love it.' My eyes are shining. 'You should play it at the festival. Really, Ned. It's perfect.'

He looks pleased. 'I don't know about perfect, but I think it has a nice vibe.' He carries on playing it in the background as we talk. 'How are ticket sales?'

'They're going fast,' I say. 'Nicole's lined up quite an eclectic – and French – playlist, I think you'd describe it as.'

Ned grins. 'Dodgy accordion music?'

I can't help smiling. 'Afraid so. But she swears only for about twenty minutes – at the beginning. It's a friend of one of her regulars.' I look at him quizzically. 'You're sure you're going to be OK doing this?' I'm only asking because of his mother's illness.

He nods. 'It's been nice having the distraction in a way.

Music...' He hesitates. 'I suppose it's where I channel a lot of what I'm feeling.'

'That makes sense.' There's no question that Ned has talent. Topping up his glass, suddenly I have to say something. 'Ned? Don't you realise you have a very real chance?'

He looks confused. 'With what?'

'Your music.' I pause. 'It's great. And it's really great you're playing with Axl's band. And that you're putting a website together...'

'Actually, Nina is,' he says. 'She's doing a great job.'

'Exactly,' I say patiently. 'Don't you think it shouldn't be Nina having to do it? That it's something you should have done ages ago? I mean, if you're as serious about your music as you say you are, you should be chasing every opportunity – not waiting for someone else to make it fall into place around you.'

He looks startled. 'You've never said anything like this before.'

'I suppose I've never felt it before,' I say honestly. 'But nothing's going to happen unless you go out there and make it happen.'

A shadow crosses his face.

'I don't mean to be brutal,' I say gently. 'I'm only saying it because I care.'

'I know.' He sighs. 'It's just that this is horribly like the conversation I had with Jessie. The one where she told me she couldn't go on propping me up.' He pauses. 'Is that what you're saying?' He rests his head in his hands for a moment. Then he gets up. 'I'm going out for a bit. I need to think.'

I gaze at him helplessly. 'I honestly didn't mean to upset you, Ned.'

'It's OK.' Turning, he goes downstairs. Then I hear the door open, then close behind him.

Panic fills me. What if he doesn't come back? Maybe he's

misunderstood where I was coming from. Sitting there, I'm wishing I'd stayed silent. Who am I to challenge what Ned does with his life? I'm just as good at hiding away from things. But I'd felt like I'd had to say something. He needs to believe in himself a bit more. Other, less-talented musicians make a living out of music. There's no reason why Ned shouldn't have, at least, a good chance.

Closing my eyes, I let the sun's warmth soak into me, swallowing the lump in my throat. What have I done? The last thing I want is to lose Ned.

* * *

I must have dozed off, because I open my eyes to hear the door closing, then footsteps coming up the stairs. The next thing I know is that Ned is standing there.

I sit up. 'Ned—' I start.

But he interrupts. 'Please, Stevie. Let me say this. I've just had the most horrible two hours thinking about what you said. And seeing as I have nothing to lose right now, I'll tell you how I'm feeling. Playing at the village festival, or at drunken birthday parties, is easy for me. But beyond that, I suppose, I'm frightened.'

'Of what?' I ask quietly.

He pushes his hands into his pockets, a freaked-out look crosses his face. 'OK. Hear goes.' He takes a deep breath. 'I'm frightened of failing.' His eyes are darting around. 'You've no idea how hard it was to say that,' he declares with his typical self-deprecating humour.

But I'm not smiling. 'If you fail, at least you'll have tried.' I try to keep the frustration out of my voice.

He looks uncomfortable. 'Everyone in my family is successful.

It feels like such a big deal that I'm not. The thought of making it worse…'

'But if you don't try, you'll never know if you could have made a success of it.' I look at him. 'This is about you, Ned. It isn't about anyone else. The only person you're letting down is yourself,' I say more gently.

Sighing again, he sits down next to me. 'Are you sure you want me to be here?'

'Yes.' I hand him his glass.

He's silent for a moment. 'I know you're right,' he says. 'I just need to find the courage from somewhere.'

I reach for one of his hands. 'You really should,' I say. 'Your music is amazing. More people should hear it than just this little corner of rural France.'

'Thanks.' The colour comes back to his cheeks. 'Actually…' He fumbles with his phone. 'There's one track I haven't played you. I hadn't planned to play it to anyone. It's about what's going on right now. For Mama.'

I'm touched that he wants to share it with me; even more as it starts to play. The music is haunting, ethereal almost, somehow seeming to capture the most powerful love. It stirs something inside me and as I listen, tears stream down my cheeks.

When it finishes, I wipe my face. 'That's the most beautiful thing I've ever heard.'

'Thanks.' His voice is husky, his eyes locked on mine.

'You have to play it at the festival.' It's head and shoulders above everything else he's played.

'I don't know,' he hedges. 'It's kind of personal.'

And I get it; that he's poured his feelings about his mother into this one piece, that so far, he's only shared with me. As I gaze at him, something seems to pass between us. Suddenly I realise I don't mind that he says *actually* a lot, or wears sunglasses all the time. I like Ned. I like him a lot. Unable to stop myself, leaning towards him, I kiss him.

Realising what I've done, I pull away, shocked at myself; my cheeks are flaming. 'I'm so sorry.'

'Don't be.' Taking my face in his hands, Ned moves closer, then he's kissing me back, the sweetest kiss, as closing my eyes, for a moment I lose myself. Pulling his chair closer to mine, Ned takes both of my hands. 'I've wanted to do that for ages,' he confesses.

It's as though I can still feel his lips on mine. 'So why didn't you?' I say softly.

'A couple of times, I almost did. But I wasn't sure you felt the same. I mean, Billy seems a really nice guy,' he says wryly.

I can't believe he's mentioned Billy. 'He is. He's a friend of Zeke's,' I explain. 'He helped me out when my car broke down.'

Ned nods. 'There's also the timing.'

'Yes.' I know he's talking about his mother. 'It's just a kiss, Ned,' I say gently. 'There doesn't have to be a right time for it.'

Hesitating, he moves closer, his eyes gazing earnestly into mine. 'What if it wasn't, Stevie? What if it was more than a kiss? I know we're friends. Really good friends. Only I have this feeling about you and me, we could be more.'

My heart leaps, this deliciously warm feeling curling inside me, a smile spreading slowly across my face. 'You really think that?'

'You're beautiful.' He strokes a lock of hair off my face. 'But it's more than that. There isn't anyone else I've ever been able to talk to. Or feel so comfortable with. You make me feel I can be myself with you. And I want to be the same for you.'

A sigh comes from me. Just a small one, of pure happiness. 'It's how I feel too.' It's true. Ned's one of the loveliest, most honest people I've ever met.

'Will you be my girlfriend, Stevie?' he says.

My heart swells with joy as I look at him. 'Yes,' I whisper.

19

FAY

August

With my family about to arrive, I spend an afternoon at the allotments where I dig up some potatoes, before gathering the ripest of the tomatoes I've grown and fragrant stems of herbs. The aubergines and peppers are still small, but I pick them anyway, casting my eye around for anything else that's ready. After packing them into my baskets, I go to find Zeke.

Seeing him across the garden, I frown. Noticeably less active these days, he's sitting on his chair with his eyes closed. Getting closer, I cast my eyes over that black weed that plagues his garden, noticing it's spreading.

'Evening, Zeke,' I call out quietly.

Opening his eyes, he looks up. 'Good evening to you, Fay. Had a good day?'

'Oh, very good, thank you.' My face is hot from the sun, but I feel a different glow, too, that radiates from inside me. Just being here in the allotments makes me happy. 'I didn't mean to disturb you, but I may not be here for a few days.'

'Hugh's coming?' Zeke raises his eyebrows.

'Yes. He flies in tomorrow.' I know I sound less than enamoured. But if I'm honest, it's how I feel.

'I'll see you when I see you. And don't worry, I'll water your vegetables. I ain't going anywhere – not yet, at least.' His eyes are twinkling.

'That's most kind of you.' I hesitate. 'But I don't want to put anything on you.'

'You won't be,' he says.

I sigh. Then I say what I'm thinking. 'I know you're doing less these days. It's to be expected,' I add as I watch him start. 'There's something else I wanted to say.' I pause. 'If you're not feeling well, or if I can do anything for you... anything at all, I want you to promise you'll call me.'

* * *

Having extracted a reluctant promise from him, I have a sinking feeling as I drive home. When I first met Zeke, he would have laughed at just the thought of anyone looking out for him. But tonight, he didn't.

Turning my mind to the days ahead, a feeling of warmth comes over me. This time tomorrow, my family will be around me. There's nothing in the world that means more to me. But my excitement is tinged with uncertainty. You see, it's the elephant in the room, looming larger than ever. My marriage.

Sighing as I turn into our drive, I notice the lights are on. I frown. I could have sworn I switched them off this morning. After parking, I get out. Then I unlock the back door and carry my baskets of vegetables inside.

'Fay?'

The voice startles me. Going through to the kitchen, I stare incredulously at my husband. 'Hugh?' I blink. 'What are you doing here?'

'I thought I'd surprise you,' he says gruffly.

'You have,' I say, stunned. 'You should have said you were coming today.'

'I brought you these.' Coming over, he passes me a huge, extravagantly wrapped bouquet of roses.

'They're lovely. Thank you.' Taking them, I stare at him. His face is pale, and there are dark circles under his eyes. 'I thought you were coming tomorrow.'

'I thought I'd come a day early.'

'Why?' Panic hits me, that something's wrong. 'Has something happened?'

'Nothing's happened.' He looks slightly impatient. 'I thought you and I could have an evening together. But it's probably getting late to go out.'

'Oh.' Suddenly I'm flustered. 'I've just come back from the allotment, Hugh.' I glance at my baskets of vegetables. 'Let me deal with these – and have a shower. There's wine in the fridge.'

'I picked some red up on the way,' he says. 'Shall I pour you some?'

I notice the opened bottle on the side. But I fancy something more refreshing. 'I'll have a glass of white.'

* * *

After showering, I pull on a loose-fitting T-shirt dress and pin my hair up before going downstairs. Pausing in the doorway, I watch Hugh. Oblivious to me standing there, I notice how weary he looks, how his short-sleeved shirt is tight around his middle, the way his trousers need pressing, and I feel a pang of something.

I take a deep breath. 'That's better,' I say briskly, going to join him. 'Shall I make us some dinner? Some fish, maybe?'

He doesn't reply for a moment. 'That would be nice.' Then he looks across at me. 'I've missed you, Fay.'

'Have you?' I speak breezily, aware of the edge in his voice.

He sighs. 'Look, I know things have been difficult between us, but I was hoping we could talk.'

I stiffen. I know, for Hugh, this is as placatory as it gets. 'If that's what you want.' I top up my glass and pick it up. 'Shall we go outside?'

Hugh looks surprised. 'Of course.'

Going out to our terrace, I wait for a critical comment about how the lawn needs mowing; how the garden's a mess, when if you look beyond the obvious, for the first time since we bought this house, the garden is teeming with life.

Pulling out a chair, I sit down. 'When did you get in?'

'Early afternoon.' Hugh sits opposite me. 'I thought you'd be here.'

'I spent the day at the allotment,' I tell him. 'I spend most of my time there.'

'It suits you. You look well.' He looks slightly awkward.

'Thank you.' Picking up my glass, I sip my wine. 'How long are you staying?'

He hesitates. 'That rather depends.'

'On what?' I frown.

'I thought you'd come back to England,' he says suddenly. 'I didn't expect you to stay.'

'I told you what I was doing,' I frown. 'It shouldn't have been a surprise.'

'I know you did.' As he stares across the garden, I wait for him to comment on the lawn.

'Why did you think I'd come back?' I look at him, perplexed.

'Because you've always been there. And I thought you'd get lonely being here on your own. But you're not, are you?'

I shake my head. 'I'm not.' I sigh. 'Life is different here, Hugh. I'm happy.'

'Did you miss me?' His eyes meet mine. When I don't say anything, he shakes his head. 'You didn't, did you?'

'It isn't as simple as that, Hugh.' I pause, trying to find the words. 'I suppose it's more that I don't miss that way of life. In Surrey, all I do is clean the house and cook meals. I was bored with shopping and going out for lunch. I suppose I was finding I had less and less in common with all the people around me.'

'But what about me?' He sounds hurt.

'Oh, Hugh.' I try to keep the exasperation out of my voice. 'You leave the house at twenty past seven every morning. In the evenings, you come home late. At the weekends, you play golf.' I pause. 'I think I stopped missing you a long time ago.' I gaze at him, wanting him to understand. 'I had to,' I add more gently.

'For what it's worth, I missed you,' he mumbles.

I sigh. 'I'm sure you did. But when you analyse it, I'm sure you'll admit it's more about the inconvenience of not finding freshly ironed shirts in the wardrobe when you need them. Having meals ready and waiting when you're hungry. Or the house being tidy. The ease of living with someone who just goes along with what you expect, unquestioning.' I shake my head. 'I don't mean to sound brutal. I'm just being honest.'

For a while, he says nothing. When he looks at me, his eyes are filled with sadness. 'What happened to us, Fay?' he says huskily.

I gaze back at the man I used to love with all my heart. 'I think we stopped trying,' I say quietly. 'Not just you, but both of us.'

* * *

Hugh sleeps in one of the spare rooms that night and the following morning, I awake early, alone. Lying there, I replay our conversation last night, realising it's the first time Hugh didn't try to talk over me.

After getting out of bed, I go over to the window and push the shutters open. Gazing across the garden, I'm astonished to see Hugh already outside with a net, cleaning the pool. I watch him stop to wipe the sweat from his face, picturing the younger Hugh for a moment. Leaner, livelier... Was he kinder? But he's never been deliberately unkind. Just blinkered.

I go downstairs, put the kettle on and make a pot of coffee, before taking a cup outside to him.

'You're up early,' I call out.

'I thought I'd get this done before we drive to the airport.' He glances at his watch. 'The kids both land just after twelve.'

'Good idea.' As I get closer, I notice the swimming shorts he's worn for years have grown tighter. 'I thought you might like this.'

After putting down the net, he comes over and takes the cup. 'I was just thinking about when we bought this place. Changed a bit, hasn't it?'

'The garden's certainly grown up,' I say, glancing at the roses festooning the terrace. 'But I like that.'

He nods. 'So do I.'

Then I notice the hose in the pool. 'There's a drought across south-west France, Hugh. I know it needs topping up, but they're talking about a hosepipe ban.'

He shrugs. 'Haven't brought it in yet, though, have they?'

Which isn't the point; if people like us go on using water less than frugally, it will impact all of us. 'I'll leave you to it.' I turn back towards the house. 'Stevie's coming later. It was supposed to be a surprise.'

'Who's Stevie?' he calls after me.

'The most amazing chef. You'll see.' I daren't tell him that it's a vegetarian menu I've asked her to cook.

Still in my pyjamas, I cut some roses from the garden – multi-petalled, sweetly scented blooms I place in vases, finishing touches to the bedrooms for Stu and Julia. After fluffing pillows and neatly folding towels for them, I change.

It's just before eleven when I go downstairs. In the hallway, Hugh's looking impatient. 'We should have left by now.'

'Does it really matter?' I say. 'If we're five or ten minutes late, the kids will be fine.'

He gives me a look, then huffs out to the car, for want of a better word. After locking the front door behind us, I follow.

Setting off, he drives too fast, unnerving me. 'Slow down, Hugh,' I say quietly. 'We're not in a hurry.'

Reluctantly he does as I ask and I sigh a breath of relief. It's a while since I've made the journey to Bergerac and as he drives, I take in the countryside, the fields and hills scorched by the sun, animals standing lethargically in whatever shade they can find.

The heat of summer has intensified in recent weeks, water levels dropping in the lakes; the land, the rivers, the animals, crying out for rain.

'I heard on the radio it's the worst drought in years,' I say to Hugh. But there's something on my mind. 'Last night,' I say tentatively, while it's still just the two of us. 'When I asked you how long you were staying, you said it depends.'

He slams on the brakes as the car in front of us stops, then accelerates away again. 'What I meant was it depends on you.'

'Oh?' Suddenly I'm uncertain. 'How exactly?'

'It depends whether you'd like me to stay.' He pauses. 'I've given it a lot of thought while you've been here. You're right. I could take some holiday – and maybe work from here.' He pauses. 'But like I said, it rather depends.'

It's so out of the blue, I'm not sure what to say. 'I think it would be a good idea,' I say cautiously. 'Whatever happens between us, Hugh, it would do you good to be here.'

He's instantly on the defensive. 'What do you mean, "whatever happens"? Are you talking about our marriage?'

Reaching across, I pat his knee. 'One day at a time, Hugh.' I pause. 'We've both had a lot to think about these last few weeks. Why don't we put it aside? Just for now? We have a rare few days coming up, with all of us here together. Let's just enjoy them. We can talk more when the children have gone.'

* * *

The airport in Bergerac is busy, but then it's the height of summer, holidaymakers flocking in to enjoy this beautiful part of France; the medieval towns; the lakes and vineyards it has to offer.

Side by side, Hugh and I wait in arrivals.

'There's Julia.' I wave excitedly as our daughter comes through the automatic doors. 'Darling.' I run towards her and fling my arms around her.

'Mum!' Pulling back, she looks at me, her eyes widening. 'You look amazing!'

I gaze at her for a moment. 'So do you!' But her skin is pale, a hint of a shadow under her eyes telling me she needs this break. 'Now, where's that brother of yours?' Just then, I see Stu appear through the same doors. Going to meet him, there's a lump in my throat. But then I haven't seen Stu for two years.

'Mother!' He sweeps me off my feet. 'It's so good to see you.'

'You, too.' I hug him again. 'I can't believe you're here!' Then I notice he isn't alone, there's a girl with him. With long chestnut hair and dark eyes, she's watching us, a bemused look on her face.

Turning, Stu takes her hand. 'Mum, I want you to meet Andie.'

My mouth drops open as I look at her, then back to him. 'You should have said you were bringing someone.'

'I wanted to surprise you.' He grins. 'Andie, this is my mum, Fay.'

'Hello.' I hold out a hand, then suddenly feeling overly formal, I hug her. 'It's so nice to meet you.' I glance at my son. 'I'd like to say he's told me loads about you. But he hasn't said a word!'

Her eyes are laughing as she smiles. 'Like Stu said, we wanted to surprise you.' Her Californian accent is cool as she smiles up at him.

It's like old times. *Plus*, with Andie among us. As we drive back to the house, I listen to the chatter; the banter between Julia and Stu; the laughter, soaking it up, these moments all the more precious for how rare they've become.

* * *

Back at the house, when they disappear off to their respective bedrooms to freshen up, I turn to Hugh. 'Isn't it wonderful, all of us being here?'

As his eyes meet mine, something passes between us. The memory, perhaps, of how we met, the child-rearing years, coming to this house that first time; all these things that make up the history of us.

He nods. 'I realised something last night, Fay. When I went to bed, I suddenly saw all of this is only possible because of you.'

I'm oddly touched. 'It's about both of us, Hugh. You paid for it all,' I remind him.

'I don't mean the money,' my husband says. 'And I should have said this before. It's about everything that goes into a house that makes it home.'

* * *

After Hugh opens a bottle of champagne, everyone cools off in the pool. It seems miraculous that even now, he hasn't mentioned the unmown lawn. Watching Stu and Andie together, and Julia taking a much-needed break, a feeling of peacefulness comes over me.

That afternoon, when Stevie arrives, she looks flustered before she starts.

'There's no rush,' I tell her. 'It's very informal – and we can eat any time – say, after six thirty. Would you like some help?'

She shakes her head. 'I just need to get started. Oh, I almost forgot.' She fumbles in her bag and passes me an envelope of tickets, for the festival.

* * *

It's an afternoon where I lose track of time in that rare way that happens sometimes when you are at peace with the world; the hours simultaneously passing too fast yet somehow lasting forever, the heat intensifying into the evening, the volume of the cicadas rising.

Taking a glass of wine, I join Hugh on the terrace. Sitting there, taking it all in, there is no need for words.

Already he looks more relaxed, his skin taking on some colour. 'Be careful. The sun is at its strongest,' I warn him.

Lost in his thoughts, it's as if he hasn't heard. 'I'd forgotten how lovely this time of year is here.' As he gazes across the lawn, he still doesn't notice how stubbly it is.

Before I can reply, we're joined by Stu and Andie. After padding off to the kitchen in his flip-flops, Stu comes back with a bottle and glasses.

I watch him pass one to Andie, the way she looks at him, suddenly realising. They're the real deal. They're in love.

'Mum? Dad? There's something we want to tell you.' He pauses. 'It's about me and Andie.'

Looking at them, my first thought is *He's proposed; they're getting married.*

He looks at us both. 'This is it, guys! You're about to become grandparents!' He pauses. 'Andie's pregnant.'

At that moment, Julia comes running in. 'You've told them, haven't you?' she says crossly; it's like she's a child again. 'I wanted to be here!'

'You knew?' I say to her, dazed with happiness, glancing at Hugh. 'Congratulations!' Going over, I hug Stu, then Andie. 'It's the best news. When is the baby due?'

Andie's eyes are shining. 'February.'

* * *

And just like that, our family shifts into a new chapter. One where just as I'm getting used to the idea of the four of us being five, we're about to become six. But I embrace it with all my heart. After all, family is what life is about.

Stevie cooks us a sublime meal that even Hugh comments on. After, she joins us for a glass of wine. Very soon, she and Julia are deep in conversation, much to my surprise as they are very different people, and I can't help hoping that Stevie's choice of a simple life might make Julia question her own fast-paced one.

As for me and Hugh… It's an evening where we put our differences aside; in which we celebrate being surrounded by family. Only when we are about to go to bed is there a slightly awkward moment when Julia comes into the kitchen.

'I meant to ask – is Dad sleeping in the spare room?' She looks at us, a little warily.

Hugh clears his throat. 'I have sleep apnoea. Terrible snoring, apparently.' He glances at me. 'Keeps your mother awake.'

'I guessed it was something like that. Get it sorted, Dad.' Rolling her eyes, Julia goes outside.

I turn to Hugh. 'Thank you,' I say quietly.

'Least I can do,' he says. 'How about a nightcap?'

He finds a bottle of cognac, and we take it outside, as I start to wonder at this more thoughtful side of my husband; that maybe it isn't over between us. I gaze up at the stars for a moment. Maybe it isn't beyond the realms of possibility that we still have a chance.

20

NED

It's the strangest juxtaposition, I find myself thinking, that in the driest, most barren of summers I've ever known, my life feels richer than it ever has, my emotions oscillating; one minute up, the next in free fall.

Love is something I've never truly pondered before, and I'm starting to believe I love Stevie. I'm also realising I didn't love Jessie. In the same way that Stevie and I seem to seamlessly fit each other, Jessie and I were like ice cream and tomato ketchup; we were a mismatch. Why we ended up staying together so long will forever remain an unexplained mystery.

Just as Stevie's house looks over her neighbours' rooftops, I discover that they, too, have an eye on what goes on in her life.

'I want a word with you, Ned.' Madame Picard accosts me on my way to Stevie's one morning. 'Do you have a minute?'

Slightly surprised, I stop walking. On the occasions I've met her before, both times with Stevie, the exchanges between us have been nothing but friendly. 'Is something wrong, Madame Picard?'

'*Non*. Nor do I want there to be,' she says cryptically. 'I want to talk to you about Stevie.'

'Oh?' I frown. 'Is she OK?' *Stupid question, Ned. Stevie would tell you if she weren't. Wouldn't she?*

'She is very OK,' Madame Picard says conspiratorially. 'That is the problem, *n'est-ce pas*? I do not want her heart to be broken.'

It's quite an ask to be charged with the safekeeping of someone's heart. But with Stevie, I'm up for the challenge. More than that, I have a vested interest in protecting her heart. 'I have no intention of doing any such thing,' I say seriously. 'Stevie's heart is as important to me as it is to you.'

'*Bon.*' She pats my arm. 'That is all.'

As she walks away, I realise she hasn't stopped to consider *my* heart. But then she hardly knows me. However, it gives me pause for thought. I mean, no one embarks on a love affair anticipating the end of it. But unless it results in a forever kind of love, at some point in time, it will be inevitable.

Deciding Stevie's more than able to make up her own mind, I knock on her door. When she opens it, her eyes are bright as she smiles at me. Taking one of my hands, she pulls me inside.

As she kisses me, all these feelings surge through me, about how beautiful she is; how brave to come here alone. How kind and caring she is to everyone in her life.

While I watch her cook lunch, her hair glistens in the sunlight through the open window. I'm starting to think that the timing of our meeting, as well as the way we met – none of it was an accident.

Together, we take the food she cooks down to Madame Picard's house. A few minutes later, Monsieur Valois turns up, followed by the fully unleashed force of Madame Bernard, who glares at me.

'This table is not big enough for five,' she says, drawing herself up to her full height and waving her walking stick at me.

Unperturbed and far more endlessly tolerant than I could ever be, Madame Picard pats her arm. 'Sit down. That is nonsense, and you know it.'

I catch Stevie's eye. 'I hope there are herbs in this?' I say under my breath.

Nodding, her cheeks flush as she smiles at me.

I still have no idea what's actually in those herbs, but they certainly have the desired effect, smoothing Madame Bernard's natural abrasiveness, bringing a smile to Monsieur Valois's typically blank face. While Madame Picard is simply Madame Picard, almost always smiling, her eyes twinkling, which makes me wonder more than ever what goes into those herbs and how many times a day she takes them.

Before we leave, she surreptitiously passes Stevie another unlabelled jar of them, holding a finger to her lips. 'Not a word, *ma petite*,' she says mischievously.

After lunch is over, that afternoon, I take Stevie back to my parents' house. I want her to get to know our family now, while we are still four.

Nina greets her like an old friend, then waxes lyrically about the dinner Stevie cooked, while my father is gracious – and somewhat surprised.

'A very lovely girl,' he declares as he watches her go out of the room. 'Remarkable, in fact.' Looking perplexed, he scratches his head as if he can't work out what Stevie's doing with me. 'Astonishing.'

It's one of the rare days my mother has made it downstairs. In a wheelchair cushioned with a quilt, she's sitting in the shade of the garden when I take Stevie outside to meet her.

'Mama?' Leaning down, I kiss her cheek. 'This is Stevie. Stevie, this is my mother, Aimée.'

My mother reaches out one of her pale, delicate hands towards Stevie. 'It's lovely to meet you, *chérie*. Won't you sit?'

'It's lovely to meet you, too.' Stevie settles on the chair nearest to her. 'Your garden is very beautiful.'

'Thank you.' My mother glances at me. 'Can you get us drinks, Ned?'

Leaving them alone together, I go to the kitchen, coming back a few minutes later with three glasses of lemonade. Noticing how their exchange comes to an abrupt halt when they see me, I crouch down beside my mother, holding the glass for her while she sips through a straw.

'What were you two talking about?' Half joking, I glance at Stevie.

'None of your business,' my mother murmurs. 'I cannot believe you have not taken Stevie to any of the lakes,' she says. 'I used to take Ned to them when he was a toddler.' For a moment, she looks wistful. 'He was not like he is now. He was chubby. He used to get into all kinds of trouble.' She winks at me.

'I think that's enough,' I say quietly, worried she's tiring herself out.

'You know he's playing at the festival, don't you?' Stevie glances at my mother. 'It would be really lovely if you were able to come.'

When my mother is silent for a moment, I can imagine what she is thinking. That the festival is a week away and how much can change in a week; that when coming downstairs exhausts her, the thought of going out must feel like as daunting as climbing a mountain.

'Yes,' she says quietly, her eyes meeting mine as she reaches for one of my hands. 'I would really like that.'

* * *

That evening, sitting on Stevie's roof terrace, after much persuasion, I get it out of her.

'If you really want to know, what your mother said was that she wants you to pursue your music.' Stevie pauses. 'And she wants you to be happy.'

'It's so strange.' I gaze across the rooftops towards the red sun that's sinking behind the hills. 'Or rather, it's the strangest time. On the one hand, I'm happy. So happy – because of you. Because of us,' I say more expansively. 'And because, for the first time in ages, I'm where I feel I'm meant to be.' I reach for one of her hands. 'But it's also the worst time, because of Mama.'

But I can't find the words to explain to her that each day seems bizarrely vivid, that each second feels as though it has its own small part in a journey that's more far-reaching. 'The days feel full, if that makes sense. In a good way – with everything that matters to me.' I shake my head. 'It's like not even a minute of them is wasted.'

Stevie looks at me. 'Maybe it's your heart that's full, Ned.'

Speechless, I stare at her. She's absolutely right. It's how my heart feels. Full, with happiness, grief, love, gratitude and more; all these emotions that have lain dormant, that I've never truly recognised.

'Can I see you tomorrow?' I murmur. 'And the day after, and the day after?' Putting my arms around her, I draw her closer.

A smile plays on her lips. 'It's the festival next week, Ned. There's so much to do!'

'I know.' Leaning forward, I kiss her neck. 'But there's plenty of time.' I kiss her behind her ear, pretending to fight her as she pushes me away.

'Tomorrow, I am so busy.' For a moment, there's panic in her eyes.

'That's tomorrow. And don't worry. I'll help you.' Taking her hand, I lead her into her bedroom.

* * *

This time, it's me who's right. Even though Nicole is more stressed than I've seen her, with everyone pitching in together, plans for the festival are in hand. As I said to Stevie, there really is nothing to worry about. With all the hard work behind it, it should be the success story of the decade. *Should* being the operative word.

A couple of nights later, Stevie shakes me awake. 'I can smell smoke.'

'Someone's having a fire,' I say drowsily.

But she's already getting out of bed. 'It's August, Ned. Everywhere's so dry. And it smells funny.'

Seeing her pull on clothes, I get out of bed and do the same. Stifling a yawn, I follow her downstairs. 'It's probably nothing,' I try to reassure her. But when we open the door and go outside, it's clear there's a problem.

As we run down the road, the smoke thickens, the sound of burning reaching my ears. Then as we get closer, through the smoke, I see flames.

'The bar's on fire,' Stevie shouts above the noise. 'Oh my God, Ned. We have to do something.'

'I'll call the emergency services.' I get out my phone.

It's one of those times in life when you feel utterly helpless; when you can see what needs to be done but are powerless to do it. As Stevie and I stand there, all we can do is watch as the flames take hold.

'I need to tell Olivier and Nicole.' Her eyes are terrified as she looks at me. 'Can I borrow your phone?' But as she tries Nicole's number, their car is already pulling up.

They come over and stand with us as a fire engine arrives, followed by another. Even in minutes the fire rapidly intensifies. As the roof falls in, Nicole's hands go to her mouth. I watch her and Olivier put their arms around each other, as I try to imagine how it feels to see everything you've worked so hard to build go up in flames.

'This is terrible.' Stevie's voice is filled with disbelief. 'How could this have happened?'

Behind us, I notice the small crowd of villagers that has gathered, a motley assortment of young and old, in pyjamas and dressing gowns, all of them looking on in shock. As I take Stevie's hand in mine, I feel it shaking.

It's dawn by the time the *pompiers* are satisfied the fire has gone out, and hasn't spread. Sitting on the grass with Nicole and Olivier, Stevie's in shock.

'We are always so careful.' Olivier looks terrible. 'There is a checklist every night. Everything is switched off and checked twice. But I must have missed something.'

'You wouldn't have.' Nicole shakes her head. 'I know you.'

'Everyone makes mistakes.' Olivier looks helpless.

The sun is coming up as Stevie and I walk back to her place.

Suddenly it occurs to me. 'They're going to have to cancel the festival, aren't they?'

'Oh Ned.' Stevie sounds devastated. 'Do you think so?'

But the fire has reduced the bar to a shell. 'They can't cater, can they? There's no power or water – and everything was inside, wasn't it?'

Stevie's silent. Then as she turns to look at me, there's a look I haven't seen before in her eyes. 'We can still do it,' she says determinedly. 'Think about it, Ned. There must be somewhere we can get chairs – and glasses. And the wine hasn't been delivered yet.'

'But there's the food to think of, too.'

Stevie looks like she's miles away. Then she turns to me. 'All we need is a grill – and firewood. Nicole and I can cook on that. I can get vegetables from Zeke... But it won't be enough. We have to find a way to make it work,' she says stubbornly as her phone pings with a message.

> We have to cancel the festival, Stevie. Olivier is making signs to put up. If anyone asks, tell them we will refund the cost of the tickets.

Staring at me, Stevie holds out her hand. 'Can I borrow your phone?'

As she walks away, I don't hear the conversation that ensues. After ending the call, she looks slightly less anxious as she comes back. 'Zeke knows a couple of farmers who sell their meat at local markets. Hopefully, they'll help. He's calling them now to explain.'

Five minutes later, Zeke calls back. As she listens, Stevie's face lights up.

'They're selling us the meat at a heavily discounted price – in return for free tickets.' Her eyes are shining at me. 'Can you believe it?'

She calls Nicole. I don't hear all of the conversation that takes place. But somehow, Stevie persuades Nicole that the festival can go ahead. More than that, in true Stevie-style, she tells Nicole that after the fire, the village needs it more than ever before.

* * *

Yesterday's conversation with Stevie has left me with a new sense of purpose. Leaving her to flesh out plans, I'm still pondering it as

I drive back to my parents' house. I'm greeted at the door by Nina. 'Just the person I was hoping to see,' I tell her. 'Only I might need your help with something.' Looking at her more closely, I frown. 'Are you OK?'

But Nina isn't. Our mother has taken a turn for the worse. Overnight, it seems; the doctor has paid a visit.

'She was struggling to breathe.' Nina's face is pale. 'But he's given her some medication – and she's on oxygen.' She pauses. 'You know what's keeping her going, don't you?'

Apparently, my mother desperately wants to watch me play. 'She wants you to know how much she believes in you,' Nina says quietly. 'She feels they haven't supported you enough.'

'I'll go and talk to her.' More than anything I want her to be there, but when it's taking all her effort just to get through each day, I'm worried the festival will be too much. However, upstairs, crouched next to her bed, even I can't change her mind.

'It will be too much, Mama. It's so hot – and there will be hundreds of people there. I'll record it so you can watch it after.'

But she shakes her head. 'It's important to me. My dying wish, Ned. You can't deny me that.' Her voice is shaky, each word drawn out. But her trademark stubbornness is still there; her determination to do what she wants, one last time.

Blinking away tears, I take her hand. 'I wouldn't dare, Mama,' I say softly.

* * *

By the time I return to Stevie's that afternoon, incredibly it seems she has everything in hand.

'I may have found you a grill,' I tell her. 'And I'm not talking about a domestic one. One of Nina's friends caters for large events. Nina's asked if we can borrow one.'

'That's great. We need to go down to the river,' she says. 'The stage is being set up.' The light is back in her eyes.

In the village, in the shade of the delicate twisting branches of the plane trees, just in front of the river, the stage is indeed halfway to being set up. Meanwhile, in front of the bar, some of the villagers are hard at work clearing up after the fire. It's a moving example of how community works, as is the supply of wine and beer that keeps arriving to quench their thirsts.

Seeing us, Nicole comes over. 'It looks as though the fire was started deliberately,' she says.

Stevie stares at her. 'Who would do that?'

'Who do you think?' Nicole sounds mutinous. 'It is that vile Dutch boy. I would bet my life on it.'

'Oh my God.' Stevie's face is white as a sheet. 'She said this would happen.'

Nicole freezes. 'Who did?'

'Madame Bernard.' Stevie looks distraught. 'She said he would do something. I should have told you.'

'Don't worry.' Nicole pats her hand. 'She couldn't have known. But I do know. Ah. The police are here.' Leaving us, she marches towards them.

* * *

The following day, it transpires that the fire was started by petrol, most likely contained in a bottle plugged with a fuel-soaked rag, thrown through a window shattered by the large stone that was found inside.

'I will kill him,' Nicole says ferociously. 'I have told the police about Merlot, too. I do not understand how someone so young can be so evil.'

But as often happens in rural communities, the devastation

wreaked by the fire draws everyone closer. There is a sense of being in it together, of having one another's backs, a determination that the festival will go ahead, no matter what.

Stevie and I pay a visit to Zeke who, like everyone else, is adamant he wants to help. But after what I've heard from Stevie about him, I'm not surprised.

Stevie's told me about the allotments. But when she leads me through the hedge into the garden, I'm utterly astonished. I must have driven past a hundred times over the years, completely missing the whole secret world that exists in here.

After introducing us, Stevie tells Zeke about the fire being started deliberately.

He shakes his head. 'Makes you wonder what goes through some folks' heads. Do they have any idea who did it?'

'A teenaged boy. Last week, Nicole took away a dog he was mistreating. It could have been his idea of revenge.'

Zeke's silent for a moment. 'Sad, isn't it, that someone would think it's OK to do such a thing. But life must go on. Come on. I'll show you what we've got for you.'

In the allotments too, it seems that everyone has rallied round. Stevie and I gather up the many boxes of freshly picked vegetables and herbs that have been assembled and load them into the car.

* * *

By the time the day of the festival arrives, what started out as an event run by Olivier and Nicole has truly become a village affair. From early on, the green is milling with people who've come to help. Like everyone else there, I do what I can, pitching in to set up chairs on the grass and string lights from the trees, before helping Stevie set up a makeshift kitchen next to the grill, while for the first time I notice the strain is getting to her.

She puts down the pan she's holding. 'We don't have anything like enough utensils, Ned. Not to cook for all the people who are coming.' A look of despair washes over her face. 'I'm not sure this is going to work.'

But before I can reply, out of the corner of my eye, I notice an odd little procession making its way towards us. Fronted by Madame Picard, there are Monsieur Valois and Madame Bernard, followed by others that Stevie has cooked for.

Reaching us, Madame Picard places the box she's carrying on the trestle table, then takes out graters and peelers and lemon squeezers and other things I can't identify. 'We have all put together some things for you. Madame Bernard?' Turning to her friend, she snaps her fingers. '*Ici, s'il vous plaît.*'

Coming forward, Madame Bernard places an enormous pan on the table, followed by an equally enormous frying pan, before the others come forward with cooking utensils and a motley assortment of large serving bowls.

'Oh.' Overwhelmed, Stevie's hands go to her face. 'You are so kind.' She looks at them in turn. 'All of you. We can cook, now. I can't thank you enough for this.'

'*Mais non.* It is our turn to help you. I must not forget this.' Madame Picard passes Stevie a brown paper bag. As she winks at her, I'm guessing it contains more of her legendary herbs.

'Nicole? Over here,' Stevie calls out as Nicole walks past. 'Look at everything our friends have brought us.'

For once, even Nicole is lost for words as she stares at everything, a dazed look on her face. '*Merci beaucoup.*' Going to each one of them, she kisses them on the cheek – even Madame Bernard. Then as she looks at Stevie, I'd swear there are tears in her eyes.

I see little of Stevie after that. On a series of trestle tables, she and Nicole prepare the food, working non-stop until early evening, by which time the bar is set up and people start arriving, the accordion music in full swing.

A far better band follows, everyone's heartfelt relief reflected in their applause. All evening, I've kept an eye out for my father's car, but when there's no sign of it, I start to worry that it's too much for my mother, and they're not coming.

Telling myself that from her point of view, it's probably for the best, I go to find Axl and the guys. But as the second band starts to play, out of the corner of my eye I notice a car slowly crossing the bridge. My father's car.

With our performance about to start, I run across the grass towards my mother. Accompanied by my father and Nina, I take in how pale she looks; the oxygen bottle attached to the wheelchair, just in case.

'Hey, Mama.' Leaning down, I kiss her cheek. 'Thank you for coming. All of you.' I look at my father and Nina.

'You'd better be worth it.' Trying to hide how worried she is, Nina winks at me.

After directing them to a place away from the crowd, I hurry back to find Axl. 'Slight change of plan.' I tell him what I'm thinking. 'OK with you?'

Taking a deep breath, I know how important this is; how my fear of failure is suddenly no longer important. How it's my last chance – my only chance – to show my mother how important music is to me; how much it means that she's come here. Moreover, it's my one and only chance to share my music with her.

The sun glows orange behind the trees as, minutes later, we walk out on the stage. As Axl strikes up a chord and our band starts to play, the vibe changes completely. It's a celebration in every sense of the word, with people on their feet, dancing on the grass with wild abandon, the fire temporarily forgotten by all of us.

When the penultimate track ends, I glance at Axl before stepping forward. 'Thank you, all of you, for coming tonight.' I wait, silent, as applause breaks out. 'This next track is close to my heart. It's also for someone very special. My mother.' Turning in her direction, I blow her a kiss.

It's the most memorable evening of my entire life, to play the song I wrote for my mother. For the most part, I keep my emotions in check, but as I finish, tears are rolling down my cheeks. The applause is incredible, but the only person I'm gazing at is the woman who brought me into this world. The woman who means everything to me. Then I glance towards the kitchen, realising how lucky I am, to now have two incredible women in my life. Standing there, Stevie blows me a kiss.

21

ZEKE

A music festival isn't exactly my cup of tea these days. But given what's happened, I go along.

The sun is already low by the time I get there. Catching the last track the band is playing, I stop and listen. It's an emotional track that brings a lump to my throat – a measure of how good they are, I can't help thinking. When it finishes, I search for Stevie, finding her hard at work behind the biggest grill I've ever seen, on which are trays of meat and vegetables which she cooks and serves in a flatbread.

'I've absolutely no idea how you do that.' I watch, awestruck.

'Here.' She passes one to me. 'There's salsa on the side, and a few other bits. Help yourself.' She turns to the woman she's working with. 'Nicole, this is Zeke. Lots of the vegetables we're using are from his garden.'

'My God, Zeke!' Nicole exclaims. 'So often I have said to Stevie she is an angel.' She hurriedly turns more vegetables. 'But we have two angels in this village. We wouldn't have been able to do this without you.'

'I don't know about being an angel, but happy to be of service.'

I nod towards her. 'And those veg would be nothing without the pair of you.'

Taking my food, I wander on; I notice Fay a short distance away. Standing there, I study her for a moment. There's something different about her. She's radiating a kind of contentedness, is what I think it is.

'Evening, Fay.'

She starts. 'Zeke! I wasn't expecting to see you here.'

'I wasn't expecting to be here,' I say ruefully. 'But I heard about that fire. It's kind of important, I think, to show support.'

She smiles. 'I couldn't agree more. This is my daughter, Julia. Julia, this is Zeke. He's taught me everything I know about gardening.'

The young woman beside her smiles at me. 'Hi! I still can't believe Mum has an allotment.'

'She's a model student – and real good at it. You have her eyes,' I say politely. 'It's very nice to meet you.'

As she wanders away, I turn to Fay. 'You look happy.'

'I am,' she says simply. Then as she glances past me, her face changes. 'I'm so sorry, Zeke. There's someone I want to say hello to. Would you excuse me? I won't be long.'

'Of course.' I watch her walk across the grass to where a family are standing around a woman who's in a wheelchair. Leaning down, Fay says something to the woman. Then as the woman briefly takes her hand, it's like there's a silent exchange between them.

A few minutes later, when she comes back, the jigsaw pieces of my mind are suddenly falling into place. 'Is that the mother of the young lad Stevie's going out with?' I remember his name. 'Young Ned?'

Fay nods. 'Her name's Aimée. I met her in the church a while back.' She looks upset. 'She's very sick now. I'm guessing she came to hear him play.'

'That was him with the band just now? They were good.' As we watch them, the family are wheeling her slowly towards a car.

'They really were.' Fay pauses. 'I haven't stopped thinking about her. You see, I can imagine too easily how she feels. Her illness has happened so fast. When we spoke last, she told me she wasn't ready. I think she feels cheated – of time with her family.'

I feel for her. Aimée's clearly younger than I am – but as I know, age is irrelevant to these things. 'Doesn't seem right, does it?' It's one thing to have made peace with the fact that time is running out, as I have. But I can understand how for Aimée, it's the opposite.

'I don't suppose I'll ever see her again.' There are tears in Fay's eyes. She dabs at them. 'I'm sorry. It's so upsetting seeing someone go through something like that. I suppose it makes me so grateful, for so many things.'

'Best way to be,' I say quietly.

I stay long enough to watch the last of the daylight fade to dusk; to affirm the belief I've always had, that in spite of all the troubles in the world, there's an abundance of genuinely good people. I catch sight of Stevie and Ned together, his arms around her. Then Fay with a man I assume to be her husband.

'Zeke? What are you doing here?' Rémy's voice comes from behind me, startling me.

'Same as you, I'm guessing.' I smile at her, taking in her silver top and calf-length skirt. 'Scrub up pretty well, don't you?'

'That is quite nice for such a rude man.' She shakes her head at me.

'I'm not rude. And you know I'm only pulling your leg. That means I don't mean it,' I explain, seeing the look of confusion on Rémy's face. 'You're a one-off. The world needs more like you.'

'Just for once, I'm not going to argue with you.' She holds her arm towards me. 'Come on, old man. I'll give you a lift home.'

I accept gracefully. I'm old enough to know when I'm beat. Leaving the festival, the lanes are quiet as Rémy drives, myriad stars appearing in the darkness. When we reach my house, Rémy offers to see me in.

I wave her offer away. 'You think I'm useless, don't you?'

'You are too bloody stubborn,' she says crossly. Ignoring me, she gets out of the car. She comes around and opens the passenger door. 'How long have I known you, Zeke?'

'Too long, if you ask me.' I wince as I get out.

'I make it twenty years,' she says, taking my arm. 'I think twenty years of friendship gives me the right to be outspoken.'

'So now we're friends, are we?' I try to joke.

Looking at me, she's silent for a moment. 'Twenty years means I know when something's wrong,' she says quietly.

I pause for a moment. 'If you've not got anything better to do, I'll make you a cup of tea.'

In the kitchen, Rémy makes me sit down while she puts the kettle on and finds a mug. 'Where are your teabags? And how come, after twenty years, I've never been in here before?'

'Because you weren't invited,' I say calmly. 'There's a jar right in front of you that says "tea" on it.' I watch her. 'You'll find another mug in the cupboard.'

'I'm having brandy.' She glances around the kitchen. 'Assuming you have some?'

Eventually, she passes me a mug of tea, then pours herself a glass of brandy and takes a large swig of it. 'I have a theory about you, Zeke.'

I look at her, surprised that I even figure in her thoughts. 'And what's that?'

'Well...' Swirling the contents of her glass, she studies it. 'I don't think you were always alone. I think something happened. Something that left you with a choice.' She shrugs. 'After, you chose to look at the world a certain way. And that's what you've done ever since.'

I nod slowly. 'Very perceptive. Just one thing. What you've just described happens to most of us. I mean, we all choose the way we see the world.'

'This is different.' She sips her drink again. 'I am right, aren't I?'

I sit there for some time. There are hundreds of things I could say right now. But they boil down to one word. 'Yes.'

She sighs. 'To do with your family?'

Unaccustomed tears fill my eyes as I nod my head.

'I am so sorry, Zeke.' There's genuine warmth in her words.

I find my voice. 'It was a long time ago.'

'Does not mean it is not painful,' she says gently.

I sigh. For some reason, words are in short supply tonight. 'No.'

'And this is why...' She stops herself. 'No.' Then she looks at me. 'You are ill, are you not, Zeke? I have thought this for some time. But you are not fighting it.' She takes a deep breath, before summing it up exactly, in just a few simple words. 'It is because you have lost your family.' She pauses. 'You are ready.'

22

STEVIE

My memories of the festival are reduced to snapshots. The mountain of food we prepared that day, then cooked that evening; the sun glistening through the trees. Ned's mother, staying long enough to hear him play that beautiful song for her; the image of her face as she watched him. Fay surrounded by her family. Madame Picard and Madame Bernard, who for once kept her strong opinions to herself; even Zeke making it here.

After clearing up, it's late, just a few people milling around as Ned and I find Nicole and Olivier, before the four of us slump on the grass with a bottle of wine.

Nicole opens it and pours four glasses. 'Thank you,' she says, raising hers. 'Thank you, Olivier; thank you, Stevie; thank you, Ned. It has been the most enormous, brilliant, resounding, heart-warming success. But none of this would have happened without you.'

'It would not have happened without the villagers, either.' Olivier raises his glass.

'*Santé*.' Ned chinks his against mine.

'And Ned. That song...' Nicole's voice shakes. 'My tears were frying on the grill. It was so very beautiful.' She pauses, frowning. 'I have to ask you, Stevie, about these herbs I notice you cook with.' She looks at Stevie suspiciously. 'Can you tell me what is in them?'

'Oh! They come from a local supplier,' I say hesitantly, feeling my cheeks grow hot. But as I'm speaking, I watch Ned's face cloud over. 'Are you OK?' I ask anxiously.

He frowns. 'I'm not sure. I have this strange feeling.' He drains his glass. Then as he gets up, a look of uncertainty crosses his face. 'Sorry to run off like this. But I should go.'

'It's OK.' I walk with him to his car. 'You're worried, aren't you?'

'It's something Nina said.' There's a restlessness about him. 'About Mama hanging on to hear me play.' He pauses, looking at me. 'I have this feeling, Stevie.' His voice wavers. 'I have to be there – just in case.'

He kisses me briefly, then I stand there as he gets into his car and drives away, before going back to the others. Nicole passes me another glass of wine.

'Ned is worried?'

I nod. 'His mother is very sick.' The elation I felt earlier has evaporated. Instead, like Ned, a sense of premonition hangs over me.

'Maybe you should go with him,' Nicole suggests.

I shake my head. 'I think he probably wants to be alone with his mother and family.'

* * *

Back at home, I realise how tired I am. Picking up my phone, I check for any messages from Ned. Finding none, I send a brief one.

> Thank you… You were amazing today. Sorry you had to leave. I'm thinking of you. S xx

It's crushingly inadequate, given what's happening to his mother. But at least he knows he's on my mind; that I care. I think back to what Aimée said to me, while she and I were briefly alone, that I've yet to tell Ned. How she regretted not being supportive enough to Ned; how she worries that people take advantage of his kindness. That what she wants most is for him to be happy.

When the time is right, I'll tell him. Still thinking of Ned, as I get into bed, the last few days catch up with me and as my head hits the pillow, my eyes close.

It's light when I open them again. Lying in bed, last night comes back to me. The wonderful music and people, before the memory of the way Ned suddenly left brings me up short. I get out of bed, open the curtains and push the shutters back.

Standing there looking across the village, I realise it's much earlier than I thought. The trees are silhouetted against the sky, the river timelessly flowing. Thinking of Ned, then of his mother, I watch the most glorious sunrise.

23

NED

The morning after the festival, it's early when I go downstairs. The kitchen is quiet, my father clearly not having made it out of bed yet. After switching on the kettle, I open the back door and step outside.

Standing there, the festival seems a distant memory as I watch the sun rising behind the trees, the dawn chorus coming at me from every direction, while the dogs sniff around the flower beds for any signs of nocturnal visitors and do dog-like things like cock their legs on the extravagantly planted flowerpots.

Back inside, as I make a cup of coffee, my father's voice comes from behind me.

'Ned.' Something in his voice makes me stiffen. Then turning, I see the look in his eyes.

The blood drains from my face, as I realise that it's the moment I've known would come. But as shock hits me, it's as though I've frozen inside; a part of me wanting to cry out 'I'm not ready.'

'When?' I say numbly.

'An hour ago.' He looks much older as he sits at the kitchen table, before telling me he sat up all night with my mother. 'I held her hand. And I talked to her.' Overcome with emotion, he rests his head in his hands just as Nina comes in.

As she looks at us, her expression changes to one of shock, then disbelief, as her hands go to her mouth. 'No...'

Tears pour down her face. Tears that I wish I, too, could cry; that yesterday, holding my mother's hand, came easily.

Going over to our father, Nina puts her arms around him. 'You should have called us, Dad,' she says tearfully.

'I thought about it.' He shakes his head. 'But it was how she wanted it. To slip away quietly.' His voice trembles. 'I closed my eyes for five minutes.' His voice is hoarse with emotion. 'Then when I opened them again, she'd gone.'

Sitting down, I can't move. Instead, a surreal feeling takes over me. Even though I've known this moment would come, nothing could have prepared me for how it feels. It's as though the fabric of time has been ripped apart, opening a portal into somewhere alien, while life as I know it has gone. Forever.

24

FAY

The morning after the festival, I awake unusually early, lying in bed for a moment. I think of my family all under this roof, how we have grown to encompass Andie; how we will soon be welcoming the baby she and Stu are having.

A feeling of warmth comes over me. *I'm so lucky*, I suddenly realise. To have them all, to be sharing this time in the house we all love; to be here in the beautiful heart of rural France.

But none of it is taken for granted; I know how fragile life is. Thinking of Zeke, then Aimée, makes it all the more precious.

I get up and go downstairs to the kitchen. After making a cup of coffee, I take it outside and watch the sunrise. It was miraculous that Aimée made it to the festival last night, but from the way she spoke, from the look in her eyes, I could tell she knew she didn't have long.

Suddenly restless, I walk across the garden. The grass is prickly underfoot, slightly damp with dew as the strangest feeling grips me. This life is intensely precious, as are the people around us – something we too easily lose sight of. I've let too much of mine simply pass me by, when I'm getting older; when I should be making each joyous, irreplaceable minute of it count for something.

25

ZEKE

The morning after the festival, it's still dark when I awake. Getting out of bed, pain comes from somewhere deep inside me. Holding myself, I grit my teeth and wait for it to subside, before standing up and walking over to the window. Pushing the shutters open, I listen to the sweet sound as the dawn chorus rings through the darkness.

I think of Stevie's young man, Ned, about to lose his mother. How it isn't going to be long before it's my turn; how our lives in the grand scheme of things are no more than a drop in the ocean.

A sense of urgency takes over me as I hobble to the chair and start to pull my clothes on. It makes it all the more important to do things, while I still can.

26

NED

The morning passes in a blur. Mama's doctor arrives, then the undertaker; then the priest – which strikes me as vaguely ridiculous, when my mother wasn't religious; and who has nothing to say that's remotely of comfort to me. As my father says, at times like this, there are traditions to uphold. Traditions I think my mother might quite possibly have broken away from, had she been given a chance to put her own stamp on things. But there wasn't time – or maybe she hadn't wanted to shock my father. Either way, I'll never know.

It isn't so much the shock, I reason as I go outside. We've known for some time this was coming. It's more the emptiness my mother's passing has left; the finality for those of us who are left behind. The coming to terms with something you're powerless to change.

Taking out my mobile, I sit on the grass and call Stevie.

She answers straight away. 'Ned? Are you OK?'

'Mama passed.' The words stick in my throat. 'I wanted you to know.'

'Oh Ned... I'm so sorry.' There's sadness in her voice. 'When?'

'Early this morning. Dad was with her.'

'Can I do anything?' She pauses. 'Would you like me to come over?'

'Can I call you later? I'm not sure what's going on here.' I frown. But the fact is, after weeks of caring for my mother, it's like everything's ground to a halt.

'I'm here if you need me,' Stevie says gently.

* * *

She comes over that evening. Putting her arms around me, she just holds me as I feel the wetness of her tears on my neck.

Letting go of her, I gently wipe her face.

'I've been so worried about you,' she says, her eyes searching mine. 'It's like I can feel you, Ned. In here.' She places a hand over her heart.

She also brings one of her home-made pies. 'I don't suppose any of you feel like eating, but just in case.'

Meanwhile, it's as though time has gone on hold. Of course, there are formalities to see to, a funeral to plan in the next few days. In France, they generally happen within a week which, as I soon find out, isn't long.

I watch my father hold his grief inside, graciously making calls to people my mother was close to; marvelling at his poise, wondering how he's able to do this, until I understand. This is his final act of love for her.

Nina cries constantly – which is probably healthier. As for my own grief, I can only describe it as a knot I can feel slowly tightening deep inside me.

As plans for the funeral come together, to my surprise, my father asks me to play the song I wrote for my mother. My first reaction is to say no; I'm not sure I'll be able to hold it together. But I agree to. After all, it came from a place of love for her.

In between, we field the calls and visits from the villagers between the three of us. I discover that casseroles are less about food and more a display of people's sympathy, while the house begins to resemble a florist's shop.

Through it all, Stevie is my constant. There when I need her, undemanding of me; shoring me up through the worst days of my life, while all I want is for it to stop. The sympathy calls, the casseroles; the forced conversations about my mother. This grinding numbness. *How do I make it go away?*

* * *

The day before the funeral, Nina and I take some of the flowers we've been sent to the church, arranging them at the front where my mother's coffin will be placed.

Then after, I go to see Stevie. 'We've just been to the church.'

'Is everything ready?' She takes my hands, her eyes searching mine. 'Are you OK?'

'I think so.' But the truth is, I've no way of knowing if I am or if something weird is happening to me. I'm functioning, going about the day-to-day, but for the most part, my emotions are switched off, as though I'm dead inside.

She looks worried. 'Are you still going to play tomorrow?'

I nod. Then I shrug. 'I have to. If I don't, I'll always regret it.'

* * *

The day of my mother's funeral will be forever recorded in my mind as one of the strangest, most detached days I will ever experience.

I'm grateful for the calmness of Stevie's presence, the feel of her hand holding mine, as somehow, our family does our best for my mother. Standing tall in his dark suit and a rather crumpled shirt, my father gives the most outstanding and dignified eulogy. Nina reads one of our mother's favourite poems, and then it's my turn. Playing the piece of music I wrote for her, I have a peculiar sense that she's watching me, until I consider that wherever she's gone, maybe she is.

There are the traditional prayers that would have made her raise an eyebrow – I'm better informed than my father about how she really felt about organised religion. There are one or two hymns painstakingly chosen by my father, time seeming to pass unbearably slowly, until incongruously, just like that, it's over.

Back at home, Stevie helps Nicole and Olivier with the catering. Somewhat lost without her, I mingle with the people filling our house, most of them soberly dressed in black that's inappropriate somehow, when my mother was one of the most colourful people I'd ever known. Many of them I haven't seen in years, but as I'm finding out, people seem drawn to mark death in a way they forget to acknowledge life, when basically, as far as the deceased is concerned, it's too late.

Throughout, I'm struck by one thought, and that's how most of us take life for granted. But we shouldn't, I'm realising. Life is terrifyingly fragile; subject to change in the blink of an eye.

As their well-wishes go over my head, I smile politely, fighting down a yearning to escape, instead making my way over to a window. Staring outside, it's yet another glorious summer day and as I gaze across the garden, for a moment I imagine my mother out there, whistling to the dogs or pausing to pick a bunch of flowers.

Sighing, I turn my attention back to the room, as my eyes are drawn to a familiar figure. Blinking, I rub my eyes.

It's Jessie.

My first thought is, *What the fuck's she doing here?*

I think about slinking away, anywhere away from here, as a memory of my mother's voice comes to me. *Life goes on, Ned. However you're feeling now, remember: your life will go on...*

Not like this, I silently shout at the universe, or God, or whoever's listening. A reminder of the life I was royally fucking up, Jessie doesn't belong here. But it's too late. Looking up, Jessie's eyes meet mine.

'I'm sorry about your mother, Ned.'

I stand there stiffly as she kisses me on the cheek; remembering how before I left, Jessie's social life was more important to her than I was. 'I didn't see you at the church. Actually, I'm not really sure what you're doing here.'

'It was the least I could do.' She pauses. 'Is there somewhere we can go to talk?'

We go outside and walk across the garden towards the lake.

'How are you bearing up?' she asks quietly.

'OK.' I shrug. 'We've been busy – planning today. I think it's still sinking in.' I shake my head, trying to explain. 'It's like she's still here – like she's gone for a walk with the dogs and any minute now, she's going to come back in, and give me one of her lectures about doing something worthwhile with my life. The other day...' I break off, realising how ridiculous it sounds.

'What?' she says gently.

I mean, this is me. Ned who doesn't talk. And what's odder still, is that this is Jessie. 'It's nothing, really. I went to the supermarket the day before yesterday. There was this woman with fair hair the same shade as my mother's. She was even wearing similar clothes. For a moment, I considered that there'd been the most terrible mistake. That she was here – and we were doing the shopping together.' My voice wavers. 'Of course it wasn't her. Just someone who looked like her – a little bit. Up close, she was nothing like her.'

Jessie frowns at me. 'You're sure you're all right, Ned?'

As I stare at her, something clicks into place. I'd always known we were different people, but this confirms just how different. Jessie doesn't get how I think, or any of the things that matter to me. And though she may not mean it, she has this way of making me feel judged, belittled. 'It's nice of you to come today, but—'

She interrupts. 'It wasn't entirely unselfish,' she admits. 'I came because I miss you, Ned.'

As she places a beautifully manicured hand on my arm, out of the corner of my eye I see Stevie coming towards us. Glancing at Jessie's hand, she freezes momentarily. Then before I can say anything, she turns and hurries back towards the house. 'Excuse me,' I say to Jessie.

I run after Stevie. 'Hey... Wait,' I call out.

She slows down and stops. Turning, her arms are folded defensively. 'I just came to see how you are.' She pauses. 'Then I saw... Never mind.'

'That's Jessie. She's my ex,' I explain. 'You have to believe I had no idea she was coming today. And you didn't see anything,' I say urgently. 'You couldn't have. There wasn't anything to see. Jessie and I are done. We were done months ago – I haven't spoken to her since. More than that, I don't think I ever loved her. Not really.' I pause, unable to bear the hurt in Stevie's eyes. 'You see, there's a reason I know this.' Taking her hands, however risky it seems to put my heart on the line, I have to tell her; I can't risk losing her. 'It's because I love someone else.' I gaze into her eyes. 'You, in fact.'

It's the first time I've said it to her. There, in the middle of the lawn, in front of all our soberly dressed guests, I don't care how inappropriate it might seem. I know for a fact my mother would approve. After all, life is for living. Putting my arms around Stevie, I kiss her.

Gazing back at me, Stevie's eyes are bright with unshed tears. 'I love you too,' she whispers.

It's the most surreally beautiful, magical moment, as I watch a smile spread across her face as she looks at me.

But as she looks around, it vanishes. 'All these people, Ned. They're watching us.'

'Let them watch,' I say quietly. 'I don't care what any of them think. I love you.' I lean my forehead against hers, as out of the corner of my eye, I see Jessie walk past. Then she's gone.

* * *

So it is that the grimmest day that's deeply entrenched in the most heartfelt sadness becomes memorable for another, rather lovely, life-affirming reason which, given the kind of person my mother was, is somehow fitting.

After the last of our guests drift away, Stevie helps Nicole and Olivier clear up. At the back of the house, I join my father and Nina on the terrace. Pouring himself a glass of red, my father turns to us both.

'I'm proud of you two.' Clearing his throat, he looks emotional as he sits down. But it's been an emotional day. 'We did your mother proud.'

He raises a glass, then after taking a sip, puts it down. Then he sighs. 'I'm not sure what we do from here.'

It's the first time I've seen him look so lost. I watch Nina get up and go to sit on one side of him, before I join him on the other. She takes one of his hands.

'We deal with one day at a time, Dad. We'll be OK.' She pauses, glancing at me. 'We have one another.'

In an unfamiliar gesture, I take his other hand. Nina's right. Moments like this are what family's about.

Nina frowns. 'What was Jessie doing here?'

I think about being magnanimous; about generous-heartedly saying that she came to pay her respects. 'I think she'd planned to catch me out, at my most vulnerable.' Which just about sums it up. If she'd really cared, she would have been in touch before.

That evening, it's as though Stevie's always been one of us. She's quietly caring towards my father, while she and Nina get on like a house on fire. She also tolerates our rapidly and weirdly fluctuating emotions. Put simply, she allows us just to be.

Aware none of us have really eaten, without asking, she cooks the most amazing French omelette and garlic bread, which my father hungrily devours.

'I wish I could cook like that,' Nina says glumly.

I ruffle her hair. 'What's to stop you learning? Stevie could teach you.'

She slumps onto the sofa next to me. 'Maybe I'll ask her.' She sighs. 'Don't get me wrong, but I'm so fucking glad today is over.' She looks at my empty glass. 'Can I get you a drink?'

'Definitely.' I have a thought. 'There's an expensive bottle of brandy somewhere.'

I get up and find it in one of the cupboards, while Nina fetches four glasses. She takes the bottle and pours some, then hands one to Stevie and another to our father.

'We should drink a toast to Mama.' None of us react as the tidal wave of her emotions rips through her again. After wiping her eyes, she raises her glass, trying to smile. 'And to all of us.'

'I should leave,' Stevie says, somewhat reluctantly, much later on.

I don't want to let her go. 'Are you sure? You could always stay.'

She sighs. 'I keep thinking you've all had quite a day.' She pauses. 'You should be with your dad and Nina. See you tomorrow?'

'Try stopping me.' Pulling her towards me, I kiss her.

* * *

'It's a strange coincidence that you met on a flight,' Nina says the next morning.

'That's if you believe in such things as coincidence,' I say more wisely than I feel. But as I sip my coffee, I'm frowning. It was odd how out of 140 seats on that plane, we ended up sitting next to each other. What's stranger still is how easy it's always been between us.

* * *

After the funeral, our family-minus-one – as I now think of us – drifts through surreal days that lack substance. Our lives disrupted, I picture grief as a drawn-out period of slowly patching them back together. A time of healing, but one after which scars fade, but remain under the surface; leave us changed.

I have an image of our father in years to come – old, frail, alone, dependent – on us. It feels incredible I haven't thought of it before. Of course, he might equally fall in love and find happiness with someone else. But right now, that's hard to imagine.

Nina's roller coaster of emotions has yet to let up. 'You'll probably laugh at me.' Her voice wavers. 'But I have this fear, Ned. Of being alone.'

Taken aback, I hug her. In an odd sequence of events that mimics what happened to Stevie, Henri broke up with Nina just before our mother died. No great surprise – they'd been drifting apart for a long time. Plus, it had always rankled that Henri lavished more love on his vintage cars than on my sister. 'Henri was a cretin – you're better off without him. There'll be someone for you. You just haven't met him yet.' Nina's smart, sassy and beautiful – it's always astonished me that yet another inadequate man has dumped her; that she's been single for so much of her life. Not that there's anything wrong with being single. It's just that I've always imagined her with a handsome, energetic husband and several equally vibrant kids.

I try to sound reassuring. 'In my limited experience, things never work out the way we think they will.'

'Oh God. Is that supposed to be a good thing?' Wiping her eyes, she sounds more like herself again.

I'm thinking of how I first met Stevie. 'I like to think it is.'

But after our conversation, I find myself watching our father more closely, taking in how lost he seems. If you didn't know him as well as we do, no one would be able to tell. On the surface, he isn't much different. He still attends business meetings and lunches, gets invited around to friends for dinner now and then. But when I catch him unawares, there's an emptiness that was never there before, as though a light has gone out.

Eventually, I check out how he feels about me staying here. 'Dad? Is it OK if I hang around here for a bit?'

He looks at me vaguely. 'Stay as long you like, Ned.'

It's so worryingly out of character, I find myself yearning for one of those awkward 'what-are-you-doing-with-your-life?' conversations. Anything for some injection of normality into my existence – until I remind myself. The old version of normal has gone forever; that out of necessity rather than choice, we're laying the most basic of foundations of something new.

27

ZEKE

After the conversation I had with Rémy, I'm grateful that she knows me well enough not to mention it again. Instead, she reverts to being her usual outspoken, slightly abrasive self, as I find out when she comes stomping over a few mornings later.

'That woman Fay.' She looks irritated.

'What about her?' I say good-naturedly.

'You have seen the mess her garden is?' Rémy demands. 'Tomatoes falling off and rotting, lettuces going to seed... And that is just the start.'

'Calm down,' I say to her. 'I happen to know she's busy – her family are staying. And she's learning. The same way you did,' I point out. 'Took you a while, if I remember rightly.'

'It is no excuse.' Rémy's eyes flash.

But there's something else I want to talk to her about. 'Rémy? Have you ever run a business?'

She frowns at me. 'No. And I have no intention of it. I am too old to learn something new.'

'You learned about gardening,' I remind her again.

'That is different.' She stands there. 'Oh, and your cat has been pissing in my vegetable beds.'

'Not much I can do about that,' I chuckle, glad the cat is still around as Rémy turns and marches away.

By chance, a short while later, Fay turns up for the first time in days.

'I can't believe it's a couple of weeks since I was last here.' She looks slightly worried. 'But I haven't stopped – what with my family being here. Then the funeral...'

I freeze. 'What funeral was that?'

'Aimée's. The mother of Stevie's boyfriend, Ned.' She looks surprised. 'I assumed you would know.'

The news doesn't surprise me; it's more that on this occasion, the village grapevine has failed me. 'I didn't know,' I say quietly. 'I'm very sorry.' Then I realise. 'Maybe that's why I haven't seen Stevie, either.' I pause. 'So are your family still here?'

'My son and his girlfriend are. Julia had to leave. She has this high-powered job,' Fay explains.

I raise my eyebrows. 'Well, nice that you had some time all of you together.'

'It really was.' Her face softens.

I'm curious. 'And Hugh?' She hasn't mentioned him.

Fay sighs. 'To be honest, I'm not sure what's going on with Hugh. He seems different in some ways – and of course, in others, he's exactly the same.' She frowns. 'I think he's trying to understand. And I think he may be staying on a while.'

'That's good, isn't it?'

'I think so.' But she doesn't sound convinced.

'Give it time,' I advise. 'Meanwhile, Rémy's just been over to have a moan about those tomatoes of yours.'

Fay looks shocked. 'Oh dear. I'd hate to think I've upset her.'

'Storm in a teacup,' I tell her. It takes more than a few tomatoes to seriously upset Rémy. 'Let's just say, it's a good thing you're here.'

I watch her hurry over to her allotment, standing there as she peruses it all before getting to work. But then I leave them all to it. There are more pressing matters I need to attend to back at the house.

Making my way home, I'm grateful to be out of the relentless heat as I open the front door and step inside.

Closing it behind me, I sigh. Lately, there's this sense that time is speeding up. I can imagine Ned's mother felt much the same.

At the same time, I have a need to get my affairs in order. Going to my sitting room, I survey the boxes I've packed, mostly of books and pictures, china and glass, all ready to go to the local charity shop. Most of what I possess is of little interest to anyone else. My parents came to France with nothing; I have no family heirlooms to pass down. Even if I had, there is no one to leave them to.

What preoccupies me most is the future of the house and all the allotments, and that afternoon, I have a meeting with the mayor of our village. His title makes me smile when he arrives in faded jeans and walking boots. But village mayors are working people, and ours just happens to be a sheep farmer.

I have a tentative plan in mind, another piece in the complicated jigsaw puzzle my life's become, but given French law, it's one I need his approval for. Over coffee and red wine, after he reads my paperwork, I feel a weight lift when he agrees to sign.

'*Bonne chance.*' As he leaves, he shakes my hand. 'And do not worry, Zeke. I will look after things.'

'Thank you, my friend.' As he walks out to his car, just before I close the door, the cat comes running in. Standing at my feet, it miaows at me. 'Thought you'd come back. There's a tin of sardines for you.'

After wolfing them down, the cat follows me like a shadow, yowling agitatedly now and then, as if it's trying to tell me something. Or maybe, with that sixth sense animals have, it's the only way the cat has of telling me it knows what's going on.

That evening, a driver from the charity shop comes to pick up the boxes. I feel another weight lift as he carries them out to his van. It feels like the right time for life to grow lighter.

'A forest fire's broken out the other side of town,' he tells me.

I shake my head. But forest fires are not uncommon these days. 'It's only going to get worse,' I say. 'The climate's changing.' It's a controversial subject to some folks. But whatever you attribute the reasons to, there's no denying the facts.

After he's gone, I stand in my kitchen. With most of my material possessions gone, it's as though I've stripped it back to the house it was when Marie and I moved in. Most of the cupboards are empty, everything extraneous now having gone to the charity shop. Except for the photos on the wall, that is.

Going over, I trace the two faces with one of my fingers. My beloved Marie and our much-loved little Dana. Sighing, I think back to the party where Marie and I met; what a coincidence it is that the house now belongs to Fay – that's if you believe in coincidence.

Staring at the photo, it's hard to believe forty years have passed since I last saw them both. And it isn't like me to dwell on the past. But for some reason, memories of that fateful day come flooding back and going over to the table, I sit down.

Resting my head in my hands, emotion surges inside me. If only I could turn the clock back. If I could have done things differently... You see, it's all my fault that they're not here. And for forty years, I've had to live with that.

There's nothing as sad as hindsight. But here's the thing. Living without them is the prison sentence I've deserved, I figure. But I've done my time. Now, I'm ready to go where they've gone.

* * *

The following morning in the allotment, Rémy's sitting on my chair waiting for me. 'You are late.' She taps her watch impatiently. 'I want to ask you something.'

I've no idea what she's on about. 'You can ask whatever you like. But it depends on what it is as to whether you get an answer or not.'

She looks at me impatiently. 'What is going to happen to all of this?' She waves her arms towards the gardens.

'Ah.' I know Rémy's direct, but this time, she's surpassed herself. Though in the circumstances, it's a fair enough question. 'I suppose when it comes to it, not that much.'

She frowns. 'What is that supposed to mean? I have a problem, Zeke. I have to think about planting for next year. I do not want to break my back for nothing.'

It's her roundabout way of asking if the garden's still going to be allotments when I'm no longer around. 'It will still be here,' I say quietly. 'Hopefully.' I hold a finger to my lips. 'But you're to tell no one.'

'Hopefully?' She stares at me for a moment.

'Trust me, Rémy.' I wink at her.

She stares at me. 'That is all I need to know.' She turns abruptly and walks away.

Across the garden, I see Fay coming towards me. But for the first time, she isn't alone. She's with a young man I'm guessing is her son, and a girl who looks a similar age to him.

Fay's face lights up as she comes towards me. 'Zeke! I'm so pleased you're here. This is my son, Stu, and his girlfriend, Andie.'

'Nice to meet you.' I shake Stu's hand, then the young lady's, suddenly almost certain she's pregnant – I have an instinct about these things.

'You too,' Stu says. 'I have to say it's a mystery how you've turned my mother into a gardener.'

'She did it all herself,' I say proudly. 'Fay, you should go and show them what you're growing.'

Her face flushes pink as she leads them to her allotment. I feel a strange surge of pride as she starts pointing things out to them. But since that first day she came here, it isn't just plants she's learned about. It's the seasons, about nature's cycles of life, how rich earth feels when you crumble it between your fingers. She's learned that there are things you can't hurry; that you can't control the rain. That some things are timeless. You see, gardening's about so much more than people think it is.

Amidst everything that's happened to her this year, family is everything to her. I kind of like that. And they may not be here, but family means everything to me, too; there are some things that will never change.

That night, Stevie turns up.

'This is a surprise.' Standing back, I let her in. 'I was sorry to hear about your young man's mother. Really sorry.'

A shadow crosses her face. 'Thanks. He was going to come with me tonight – but he isn't himself just now.'

'Come through. I'll put the kettle on.'

Following me into the kitchen, she looks around, taking in the empty shelves and windowsill, the half-packed boxes on the floor. Turning to me, she looks anxious. 'What's going on?'

After making the tea, we sit down and I tell her about my illness, watching her face turn pale.

She looks as though she's about to say something. But then

her eyes shift to the photos on the wall. 'I've never asked. But they're your family, aren't they?'

When I nod, she looks troubled. 'What happened to them?'

I've come close to telling both Fay and Rémy about what really happened that day. Only with Stevie do I at last drop my guard. After all, she may as well know.

'I was driving them to Paris,' I say. 'Marie, my wife, had never been there. She had it in her head that Paris was this romantic place... I didn't want to go. But because she did, I booked us a few days in a hotel there. Dana, our daughter, was four.' I glance briefly at the toddler in the photo. It seems inconceivable that had she lived, she'd be in her forties. 'We stopped on the way for some lunch. I had a couple of glasses of red wine... I rarely touched the stuff. But we were on holiday, so I did.' There's a lump in my throat. Even now, I vividly remember that afternoon. 'After, we went for a walk. Then we got in the car and carried on towards Paris.' I remember Marie's excitement, the list of sights she wanted to see. 'Marie loved the city,' I say softly. 'We were five miles away when she dropped her lipstick on the floor.' The bright red Chanel lipstick she always wore. 'I reached down to pick it up. In the split second I looked away, a car swerved in front of me. I hit it. Then another piled into us.' I remember how fast I'd been driving; the multiple impacts that followed; Marie's terrible screams, until they stopped. 'Marie didn't make it. My daughter survived the crash. But she died a week later from head injuries.'

Taking the tissue Stevie passes me, I hadn't noticed my tears.

'And ever since, you've had to live with it.' Stevie's eyes are filled with tears of sympathy. 'How awful for you, Zeke.'

'Oh no.' I shake my head. 'It was awful for Marie and Dana. Afterwards though, I was in hell. But I figured I got what I deserved.'

Stevie looks distressed. 'You mustn't say that. It was an accident. You could blame the car that hit you just as much.'

I shake my head again. 'If I hadn't taken my eyes off the road... It's just one of those things. There's no one to blame but myself.'

'It was still an accident.' She's silent for a moment, then gets up, goes to the fridge and opens it. 'It's empty.'

I gaze towards the window. 'I'm not that hungry, to tell you the truth.'

'You still need to eat,' she says firmly. 'Do you mind if I help myself from your garden?'

'Be my guest.' She may as well, while she can. 'It's not going to be mine for much longer.'

She stares at me. 'What do you mean?'

Mentally, I kick myself. 'Forget I said anything. Go and see what you can find.'

After taking the single remaining bowl from one of the cupboards, she goes outside. I hear the latch on the gate at the side of the house click open as she goes around to the back. Ten minutes later, she returns with a bowl full of salad and greens.

'I saw your neighbour while I was out there. She gave me some cheese – and a baguette.' Turning her back, Stevie gets to work. A short while later she presents me with a sandwich and a mixed salad dressed with olive oil, before making another for herself.

'This is really good,' I tell her when I've finished eating. 'Hear me out.' I carry on before she can say something self-deprecating. 'You see, it isn't just the food on the plate. Well, partly it is, but it's how focused you are when you prepare it. The thought you put into it, I guess.' I'm not sure I've explained very well.

But Stevie knows what I mean. 'Anyone can throw a plate of food together.' Pausing, she looks at me. 'The difference is cooking with love,' she says simply.

28

FAY

September

The heat of summer passes, but the drought continues, the countryside desperate for rain. Instead of clouds rolling in, a thermal wind picks up and when a forest fire breaks out, it isn't long before it's out of control.

One night, as I stand in the garden watching the smoke on the horizon, I feel a raindrop on my skin. It's followed by another. Then as I look up, the heavens open. Standing there, I close my eyes and stretch out my arms, revelling in the feeling as the water soaks into me.

Where the efforts of a team of firefighters have failed, it takes the rain to extinguish the last of the forest fires. And for the next few days, the rain continues. One day, I brave it to the allotments in waterproofs to salvage what I can of my tomatoes. But there's no sign of anyone else.

Standing there, I wonder what will come next. Whether next year, I'll come back for a few months again, or maybe this summer was a glorious one-off. But by then, Stu and Andie will be parents; maybe Hugh and I will go to the States.

As I look around the allotments, I know a part of my heart will always belong here; that I feel more at home here in this village than anywhere else in the world. And I have choices, I know that now. Choices that have implications for other people, but I'm the only person who knows what's right for me.

Deciding at this point that I simply have to trust it will work out as it's meant to, I drive back to the house. In the weeks that have passed since Hugh left, I've adapted to being alone again. We've a long way to go, Hugh and me. But this summer, for a while, the sun and nostalgia drew us together. Only time will tell if it's going to last.

But at the very least, it felt as though we reached a fragile understanding. And now that the weather has changed, that the seasons are turning, I'm surprised to find I miss him in my life. Just a little, but enough to make me wonder.

Maybe it's time to think about going home.

29

NED

October

From Stevie's terrace, we watch the river swell after the rain, colour returning to the landscape; the faded green of late summer turning to the rich red browns of autumn.

'Thank goodness,' she breathes as she gazes across the village.

'I guess the bar will stay closed until next year, now.' Standing behind her, my arms are around her waist as I kiss her neck. 'What will you do this winter?'

'I haven't really thought. I guess there'll be some dinner parties. Then there's Christmas, too.' She turns to face me. 'What about you?'

I'm silent for a moment. I've been waiting for the right time to broach the subject. 'Axl's asked me if I'll go on a tour with him. In Italy.' My voice is husky as I look at her. I take hold of both of her hands. 'He has family there. He reckons there's money to be made in the run-up to Christmas. Then after, I guess we'll see.'

Shock registers in her eyes. 'Are you going?'

I hesitate. 'I haven't decided.' It's the truth. Since Axl first mentioned it, I've been weighing everything up. The chance to see where music will take me, versus staying here, with her.

'You have to go,' Stevie says quietly. 'This could be the chance you've been dreaming of.'

It could be – or at the very least, it could be a step up the ladder in my career. As I know only too well, chances like this don't come along very often. But nor do girls like Stevie. 'If I go, would you come with me?' I say softly.

She sighs. 'I don't know, Ned.'

I look at her for a moment. 'You know how a little while back, you told me I should confront my fears?'

Alarm fills her eyes. 'This is different, Ned. You know how I feel about flying.'

Disappointment washes over me. But I'm not giving up. 'We can go by train,' I urge her. 'We don't have to fly!'

Smiling slightly, she sighs. 'It isn't that simple.' She pauses. 'This is my home. There are all the people I've come to know here. And I'm trying to get my business off the ground. These are things I need in my life. I can't risk losing them.' Her voice wavers, a tear rolling down her cheek. 'But I don't want to lose you, either.'

There's angst in her voice, in her beautiful blue eyes. Angst I wish I could take away, but I'm torn. I have a feeling this could be my chance to prove something to myself. I stroke her hair off her face, trying to hide my disappointment. But I know how important her life here is to her; that unlike me, she has no fallback. That this is one of those times when there is no decision that's right for both of us. 'I understand,' I say softly.

'When will you go?' she asks quietly.

I take her hands in mine. 'He wants us to leave at the end of October.'

Her eyes widen. 'That's a week away.' She's silent for a

moment. 'You must go, Ned. You can't let anything stop you. This could be the chance you've been waiting for.'

* * *

Love is all-defeating, I keep telling myself. If it endures after death, it can survive a few hundred miles for a few months – that's if Stevie and I want it to. But the knowledge I'm leaving puts a strain on our relationship, so much so I wonder if Stevie's having second thoughts.

Preparing myself for the worst, I'm nervous when the day before I leave, she turns up unexpectedly.

'Are you busy? There's something I want to say.' She sounds breathless.

A strand of hair has fallen across her face. Suddenly I want to stroke it back, then sweep her into my arms; to tell her I'll love her forever. But another, more defensive side of me just feels guarded, my heart filling with dread that this is the moment I've been fearing. 'Not really. I've just finished packing.' For once, I'm organised. 'Want to come in?' I stand back to let her in.

But she hesitates on the doorstep. 'I don't want to disturb anyone.'

'You won't,' I reassure her. 'My father's gone out for one of those lunches that will go on for hours and blend into dinner. And Nina's gone to Marseille.'

'Oh.' Stevie looks relieved as she comes inside.

I stand there slightly awkwardly. 'Would you like a coffee? Or something stronger?'

'Coffee would be nice.' She seems oddly restrained as she follows me through to the kitchen. Leaning against a worktop, she's silent as she watches me make two cups.

I pass her one, before asking, slightly trepidatiously, 'Er, you said there was something you wanted to talk about?'

Sighing, she puts the cup down. 'I had it all planned out in my head. But it seems to have gone now.' She pauses. 'I suppose what it comes down to is this. I really want you to do this, Ned. Go away with the band, I mean.' Coming over, she takes one of my hands. 'Sorry. I've been so miserable since you told me about this. But it's only because I know I'm going to miss you.' She pauses. 'There's something else, too. Something I should have told you, but it's never felt like the right time. It was when I met your mother.' Her eyes gaze into mine. 'Remember you left us alone for a few minutes? Anyway, we talked – about you, obviously.' Stevie pauses. 'You see, I know she'd want you to do this. But it isn't just her. I want you to do it, too.'

I gaze at her, lost for words, as in that moment I feel a gigantic weight lift, my doubts completely evaporating along with the guilt I've felt at leaving Stevie. 'You're sure?' I say huskily.

'Completely.' There's a light in her eyes I haven't seen before. 'It's important to do what you want with your life. Music feeds your soul, Ned. While for now, maybe because I have nowhere else, being here feeds mine.' She pauses. 'Go to Italy. Have the best time.' She smiles. 'When you come back, I'll still be here.'

* * *

Just like that, my road map changes, so to speak. Not only is the road itself straighter, but it's as though someone has taken an eraser to it and rubbed out the obstacles, potholes and traffic jams. When the day of my departure arrives, Stevie doesn't come to say goodbye. Last night, she told me we'll keep in touch. That if we're meant to be together, as it was when we met on the plane, the universe will conspire to make it happen.

I'm still not that sure what the universe has to do with anything, but unimaginable, surprising things have happened in the last few months, and I have the strangest feeling things are going to work out between us.

'I'm proud of you, Ned,' my father says as he stands on the doorstep. Then to my surprise, he hugs me.

Taken aback, I swallow the lump in my throat. It's the closest to acceptance of my music career that my father's ever come.

'Don't worry. I'll look after the old man.' Nina hugs me tightly. 'Come back soon. Not too soon, though.'

I linger for a moment. In his car, Axl hoots impatiently. Turning, excitement ripples through me as I walk down the steps and across the drive towards him. With my guitar on my back, my battered old barrel bag over my shoulder, sunglasses perched on top of my head, I'm older, and I like to think a little wiser – and more purposeful, but otherwise almost exactly as I arrived several months ago.

30

FAY

November

The day before I leave France, the sun makes its first appearance in days and I drive to the allotments. The soil is waterlogged, the ground covered in sodden leaves and as I make my way to Zeke's corner, I have an urge to clear them up, one last time.

As it comes into view, I stop, frowning. Zeke's sitting on his chair. But there's something about the angle of his head that doesn't look right.

I hurry towards him. 'Zeke?' Noticing the colour of his skin, I take his hand to feel for a pulse. Then slowly, I put it down again. A tear rolls down my cheek. Then as I glance at his flower beds, I freeze suddenly. The black weed that's plagued Zeke for so long has gone.

I pick a flower and place it on his lap, then stand there a moment before calling an ambulance. But however sad I feel that he's left this world, I know he wouldn't have wanted it any other way.

He's at peace now. Moreover, he's gone to join his family.

31

ZEKE

December

1st October

To all of you,

Funny, isn't it, when you are the holder of something magical, how it means the world to share it with folks who feel the same. For some, that's family. But family is about more than blood, as I've found out. It's your soul tribe, as I've come to call it.

I'm talking about the allotments. The value each of you places on them, the respect you show the earth. I think that's what this garden was always about. It found me my tribe. And that's you. Rémy, Fay, Stevie. The closest I've had in a very long while to family.

You know that way life has of coming up with the unexpected? So now it's your turn. I won't spin it out any more. The allotments belong to you. I have my own ideas about what you could do with them, but I'm not here any more, so it's up to you.

About the house... I don't know how long Nicole and Olivier are going to be without premises, but I've always felt it would make a pretty nice bar. Stevie, that's in your hands. Or maybe a cookery school. I reckon between you, you'll find a way to make it pay.

Maybe I'll see you on the other side one day. But for now, au revoir, my friends. You were my greatest blessing. I'll never understand what I did to deserve that.

Oh, and before I sign off, please look after my cat. Though come to think of it, I haven't seen him for a while. But I'm sure he'll be back.

So now, it's time for a brand-new chapter. Bring it on, I say! And embrace it. But I know you will. It's what brought you here in the first place. Endings lead to new beginnings; when winter ends, there will be another spring.

EPILOGUE
FAY

December

'Oh dear.' I gaze at the letter that's put the cat among the pigeons. What do I say to Hugh? Just when I thought I'd worked things out, suddenly I'm realising I haven't.

'He was sick. Maybe it affected his mind,' Rémy says disrespectfully.

'*Madame.*' The mayor who's summoned us today glares at her. 'I can assure you this is not the case. Zeke's mind was better than most.' He holds her gaze a little longer than necessary.

'Maybe we should just think about it for a while.' Stevie's voice is quiet and clear. 'It's winter. The garden is sleeping. We don't have to rush into anything.' She pauses. 'Actually, I think we're really lucky. It could be amazing.'

'It is more work.' Rémy sounds cross. Then she sighs. 'You are right. It is nice of Zeke to leave us the garden. It is just I was not prepared for this, or for anything like this.'

'I don't think any of us were.' I'm quiet for a moment. But my mind is already wandering, imagining keeping chickens and goats, perhaps, on the scrubby patch of land at the edge of the garden. Extending the reach of Zeke's philosophy of caring for the land, at the same time living and eating with the seasons. 'Shall we put the garden on hold while we all think about this?'

'I thought you were going back to England.' Rémy looks at me accusingly.

'I was.' I look at her, then at Stevie, frowning. 'In fact, I still am. But I'll be back in the New Year.' I'm not sure why, but Zeke's letter has given a new – if rather odd – clarity to everything. 'I think you're right,' I say to Stevie, feeling a flicker of excitement. 'This really could be the start of something amazing – whatever that is.'

'I think it could. It's exciting!' Far from excited, there's a distant look on Stevie's face. 'So we meet up again in January? Because before we get started, I have to do something.'

* * *

Stevie

You can do this, I tell myself. Ned faced his fears; it's my turn to do the same.

Sitting in the airport on the day before Christmas Eve, as I watch a plane take off, the familiar fears engulf me. *Stop it,* I tell myself. *There's no point in frightening the hell out of yourself. You're doing this.*

I picture Ned's face; remember the first time we met, in another airport, when life was different, just under a year ago. Less than a year. How is it that in such a short time, so much has changed?

I listen as my flight is called, taking a deep breath before getting up. This time, I will not be last to board. My hand will not shake when I hand my passport over. I will walk out there with my head held high. *You can do this*, I tell myself again.

Just before I reach the gate, I stand to one side and take out my phone to make a call. I've waited until now – just in case.

It's answered straight away. 'Stevie?'

'Hello.' I hesitate. 'OK. I'm going to tell you this quickly because I probably shouldn't dwell on it or I'll freak myself out and probably change my mind. But I'm at the airport – in Bergerac. I'm about to get on a flight...' I break off as I say the word 'flight'.

'That's brilliant.' There's a silence at the other end. 'I'm proud of you,' he says softly. 'For conquering your fear. For doing what you said you were never going to do.'

'I haven't exactly conquered it but I'm trying.' I try to keep the panic out of my voice.

'You haven't told me where you're going.' He sounds unsure.

'Oh.' Suddenly I'm realising I haven't. 'I'm coming to Rome. To see you, Ned.'

And just like that, my nerves vanish. You see, there will always be risks in life. But sometimes, you just have to take them. They don't all end in disaster. Quite the opposite. Sometimes, taking a risk can lead you somewhere magical. And more often than not, risks are all in the mind, while risks you walk away from will, in a matter of time, almost certainly become regrets. And I don't want my biggest regret to be stopping myself from being with the man I love.

'I land at four thirty.' Holding my breath; crossing my fingers he still wants me to come.

'I'll be there,' Ned says softly.

ACKNOWLEDGEMENTS

This book was inspired by the months we spent living in a tiny village in south-west France. It's true that in these places, life is simpler. It's definitely slower, too. In winter, you'd drive through and, quite understandably, imagine nothing ever happens there. But even in these quiet places, everyone has their own story. *The Making of Us* is about a number of such stories and the way they overlap, during one beautiful summer set amidst the glorious countryside of rural France.

There are so many brilliant people behind the scenes of every book that's published, and I'd like to say a huge thank you to the wonderful Boldwood team for everything you put into getting mine out in the world. Through the various stages of editing and proofreading; from cover design to marketing to social media promotion, I'm so grateful to each and every one of you.

Huge thanks also to my editor, Isobel Akenhead, for helping to make this novel as good as it can be.

And as always, to my superstar agent, Juliet Mushens.

A massive thank you and much love to my family and friends for supporting each one of my books. To Georgie and Tom, to whom this one is dedicated. And to Martin for understanding those weird days writers have when all I can think about is the story in my head.

And to you, my readers. Thank you from the bottom of my heart for reading my books, for sharing them and for loving them.

For your many wonderful reviews; for your thoughtful messages and emails. You are the reason I keep doing this.

ABOUT THE AUTHOR

Debbie Howells is a Sunday Times bestseller, who is now fulfilling her dream of writing women's fiction with Boldwood. She has perviously worked as cabin crew, a flying instructor, and a wedding florist! Now living in the countryside with her partner and Bean the rescued cat, Debbie spends her time writing.

Sign up to Debbie Howells' mailing list for news, competitions and updates on future books.

Visit Debbie's website: www.debbiehowells.co.uk

Follow Debbie on social media:

facebook.com/debbie.howells.37

x.com/debbie__howells

instagram.com/_debbiehowells

bookbub.com/authors/debbie-howells

goodreads.com/debbiehowells

ALSO BY DEBBIE HOWELLS

LOVE NOTES

LOVE IN EVERY CHAPTER

WHERE ALL YOUR ROMANCE
DREAMS COME TRUE!

THE HOME OF BESTSELLING
ROMANCE AND WOMEN'S
FICTION

 WARNING:
MAY CONTAIN SPICE

SIGN UP TO OUR
NEWSLETTER

https://bit.ly/Lovenotesnews

Boldwood

Boldwood Books is an award-winning fiction publishing company seeking out the best stories from around the world.

Find out more at www.boldwoodbooks.com

Join our reader community for brilliant books, competitions and offers!

Follow us

@BoldwoodBooks

@TheBoldBookClub

Sign up to our weekly deals newsletter

https://bit.ly/BoldwoodBNewsletter

Printed in Great Britain
by Amazon